THE HOUSE OF GOLD

A James Geraldi Trio

Other Five Star Titles by Max Brand:

Sixteen in Nome
Outlaws All: A Western Trio
The Lightning Warrior
The Wolf Strain: A Western Trio
The Stone That Shines
Men Beyond the Law: A Western Trio
Beyond the Outposts
The Fugitive's Mission: A Western Trio
In the Hills of Monterey
The Lost Valley: A Western Trio
Chinook
The Gauntlet: A Western Trio
The Survival of Juan Oro
Stolen Gold: A Western Trio
The Geraldi Trail
Timber Line: A Western Trio
The Gold Trail: A Western Trio
Gunman's Goal
The Overland Kid: A Western Trio
The Masterman
The Outlaw Redeemer
The Peril Trek: A Western Trio
The Bright Face of Danger: A James Geraldi Trio
Don Diablo: A Western Trio
The Welding Quirt: A Western Trio
The Tyrant

THE HOUSE OF GOLD

A James Geraldi Trio

MAX BRAND™

Five Star • Waterville, Maine

Additional copyright information can be found on page 316.

Five Star First Edition Western Series.

Published in 2001 in conjunction with
Golden West Literary Agency.

Cover photograph by Jillian Raven.

Set in 11 pt. Plantin by Al Chase.

Printed in the United States on permanent paper.

Library of Congress Cataloging-in-Publication Data

Brand, Max, 1892–1944.
The house of Gold : a James Geraldi trio / by Max Brand.
p. cm.—(Five Star first edition western series)
ISBN 0-7862-2757-5 (hc : alk. paper)
1. Geraldi, James (Fictitious character)—Fiction.
2. Western stories. I. Title. II. Series.
PS3511.A87 H68 2001
813′.52—dc21 2001040524

TABLE OF CONTENTS

Editor's Note

Frederick Faust wrote a total of ten stories about James Geraldi, all of which appeared in various issues of Street & Smith's *Western Story Magazine* under the byline Max Brand. Two of the Geraldi stories were published as serials in a number of installments. "Three on the Trail" appeared as a six-part serial in *Western Story Magazine* (5/1/28–6/16/28) and was the first of the two serials to appear in book form as *The Killers* (Macaulay, 1931) by George Owen Baxter. "The Geraldi Trail" appeared as a four-part serial in *Western Story Magazine* (6/11/32–7/2/32), but its first book appearance was complicated by the fact that Dodd, Mead & Company, which was publishing Faust books at the time under the byline Max Brand, did not want to publish a Max Brand novel featuring a character that had already appeared previously in a George Owen Baxter novel issued by a competitor. Therefore, the character's name was changed from James Geraldi to Jesse Jackson, and the book published by Dodd, Mead in 1932 was accordingly titled *The Jackson Trail.*

Gunman's Goal (Five Star Westerns, 2000)—as the serial, "Three on the Trail" has now been titled—is the first story in the saga about James Geraldi. *The Bright Face of Danger* (Five Star Westerns, 2000) contains the first three interconnected stories in Geraldi's pursuit of several priceless Egyptian jewels. *The House of Gold* continues

Geraldi's adventures in the next three stories. Once the James Geraldi stories have all appeared in Five Star Westerns, they will at last have been published for the first time in book form in definitive texts so they can be read as parts of a continuing saga—which was ultimately the author's intention in writing them.

The House of Gold

I
"TWO SAILORS ASHORE"

Having put her hand to the plow, Emily Lucile Ingall has never been one to turn back, so I am still in this Wild West with my poor niece, Mary Ingall. And, indeed, what with my anxiety about her, my worry about the golden box, the diamond, the missing emeralds, I have had but little time to think of my dear and distant Boston.

Mary has been frantic ever since we saw James Geraldi pitched from his horse. I've tried to reassure her by pointing out that, if he had been killed, the Winchelmere gang never would have taken the trouble of carrying him off, in spite of the pursuit that they knew would start after them, instantly.

I induced her to come on to San Felice again, with me. After the wilderness in which we had been living—like human bait in a trap—San Felice seemed like a metropolis to us, and a center in the safe middle of civilization. But even that did Mary little good. Her mind was casting back, always, to James Geraldi. She even suggested that she should advertise that the golden box of Horus, and the yellow diamond, and the fourth emerald, would be freely given up to the man or men who returned Geraldi to her in safety.

I managed to point out to her that, no matter how great her heart was, it would be useless to advertise on such a matter—that already Winchelmere knew well enough that she would pay any price for Jimmy. And, finally, that by such an advertisement she would probably bring down on us a great deal of unpleasant, official attention upon our affairs, and upon her poor father. Now that he is dead, we must do our best to preserve his reputation pure and spotless in the eyes of the world. Pure and spotless, too, in my eyes; for I know that he never would have taken that fatal treasure out of Egypt if his mind had not been unbalanced by more than a touch of a strange, religious mania. And if ever we can restore the wretched golden box and all its ornaments to the Egyptian government, and put the thing safely in the hands of the ruler, we shall have left the fame of poor Robert Ingall brighter than ever.

When strength came back to my dear Mary, she grew tremendously uneasy and wanted to do something—she hardly knew what. I think she would have climbed on a horse and gone adventuring to find Geraldi in the wilderness, if she could have done so. But she was restrained by a saving touch of common sense when I was in despair.

I thought that I had an inspiration, and, although I have been rather untrustful of all of my thoughts since the last tragedy that I caused, still I felt this idea was good. The owner of a little cottage at the edge of the town was moving away. He was a part owner of the bank, and through the bank I heard about the opportunity. We had noticed the place before, particularly because of its bright little garden, with a flaming hedge of sweet peas raised on brush, and wandering all around the edge of the garden.

It was very comfortable and very cheerful, and—since we couldn't leave the community until we had some news of Geraldi—I begged Mary to consent to moving into it.

She became extraordinarily practical and thoughtful at once. "Here in the hotel," she said, "we have a certain amount of protection around us. On the other hand, in the cottage. . . ."

"Here in the hotel!" I exclaimed. "Wasn't it from this very hotel that you were abducted?"

"Well," said Mary, "that was long ago."

Strong-minded and clever as Mary is, she can be as bafflingly feminine as any one in the world, when she wishes to be so.

"Humph!" I said.

"Besides," said Mary, "nothing came of it."

"Only," I reminded her, "because the one man in the world who could have saved you happened to be there. If it hadn't been for Jimmy Geraldi. . . ."

I stopped and bit my lip. Her face had grown crimson, and her eyes widened in a painful manner.

However, she said at once, with her usual courage: "You don't have to shrink from naming him. I'm not an Eighteenth-Century baby. I'm not going to faint, Aunt Emmy."

I went on, at that: "Also, from this very hotel, wasn't the box stolen away?"

"But that was by Jimmy," she said, smiling at me.

"You're being very silly," I couldn't help telling her.

"But *what* protection would we have in that cottage?" she asked me.

"We're neither of us helpless," I assured her. "I know you're not, and I know that *I'm* not!"

"Against his lordship?" she asked.

That spiked my guns, as one might say, but I answered: "I've thought it all out. We'll have to have a cook. We'll have to have someone to look after the horses and the garden."

"Well?" she said.

"And I'll simply hire men . . . at double wages, if necessary . . . who will be able to take care of themselves and of us, too."

"Against Lord Winchelmere?" she repeated.

I pointed out to her, in some irritation, that clever and wicked as his lordship was, he was not absolutely superhuman, and that we would undoubtedly be a match for him if we did everything carefully. She finally agreed. The picture of that charming little garden was in her mind's eye and tempting her, although she said that it was against her better judgment to yield.

I went that same day to the employment agency. It was the roughest place I've ever seen, filled with ruffian-looking lumbermen, and miners, and cowboys. They stopped their swearing, however, when I came in. These Western men are strangely courteous—to women, I mean to say.

I told the head of the agency, who wore a sombrero with a brim that flopped down over his eyes, that I wanted two good men, and I told him what I needed them for.

"A cook," he said. "That'll be a chink, I suppose?"

I asked him if white men never cooked in this country. He replied that they did—for themselves. And at that a hardy-looking wretch with the face of a pirate spoke up and declared that he was tired of breaking bronchos, and that he would be glad to take a job slinging chuck.

I hope I have remembered the way he expressed it. I turned on him and asked him if he could shoot straight and fast.

At the very mention of shooting, he grinned with joy, then he banished that look and admitted modestly that now and then he could hit his mark, although he wouldn't set himself up, he said, to be any expert. "Not like Champ, yonder."

He pointed to a gray-headed fellow who was just as villainous-looking as himself.

"Champ," I said to him, "will you come and look after two horses and a patch of garden?"

Champ stood up and touched his hat—just high enough to let me see iron-gray hair, and his face, too, was misted over with three or four days' stubble of the same color.

"Hosses, ma'am," he said to me, "I take to right kindly. If they'll take to me. Gardens, ma'am, is something that I have seen, occasional . . . but I dunno that I ever looked at one from inside of the fence."

"Belay that, Champ," said the first man. "There ain't anything that he can't lay his hand to. He's been a sailor, ma'am."

"Are you two friends?" I asked the first fellow.

Champ answered: "Mike and me sailed together in the old days. Mike, he taught me everything up to how to cross a royal yard."

That meant nothing to me, of course, but I was very glad to know that they were friends—if they had to work for me.

"Mike and Champ," I said to them, "if you will come to work for me, I'll pay you whatever you would make on the range . . . and a little more. The work won't be hard."

"But including shooting?" asked Mike of the iron face.

"Suppose we talk it over in the open air?" I asked.

Without another word, they went outside with me.

"I don't mind a dash of pepper," admitted Champ. "Only I don't like to ship for Guam."

"He means to say," Mike said, kindly interpreting, "that he wants to know what the trouble is all about?"

I thought it over briefly. As a matter of fact, I had thought beforehand what I should say. I couldn't tell them a great deal. I said at last: "I can tell you briefly how most of the people appear . . . the ones that I expect may make the trouble, I mean to say. Outside of that, I can't tell you anything."

"It's a mystery," said Mike.

"Crossing three sky sails," said Champ.

They looked at one another.

"My niece will be with me," I told them. "We need two steady, courageous, dependable men. And . . . I'll pay you five dollars a day."

They both started.

"Five bucks!" said Champ.

"Five iron men," Mike said, nodding, with a faraway look in his eyes.

"What time do we move into our new bunks?" asked Champ.

"When do we sign?" said Mike.

I looked them over for the last time before making up my mind. After all, I knew that I could not pretend to read character accurately here in the West. Finally I said: "You can move in today, if you please, blankets and all."

"All ain't much," said Mike with his dreadful grin. "You tell us where the job is docked."

I told them where to find the house, and they touched the brims of their hats—which serves for hat tipping here in the West. Then they marched off. They had not so much as asked my name.

I went into the employment agency then, and gave my name and address, and went back to the hotel. Two hours later we were installed in the cottage where things were to happen to us much faster than I wished.

II
"A WELCOME VISITOR"

Our landlord wanted to sell his house furnished, and we were renting it under an agreement that we would move out as soon as he could make a sale. For that reason we had been able to get him to agree to a lease as short as a month—which, of course, was ideal for us. We found everything tidy and neat. The furniture was rough, but convenient, and strongly made; the walls of the place were solid, and the stairway to the two upstairs bedrooms did not creak a bit. Altogether, though we had rented the place because of its pleasant face, we were delighted with what we found inside.

There was a neat little kitchen with a sufficient array of pans; there was a small dining room opening out through a side door into an arbor drenched with honeysuckle; and we also had a living room, and a bedroom which Mary and I agreed to occupy together for the sake of security and company.

The two upper rooms we offered, one apiece, to the two men, but they refused. As Mike said: "Champ and me have bunked together in the same forecastle eight voyages before the mast, and I dunno . . . we'd feel a little mite queer, switching things over to different parts of the ship."

I was glad enough to have that much extra space, and gladder still the evening of the second day when the first great event happened.

There were other things, but I can't dwell on them. Although I must mention Champ's idea of weeding the garden, and pulling up more flowers than weeds! I saw that Mary and I would have to attend to that business, while Champ was wonderfully good-humored and willing to carry water in countless buckets. He rigged a pole over his shoulders—"chink fashion," as he called it—and he used to carry two five-gallon pails at once from the mill. There was a well and a windmill whirling and singing behind the house.

He was inventive. All sailors are, I believe. And, before noon, he had arranged a little system of irrigation, running the water directly from the windmill through little troughs and trenches into the garden. Soon he had such a head of water that he could have flooded every inch of the place in half a day. He was very contented with his work and declared that he had not enjoyed himself so much since he'd last "run his easting down," whatever that may mean.

Mike proved a queer cook. He fell to work at once, and we discovered that he could not work without making noise. Everything that he touched crashed and banged under his iron fingers, and he kept time to this jargon of metal, as it were, by roaring out sea songs in an enormous voice.

And what songs! I was crimson with embarrassment before I had listened to half the first one. Mary and I, red in the face, hurried into our room and stared at one another.

"He won't do," I said. "I'll have to discharge him."

"Champ will go with him," said Mary.

"We'll have to do without him, too."

"But what of the garden?" asked Mary.

I thought of what Champ already had done to the garden, the flowers he had uprooted, and the great, muddy trenches that he had excavated until it looked like a small irrigation system. I broke into laughter, and Mary joined in with me.

We went out into the living room; a huge torrent of frightfulness came thundering from the kitchen. I clapped my hands over my ears.

"But," said Mary, "he hasn't the slightest idea what he's singing."

I thought she was right. Mike didn't know what the sounds meant; he repeated what he had heard, and there's an end. His food was odd. He made for us what he called "duff." It was a sort of boiled pudding. Flour and dripping, and heaven alone can tell what else. But it was as good as it was strange.

When I told him it was excellent, he put his hand on the back of my chair and leaned over me in a brotherly fashion.

"I seen the time, ma'am," said Mike, "when a duff like that there would 'a' been the savin' of fifteen lives." Table talk furnished by the cook. He added, as he straightened: "But some was better dead . . . and I dunno as any of them missed much." He went back to the kitchen.

"How odd!" I said to Mary.

"How delicious!" said Mary to me. And she laughed, the first real laughter that I had heard from her in many, many days—since Jimmy disappeared.

I encouraged work on the garden. Anything to keep her hands so busy that she would not have any time for thinking. And on the evening of the second day we were grubbing like two gophers in the cool of the dusk. Mike complained from the side door that the soup was growing cold.

"The outbeatingest soup you ever throwed a lip over," said Mike. "It's the kind of a thing that I invented myself, when there wasn't anything on board but some spoiled cabbage, and canned tomatoes, and mighty tired-looking pork. . . ."

This was to raise our appetites, I suppose. Mary made a face at me, sitting upon her heels.

"Isn't he terrible?" she said.

But I knew that she felt as I did—half horrified, but more amused. And then she looked past me, and rose up to her feet as though a hand were drawing her.

"What is it, Mary?" I asked.

She said nothing, simply reached a hand toward me and seemed to be fumbling for support.

I stood up beside her and put my arm around her.

"Oh, Aunt Emmy," she was whispering. "Oh, Aunt Emmy, is it? Is it?"

I strained my eyes through the shadows. They're not such eyes as they once were, but they're strong enough, and finally I made out a horseman coming up the street on a fine, tall horse. There wasn't much light, but that horse was lighted from within, if I may say so. He danced over the ground as though he scorned it. He came steadily on.

"*Can* it be?" said Mary.

I knew what she meant. There were not so many horses in the world like this one. There could not be. And the only one I had seen before like him was black Peter, that beautiful stallion that Geraldi took from Lord Winchelmere and for the sake of which, I think, Winchelmere hated him more than for any other reason.

"Will it stop at the gate?" asked Mary. "Will it stop here?"

You would have thought that the horse could have acted of its own volition. I felt Mary trembling and drew her a little closer. We were like two infants watching an eagle drift through the sky. *Could* it be Geraldi?

They came opposite the gate, and suddenly the big horse stopped, and the rider leaped down.

That instant we both knew. No other man in the world moves with just that cat-like lightness of foot. The garden gate groaned open under his hand, and black Peter stretched his head over as far as he could and began to crop the top sprouts of a climbing rose.

I didn't care. I would have let him eat the entire garden, such a flood of relief and joy was pouring through my heart.

"Jimmy!" Mary cried, and she started for him.

I clutched frantically at her. But she slipped away, and in another moment I blushed to see that her arms were around his neck. Good heavens! I was between laughter and weeping—for pleasure of seeing that young rascal back, and for vexation and sorrow to see Mary wear her heart on her sleeve so openly.

He came on to me and disentangled himself from Mary without seeming to do so. He took my hand; I heard his soft voice saying something.

"Jimmy," I said to him at last, "I can't hear you. My head is whirling. I can only say . . . thank goodness that I have your hand again!"

They led me into the house, laughing heartlessly at me, and sat me down by an open window.

"Don't say a word to me," I told him. "Don't speak. Just sit here and let me hold your hand and make sure that you're really not a ghost."

"No ghost ever could carry so much dust," said Mary. "He's drenched with it."

"Heavens!" I exclaimed. "The rug! Go brush yourself off at once, Jimmy!"

He went away with that soft, soft laughter—barely audible, a mere pulse of sound. When he came back, I was myself again, and we all went in to the supper table, Mary shining like a fairy princess, and with her voice continually melting into the sweetest laughter.

We did the talking. Oh, we asked questions, of course, but almost as though we were afraid to hear the answers; we interrupted him before he could speak and rattled on breathlessly, with Mike drifting in and out of the room and fixing a curious eye upon the visitor. He couldn't make out Geraldi. How could anyone at the first glance?

For my part, I watched him carefully, and, as far as I could see, he was exactly the same as he had been before. There was not a wrinkle on his brow; there was not a shadow beneath his eyes. No one could have guessed that he had spent the time since we had seen him—or some portion of it—in the hands of men who would have taken his life as freely as they would have drawn a breath.

We had great cups of black coffee to end the meal—coffee and wedges of pie made from dried apples. Mike was hugely proud of it.

"A thing like that was never seen aboard a ship," he assured us.

And as he went out, Geraldi passed a twist of paper to Mary. "Here they are," he said.

Mary, lips parted, fingered the paper. I saw her thumb press it three times, and I knew that the miracle had happened. Jimmy had brought himself safely back to us. He had brought the three stolen emeralds, as well!

III
"COINCIDENCE?"

Just then, Mike drifted back into the room, with an expectant grin on his face, ready to drink up praise for his pie. Poor fellow, Mary and I had something else on our minds, and only Geraldi would pay any attention to our cook.

"You don't know me, do you?" asked Jimmy. "My name is Winslow." He stood up and shook hands with Mike. No one could be more democratic than Jimmy.

I, watching him with awe and wonder, trying to understand that he actually had slipped through the hands of Winchelmere and his master crooks, and, indeed, had taken the spoils of war when he came, full of questions to the teeth, marveled when I saw him chatting easily with Mike.

"You're a man in a thousand for a cookhouse, Mike," he said. "But still I see that isn't your usual work."

"How do you see that?" asked Mike.

"By the inside of your hand and the outside of your eye," said Jimmy.

Mike looked at him for a moment. "I've handled a rope a little," he admitted. "I've built a noose or two and dabbed it on a cow, now and then. That toughens up your hands."

"You've been working this range?" Jimmy asked, sitting down.

"I been doin' the Wentworth place," said Mike. "I been a

sort of a handy man up there . . . roustabout . . . any odd thing. Me and Champ, we turn a hand to anything."

Jimmy nodded and smiled, and Mike went back to the kitchen.

"He's a good old chap, isn't he?" I said to Geraldi.

And Jimmy smiled and nodded.

At that moment, Mary shook the contents of the paper into her hand, and we saw the three emeralds, glimmering and glowing with green fire.

We went silently into the front room, and Mary said: "It's all accomplished, now, and you've done every stroke of the work, Jimmy. You've done it all. . . ." She paused, and her lips trembled.

"No job is ended until you've come to the finish," Jimmy said coldly. "You haven't built a house until you have cashed the pay check. There's a good deal to be done, still."

I thought, at the time, that he had assumed that chilly, practical tone merely for the sake of keeping Mary impersonal, and I was grateful to him—enormously grateful. I was ashamed of Mary. I was heartily ashamed of her. Never in my life have I seen a woman wear her heart so openly on her sleeve as she did that evening. If she had been the wife of an Arctic explorer just back from a four-year voyage, she could hardly have been more emotional.

Geraldi handled the situation very well. He acted in what I can only describe as a "brotherly" way—cheerfully friendly and sympathetic, I mean, but without a trace of sentimentality. I could have thanked him on my knees for acting in that manner. Mary began to get control of herself. She could watch him, at least, without quite such a calf look in her eyes.

"What still remains?" I said. "We simply have to get the box from the bank, fit back the emeralds, and take a train for the East. It all looks simple enough to me."

"Think of it in stages," Geraldi said. "You have to keep these emeralds until the morning, it appears."

"That should be easy enough," I laughed.

"Of course it should," said Geraldi. "And then, after that, you have to get them down to the bank."

"I'm strong enough to carry them," I suggested.

"No doubt," said Geraldi. "And yet I have an idea that a good many other people will be offering to help you . . . almost insisting on helping you, in fact."

I stared at him. I understood, at last.

"You mean that the gang of Winchelmere, and Asprey, and the rest of those scoundrels are already about us?"

He considered for a moment, very much as though he doubted whether it were best to tell us everything, or to tell us nothing.

Finally he said: "Three weeks ago, and a day or two over, I left them."

"Three weeks!" I said.

"I couldn't come the straightest way," said Jimmy. "I had to swing from side to side, now and then. Hunting for easy going, you know."

Mary said earnestly: "They were after you, Jimmy?"

"They were," he admitted. "And after a good deal of dodging, I managed to get back to you. But they've had plenty of time to guess where I was bound, and to send their warning on ahead."

"Very well!" snapped Mary. "There were six of them. Now there are only five. And we have the power of the law with us . . . and we have you, Jimmy, and we have two really safe, true, strong men that Aunt Emmy has hired. Why haven't we huge odds in our favor?"

"Perhaps we have," said Jimmy. "Perhaps we have the odds in our favor. Particularly since there are no longer five."

"Strozzi is dead," Mary said, with a really fierce pleasure in her voice, in her eyes. "And who else?"

"Poor Oñate was shot," Geraldi explained. "Officers of the law interrupting a little journey on which they were taking me . . . and then, on the way back, Rompier insisted on getting in my way. There are only three, now."

"Three!" cried Mary. "But, then, that's perfectly simple, isn't it? Three! We already are as many as they, and besides, we have the law. . . ."

Jimmy smiled. "I don't think, Mary," he said, "that we'd better rest our backs against it too confidently."

Mary was on fire with confidence. "The thing is as good as done!" she insisted.

"It worries me to hear you say that," I told her frankly. "Don't do it, Mary. Don't count your chickens, you know."

She simply laughed. "Jimmy has beaten them so many times that there will be no heart left in them. He has killed two of the six with his own hand. And the law, he says, has taken off another of them. Half of them are gone."

"The brains are still there," answered Jimmy. "And brains always can find hands. It's like the story of the chimera. Cut off one head, and the remaining ones have stronger fires to breathe at you. Hands always can be hired."

"Why did you say that so significantly, Jimmy?" I asked him, for he had glanced at me as he spoke.

"Ah, well," said Jimmy, "just tell me how you happened to hire these fellows of yours?"

That startled me. It angered me a good deal, too, to have any shadow of doubt cast upon my rough-and-ready cowpunchers. Geraldi had risen from his chair as he asked the question, and, when I began to answer, he stepped like the noiseless cat that he is to the door, and pulled it suddenly open.

There stood Mike in the hall.

"Thanks, boss," said Mike. "I had both hands full, you see?" He walked in with a platter of steaming fudge.

"It ain't quite cold enough yet, ma'am," Mike said to me. "But you lay a tooth in that candy about five minutes from now and you'll be sittin' pretty!" He went out of the room.

"You see?" I challenged Geraldi. "You see how it is? He simply happened to be there at the door. You haven't proved a thing against him."

"I hope not," said Geraldi. "I don't want to prove anything against them. I want to prove things in their favor. Only . . . I don't like what I've heard so far."

"Why don't you like it?" I asked him.

"In the first place, I find out that he's only playing at cook. He has the hands of something else."

"With a talent for cooking, of course," I said.

"He's a common ranch hand, he says," remarked Geraldi.

"Yes. Of course. It's printed large on him, the poor old dear," I said.

"He's a cook who can make pie crust and candy. Very good candy it is, too," Geraldi said, taking a piece and nibbling a corner of it, with his eyes turned a trifle up. "Furthermore, he can turn out a beautiful omelet, you've said, and his supper tonight was excellent. My own observation is that no man can be a cook unless he has a strong touch of imagination, plus a little touch of culture in the brain. . . ."

We both stared at Jimmy. I didn't want to believe him.

"Then I asked where he had been working," said Geraldi, "and he told me that he came from the only ranch in the range which is fifty miles from a railroad."

"And what of it?" I asked.

"Oh, it's probably not an important point," said Jimmy. "But I want you to see that if we were to attempt inquiries, it would take us ten days to get an answer." He went on: "But tell me how you found these men. Did someone in the hotel recommend them to you?"

"As a matter of fact," I said, "I simply stumbled on them. I went to the employment office, and there I asked about a cook, when Mike happened to hear me and spoke up. And when he heard that I wanted another man, too, he naturally recommended his Bunkie and old shipmate, Champ. Could anything be more a matter of course than that? Except that it's never a matter of course to find a good cook."

"You're perfectly right," Geraldi said. "But it's also interesting to notice, don't you think, that these men introduced themselves to your attention?"

"They simply happened to be there," I said.

"A coincidence," Geraldi stated, with that white flash of a smile that I dreaded. It was one of the few things about him—that and his silent, cat-like step—that I thoroughly disliked. "Also," he said, "it's a coincidence that a ranch hand can cook so well, and there was another coincidence . . . that he should have been standing there at the door, when I opened it."

"His hands were too full to open the door . . . ," I began.

"Nevertheless, his ears were free," said Geraldi.

IV
"KISMET!"

I looked at Mary, and Mary looked back at me. We both were irritated more than alarmed. It seemed very unpleasant that the least shadow of suspicion should fall upon our rough cowpuncher.

"He's so free and easy and blunt!" exclaimed Mary with a frown.

"So was Iago," answered Jimmy quickly.

There was nothing to do with that man. He had his answers by heart, as it were.

Mary stood up impatiently. "Let's go outside," she said.

"It would be a great deal safer," said Geraldi.

There, you see, was his way of forcing our thought along one line.

We sauntered out into the garden. Poor Champ had so thoroughly drenched it that day that the water was still standing in the trenches he had cut, and the first step I took was ankle-deep in mud. After a moment, our eyes grew used to the night light, and we could see the standing water glimmering under the stars.

We stood very still. The breath of the sweet peas was miraculously strong, stealing across to us without a touch of wind. It was like the coming of a pleasant spirit on that windless night.

I said at last: "And what are we to do, Jimmy?"

"You and Mary," he answered me, "should take the box from the bank tomorrow, and take the first train, and go on East."

"And you?"

"I have other things to do here," he answered. "I'll have to stay."

Mary exclaimed softly.

"What is it?" I asked.

"What I think is no use. He wouldn't care to hear me," Mary said bitterly. "But I know why he'll stay."

"And why?" I asked her.

"There are still three of them living," answered Mary. And she added: "He wants to go on tempting Providence, rioting in danger, begging for peril . . . until at last they find a way to reach his life."

"Ah, Mary," he said, with an attempt at lightness, "I haven't any volition about this matter. I can't guide myself. I'm simply in the hands of Horus, you know. Golden Horus . . . Horus of the two horizons. . . ."

"It's very bad taste for you to speak like that," Mary said, her voice trembling.

"It is," Geraldi agreed, filled with compunction. "I'm sorry. I shouldn't have said that. Forgive me, Mary."

She seemed too deeply disturbed to answer him at once, and presently she said: "I'm going back to the house. I'm going to bed. I'm dreadfully tired." And she yawned as she spoke. She said good night to me. Then she went to Jimmy and put her face to him.

Ah, the girls of this century.

He held out his hand and said good night.

"Don't be so difficult, Jimmy," she said. And she drew down his head and kissed him. Then she put something into his hand. "You'd better keep these," she said, and went back to the house. I remember that she stood for a moment with the door open. "How still it is," she said. "One could hear . . . a heartbeat." She went in. The door stuck, and she had to pull it to with a jerk.

"Is she armed?" Jimmy asked gravely.

His question came chiming into my own thought so suddenly that I was startled.

"She always carries a revolver," I told him.

"That Thirty-Two caliber thing never would stop a charging man," observed Jimmy.

"She couldn't manage a full-size Colt," I said.

"I have in mind a little bulldog . . . a brute of a weapon. She needs something that will knock a man down."

"Do you think that she should be specially armed this night?" I asked him.

"Ah, Miss Ingall," he answered me, "this night above all nights. We're living, breathing, thinking danger. There's poison in the air and dynamite under our feet." He said it in his quiet way. So often there is no expression in his voice; only the words in themselves have any significance.

"They *are* around us?" I asked.

"They *are* in the town, beyond any doubt," answered Geraldi.

"And Champ and Mike?"

"I don't know. There's one chance in ten that they are honest," said Jimmy.

It did not occur to me to doubt him. So many times I had found him right—totally right.

"Jimmy," I broke out at him, "for heaven's sake don't stay here in this danger. Come East with us. Escort us safely home. Please say that you'll do it!"

"There's hardly a safer escort than an American railroad," Jimmy said lightly.

"You don't mean that. You really must come with us, Jimmy!" I begged.

He astonished me by answering gravely: "There's nothing that I want to do as much as that."

"Then it's settled," I assured him. "My gracious, what a weight you lift from my mind."

He did not reply at once.

So I urged him: "Please commit yourself, Jimmy!"

"You want me to go?" he asked.

"Haven't I said so?"

"Do you realize," he replied, "that it would mean sitting beside Mary or opposite to her for four long days?"

I wished mightily that I could see his face. The darkness prevented that. And, as I've said before, he can make his voice totally expressionless.

"I *have* thought of that," I said. "But Mary already has been with you longer than that."

"Just now," he replied, "I'm not thinking of Mary."

I couldn't understand what he meant. I grappled with his words; my mind wouldn't believe them.

"Will you say that again?" I asked him.

"Do you think I'm an inhuman machine?" said Jimmy.

"I've been tempted to think that," I admitted frankly. "But I've seen you do so many generous and heroic things, Jimmy, that I have had to revise my ideas. I don't know what to think, really, where you come into the picture."

"At least, don't flatter me," said Jimmy. "Flattery numbs a fellow's brain, and I want to think. And I want to have your help in the thinking."

It was a staggering moment for me. I have a sufficient share of pride and conceit, but that quiet remark I took to be the greatest compliment that I ever have received. It took my breath away. Then I was able to say: "How can my brain help you, Jimmy Geraldi? Certainly you can use it for whatever it's worth."

"I'm in a fog," he told me. "I'm no longer sure of myself. I'm looking through a mist."

"Sharply enough to suspect Mike and poor Champ," I suggested with a little pique.

"Oh, I can see the sun at noon," he replied impolitely. "But my brain is spinning."

"What in the world is the matter?" I asked. "Are you ill?"

"Of course, I am," he replied.

"Of course? I don't understand that."

"You have your share of imagination," he said. "Imagine, then, that you are a man, and that a girl full of beauty, and gentleness, and courage, and grace, makes open love to you whenever you're near her, and kisses you good night, and looks at you with her heart in her eyes . . . well, Miss Ingall, if you were a man, what would you do about it?"

What answer could I make? I could have burst into tears, it wrung my heart so.

But I never guessed that he was actually as human as this. I wanted the whole truth. I said bluntly: "Jimmy, do you love her?"

"I do," he said.

"Oh," I suggested, "of course, any man will have a quiver of the heart when such a lovely thing as Mary loses her head. But I mean . . . do you really love her with . . . well, greatly?"

"I won't talk about it," Jimmy Geraldi said shortly. "Because words are like drinks, you know. One leads to another."

Think of it! That fellow of steel nerves and machine-like mind was afraid to talk of Mary. It struck home to me suddenly that as he loved, perhaps not one man in a million could love.

But I had to think for both of them. I talked. I was simply

thinking aloud: "Here's my dear Mary," I said, "gentle, and true, and good, and beautiful. Here's Mary on the one side. And on the other side there is. . . ."

"A professional criminal," he offered.

"Yes," I said. "But a criminal not for the sake of the money he can make, because that sort of criminal could be reformed. No, you live for the joy of danger, Jimmy. You don't match yourself against the law. You simply live above it . . . outside it."

"I admit it freely," he said, with such humility that I was touched to the quick. But I carried on my thoughts, as I was bound to do for the sake of both of them.

"You have a great and a noble heart, Jimmy," I said. "And you love Mary, and heaven knows that Mary loves you. But I think she could get over that. I would risk it, at least . . . the attempt at a cure. A year or two . . . and then perhaps some other man. I don't know. But I hope. And as for you . . . well, I know that you care for her. But though a Bedouin often loves a woman, he never loves her as much as he loves the desert."

"True . . . true," poor Jimmy said thoughtfully. And how I loved him for his honesty, poor fellow. Then he added, so that I hardly could hear it: "Kismet!"

V
"THE 20TH-CENTURY GIRL"

I went into the house from that garden feeling very dark and miserable and wretched, and the sky turned black, and the stars were mere pinpricks upon the surface of the night.

When one has to say a disagreeable thing to another human, it's a great deal pleasanter if one can feel actually hostile to him. But to speak as I had had to speak to James Geraldi, knowing that I had owed my very life to him, and that he had saved Mary from I can't say what, and that at least he had replaced a stolen fortune in her hands—ah, that was hard, indeed! And hardest of all was to have him agree with me so gently.

When I went into my room, I found Mary dressed, and lying face down on her bed. I guessed that she had been crying, but I didn't trust my voice at that moment. I arranged my writing materials, and I began a letter. I don't know how long I had been at work, when I heard the springs of her bed creak, and she was sitting up.

I steeled myself against a scene of some sort. I guessed, in a way, what was coming. But in the meantime I had recovered a little from the torment I had been in. The writing table was in front of the window, which was open, and through it came a rising breeze that touched my face with its ghostly fingers. Besides, I had been writing, and words are like a current of water—they carry away our old ships of thought and bring the new ones drifting home.

"Aunt Emmy," Mary said, behind me, "you don't need to pretend that you're too busy to think of me."

There was the hateful voice of the 20th-Century girl speaking. I turned a little in my chair.

"You mustn't be rude, Mary," I said to her very sharply.

She stifled a yawn. She was woefully bedraggled. Her eyes were still swollen and red from crying, and her lips looked a little puffed as they do when one has been sobbing. Her hair hung in tatters, so to speak; and she looked, indeed, like nothing at all. And still she was pretty, even then.

"Where does Jimmy sleep?" she asked me.

"Upstairs," I answered. "In the room across from Mike and Champ."

"Is that safe, I wonder?" she asked.

"Safe for whom?"

"Safe for Mike and Champ," she answered. "For just suppose that they were the hired men of Winchelmere. And suppose that they know Jimmy suspects them. And suppose that they try to make a secret attack on him this evening. . . ."

"Well? Well?" I asked.

"He would shoot them to bits, I dare say," Mary said dreamily.

"Mary," I said, striking my hand on the arm of my chair, "do you speak of the killing of two men as though it were the shooting of . . . of a dog?"

She paid no attention to me. Her mind had drifted on to other things.

"What did you think?" she asked me.

"About what?"

"About what he thought."

"I don't know what you're thinking of, Mary," I said. "I

only know that you're making a huge tangle of your words."

"About me?" she asked.

"What about you?"

She stared at me hopelessly. "You know perfectly well. You're just dodging a disagreeable subject," she declared.

I tapped the arm of my chair with dignity and finally hunched my chair about a little as though I would resume the letter. At that, she came to me and sat on the arm of my chair. She began to smooth my hair, and I felt my heart melting, and the pain running back into it.

Poor Mary! Poor Jimmy! And how insoluble that problem seemed.

"Has Jimmy come in?" she asked me.

"No," I said shortly.

After a time, she sighed. "Out there . . . watching over us," Mary whispered.

"The stars, I suppose you mean," I conjectured.

She sighed again. "After I came in, what did you talk about?" she asked.

"About the garden," I lied.

"Did you, really?"

"Naturally. The flowers were at our feet."

"So was I," she said.

"What do you mean?"

"Well, just that, of course. I did as much as I could to introduce myself as a subject."

"You mean by acting so shamelessly, Mary?"

"By kissing him good night?" she asked, still dreamy.

"Extraordinary conduct!" I responded sharply.

She sighed once more. "He only touched my forehead with his lips," she stated.

"Mary," I broke out, "you were properly raised. I don't understand it."

"Don't you?" she said. That was all.

"I want to finish this letter," I told her.

She paid no attention to me again, and there was another breathless silence. I wondered what blow would fall next. My mind whirled.

At last she said: "What is he thinking of now?"

"About getting us safely aboard the train, perhaps."

"And what else?"

"The stars, perhaps."

"And?"

"No doubt they bring faces into his mind. He's still young enough to be sentimental."

"Sentimental my hat!" said Mary roughly.

"I *wish* you'd watch your language, my dear," I said, keeping as stiff as possible. I didn't dare to unbend and become sympathetic.

"What faces?" she broke out.

"He's seen the beauties of a good many lands, no doubt," I said, pretending to yawn.

"Well," she declared thoughtfully, "I'm not so hard on the eyes, when it comes to that. Am I?" she persisted, when I didn't answer.

"You're a strong, vigorous, healthy girl, Mary," I said.

"Look at me," said Mary.

I did—frostily.

"I know I need a cold bath," she said. "But even now I'm not ugly. I know all about myself," Mary said, with terrible self-assurance. "Admit that I'm good to look at?"

"You're a bold, complacent, young . . . ," I began.

"You dear!" Mary exclaimed, beaming at me. "But you do agree? They turn to look when I go by," she went on. "They always have!"

"Who?" I asked her, full of trouble.

"The men, of course," she replied. "But not Jimmy. Not Jimmy . . . never once."

I closed my eyes. I couldn't meet her glance. And in that moment I wondered at him almost more than I ever had wondered before. I mean—his imperturbable calm, which had enabled him to disguise all that he felt from her.

"I thought tonight," she said, "that I would play all my cards in one heap and try to win a trick or two."

"Mary," I said, "are you thinking aloud, or are you really trying to tell me something?" But nothing would put her off the track. She went on: "I made love to him all evening . . . with my eyes, I mean. I wanted him to see that I was simply shuddering for the joy of seeing him again."

"It was perfectly obvious," I couldn't help rejoining.

"And then, when that didn't disturb him, I kissed him good night. Not in a sisterly fashion, either. But loving him. Almost saying so in words. But, do you know? He wasn't a bit bothered. It didn't unbalance him a bit. There wasn't a quiver in his lips when he kissed me. It was heartbreaking, Aunt Emmy. That's why I had to come in here and cry. Heavens, what a sad time I've been having. And how do you explain it, Aunt Emmy?"

"I've never been a man," I said dryly.

"But," said Mary, "it's mysterious. He's not a creature of steel. He's made of flesh and blood. And here am I. Young, pretty to say the least, and pouring myself out at his feet. And yet never the least sign of any feeling from him." She started to her feet. "I don't believe it!" she said fiercely.

"What don't you believe, silly child?" I said.

"It isn't possible!"

"Perhaps," I said, "men don't like to be treated so boldly, Mary. They like to see a girl maintain a little distance. . . ."

"Nonsense," she said. "That's the idea of the novelists of

fifty years ago . . . or less. The hero was always patiently devoted. The girl was always wiping her shoes on him, and he was changing his coat and coming again . . . to take more mud in the face. But it doesn't work out that way. Not a bit! Your chilly girls can stay on their cakes of ice. Men can't be bothered. The world is turning too fast, and Sunday afternoon is not the only time for making love. If you want a man to be good to you, you have to be good to him. I've always done that. It's never failed to. . . ."

"Mary!" I gasped.

"Oh, I don't mean that I've had to kiss them good night," she answered carelessly. "But just to be jolly, and kind, and glad to see them. That was enough. Smiling in a particular way does a girl a tremendous lot of good with a young man."

"Heavens, Mary!" I said. "Do you mean to say that you have been living through one continual procession of . . . of . . . ?" Modesty would not let me find a word.

"Flirtations?" suggested Mary. "That's an old-fashioned word. Nearnesses, you might say. That's more like it. You meet some interesting young fellow with a head on his shoulders and a certain something about him, and a delicious chill crawls up your spine. . . ."

"Mary," I snapped, "I think you had better go to bed."

"I couldn't sleep," she said. "I haven't quite talked myself out."

"I don't care to listen any longer," I told her.

"But they all were easily handled," declared Mary. "I've had a lot of friends. And then I met Jimmy. And . . . I went crash!"

I drew a great breath. "I don't think that this talk is leading you anywhere," I suggested to her.

"Don't you see?" Mary insisted. "Of course, he may not love me as I love him, but he has to think more of me than he pretends. He acts as though I were just another man. Well, that won't do. I'm not a man. Not by a million miles. And he *does* like me. And he doesn't show it. And that's the proof that he's pretending. And if he's pretending a little bit, he may be just as much in love with me as I am with him."

So, you see, suddenly, with a terrible logic, she had arrived at the truth, and left me unable to say a single word.

But she went on in enthusiasm: "And this very minute he may be standing out there under the stars just as empty and wretched and sad-hearted as I am. And I'll wager that that is what he *is* doing. And I'm going out to find him, and to ask him if I'm not right." She whirled for the door.

I could not stir. I only cried: "Mary!"

She paused and turned slowly toward me. "I suppose you're right!" she concluded. "I'll have to wait till to-morrow."

VI
"THE OPENING DOOR"

I sat up late that night, finishing that letter, but there was a great deal to happen before the morning came. Oh, I wondered when this madness will end, and when I could bring poor Mary back to safe Boston streets and Boston houses, where things are fixed and simple, and everything is not adrift and aflame.

The night turned chilly. The last heat of the day was gone. The wind whistled a little more sharply. My fingers grew cramped around the pen before I finished. And then I went to bed and lay shivering for a while. How hard it is to get to sleep when one's feet are cold, and one's legs almost to the knees. That was the way with me, and, if it had not been for that wakefulness of mine, heaven alone can tell what might have happened during that dreadful night.

The wind increased a good deal in force. It began to whistle through the window with such strength that finally I got up and closed the window, or, rather, tried to. It stuck fast, halfway down. I leaned out to make sure what was holding it, and, as I did so, I saw a faint smudge of light farther up the face of the house. It came from the little imitation balcony that ran beneath the window of Jimmy Geraldi's room, and it was no stronger, say, than a tenth of the power of a lighted match. But how odd that it should be there.

A moment later, I could make out that fumes were rising

in a thin, white breath above it. When I was sure of that, I was worried, of course. Something was on fire. But how could a mere spark like that persist?

Then, it seemed to me, a faint breath of sweetness came to me. Not the sweetness of the garden flowers, but a fragrance yet rarer and more delicate—which instantly made my heart throb and my brain spin. And there was a dreadful sense of danger that instantly possessed me. Something was wrong!

I stood back from the window and wondered what I should do. The obvious thing was to go at once and waken Jimmy, and then tell him that there was something wrong outside his window.

But, first, I borrowed Mary's revolver, and then opened the door into the hall. The wind whistled around me. I had to press hard to close the door behind me, and there I stood in the intense darkness that kept floating up blacker and blacker before my eyes, like a hand about to be pressed over them.

I crossed the living room, moving by inches. I found the stairs and went up them, thanking heaven that they made no creaking.

Why didn't I make an outcry? Why didn't I rouse Mike and Champ and try to get their help in this time of terror? Why didn't I call out to the keen ears of Jimmy himself? I don't know. Perhaps because I'm rather proud of the strength of my nerves. I like to be referred to as a woman without fear, although, possibly, I don't deserve any such name. But, at least, I thank goodness that I made no outcry. Devoutly I do so, and you'll soon learn why.

Halfway up the stairs, I thought I heard, distinctly, the sound of a lock clicking. I stood still and listened. There was not another sound. Not a whisper. No creaking of a foot on the boards of a floor. What had made that distinct, metallic sound, then?

I reached the hall above. I fumbled, and found the door of Jimmy's room. And I had a frantic impulse to wrench it open and then to leap inside. For it seemed to me that dim shadows were speeding up the stairs behind me, and then that they were crouching to leap at me. Nightmare emotions, of course. I've never been more frightened, and never with less actual reason. Never shall I cease to believe in mysteriously forewarning instincts, after that experience.

When I found that door, instead of jerking it open, I turned the knob softly, softly. The door came open just a fraction of an inch—an inch—a breath of thin sweetness poured out on me, and, as I breathed of it, again my heart raced, and my brain spun. And then I realized, clearly, swiftly, what had happened. That dim light outside the room of Jimmy Geraldi was burning some peculiar and deadly poison, and the gas of it was what I had smelled as I leaned from the window of my room.

I moved quickly enough, then. I swept the door open and left it standing, so that the fumes might blow through. I ran to the window and leaned over the burning thing—it glowed like a dim phosphorus. The fumes of it made my brain reel. I dashed it from the balcony to the ground, and the pure air blew kindly into my face.

Then Jimmy. He lay on his side in his bed. I touched him. To touch him, asleep, would have been like touching a wildcat, ordinarily, but it was not that now. He lay like a log. I laid my hand on his face. It was wet and cold! What dreadful thoughts rushed over me. Jimmy dead and gone. Mary alone with me in that house. And Winchelmere waiting to strike at us any moment.

But Jimmy *could* not be gone. The rushing current of the air had swept the room clean of the poisonous gas now. I ran to the door and closed it. Then I hurried back to Jimmy.

Using all my strength, I tugged him out of the bed. The clothes slid with him. He's not a bulky man. I was able to drag him to the window. There I raised him up and sat down behind him, bracing him so that the wind would blow in his face. Holding him like that, I fumbled for his heart. I could not be sure. It was the faintest tremor, perhaps my own pulse in my fingertips? No . . . then I was sure of it, and in a moment it seemed to be beating strongly.

I looked wildly behind me, feeling that I should have run home the bolt in the door, but I would not leave Geraldi now. Besides, I had the gun. And every moment Geraldi was recovering. Presently he sighed. To me, the most heaven-sent sound that ever I had heard!

Almost immediately after that he stirred, writhed, and then got up to his knees. I don't know where he got them, but in either of his hands I saw the long, cold glimmer of a revolver. He was armed. We already were nearly safe.

"Who's there?" he muttered hoarsely.

"It's I. Emily Ingall." I had to repeat it two or three times.

He dragged himself to his feet. He staggered, and braced his legs wide apart.

"Emily Ingall. Emily Ingall," he repeated it two or three times. And then he seemed to understand. He drew a great, gasping breath. "And Mary? Mary?"

"I don't know," I said to him.

"You don't know?"

"No."

He started for the door unsteadily. But in a moment the movement seemed to bring him back to himself. He was his old swiftly gliding self when he reached the door. He opened it and was gone through it.

And there sat I, alone. I could not move from the floor. I had begun to shake violently. My face was cold.

Geraldi was gone from me—Mary was in the room downstairs—and I, sitting alone in the room beneath the window, unable to move from terror, waited for I don't know what.

And now, slowly, silently, I saw the door beginning to open.

VII
"DEATH AT THE DOOR"

To me, the opening of that door was like the yawning of a cannon's mouth. I cowered closer against the wall. I managed to drag the revolver up and steady it across my knees to cover the growing gap of darkness.

I thought, at first, that it was Geraldi, standing in the hall as one will often do, listening to something, gradually pressing the door wide. But this movement was different. It was not like the caution of an absent-minded man. It was rather the caution of a man who has a dangerous motive. I gripped the revolver with all my might. The roughening of its handle pressed into the heel of my palm, and comforted me, and gave me a greater feeling of strength.

I don't know what had unnerved me so totally. I've had my share of dangers to face, and I believe that I've managed to play my part fairly well. But this was very different. I think it may have been the dreadful sight of Jimmy Geraldi lying weak, helpless, at the very door of death. It was inconceivable to me. Anyone else could be overcome by poisonous fumes, but not Jimmy!

That door swung gradually wide. I thought that I made out a shadowy form on the threshold, but then the door was brought to, and this time with enough violence and speed to send a faint whisper through the room.

The wind, which had been whistling so strongly, had fallen away as though ordered to stop. Now, I don't think there was a stir in the air. But what was at the door? Who had opened it? And did he stand now outside or inside? And, if inside, could he not see me, even in the dimness of the starlight that streamed through the window?

Once more the door opened with a whisper, and a shaft of light, hardly bigger than a needle, stabbed into the room, and settled fairly on my face. I set my teeth and prepared to fire at that spot of light.

"Are you here?" asked the voice of Geraldi.

I leaped up to my feet, with my courage restored at one stroke. Geraldi back—his voice—safety.

"Thank heaven, Jimmy," I whispered. "Is there anyone else in the room?"

The needle of light had flashed out. Now it came on again and traced a stroke around the room and up and down, almost swifter than I could follow with my eye.

"There's no one here," Geraldi assured me. "Why did you ask that?"

"Because, that door opened and closed in a very stealthy manner. I've been frightened to death since you left. . . ."

"Poor Aunt Emmy," he said.

I fumbled and found him in the dark and gave his arm one squeeze.

"Are you all right, Jimmy?" I panted.

"I'm almost all right. I will be in another moment," he said. "Mary is sound asleep," he added.

"What happened?" I asked.

He did not whisper the answer. His rage seemed to master even him for a moment, and he muttered: "I've played the game as squarely as any man could ask. And in return . . . they've tried this. Poison. Poison by night!"

My fingers still touched his arm, and I felt a shudder go through him. It went through me, too. I suddenly had no more fears for any of us. I simply pitied those men who had done this dastardly thing to Geraldi. What would he do to them?

"We'll see if your friends, Champ and Mike, are in," he said. He crossed the hall and tried the door. It was locked. Then he took something from his pocket and began to work, bending over the lock. Once I thought that I heard the scratching of metal against metal, but it was so faint a sound that I could not be sure. All I know is that the unlocked door at last opened under his hand, and he sent the thin ray of his electric lantern into their room.

With a magic touch, he ran that pencil of light across the upturned face of Champ, who lay on his back, his arms thrown out crosswise and his mouth wide open in sleep. Mike, on the farther side of the room, was doubled up on his side. The window was only open an inch, as though the pair of them got enough open air on the range and were unwilling to trust to the night damp when they slept in a house. There was a distinct smell of stale tobacco smoke that had not yet drifted out through that meager crack beneath the window.

Geraldi flashed the torch on to its full power, which was enough to make Champ sit straight up in bed, blinking, gaping.

"It ain't five, is it?" asked Champ.

He must have thought that he was back on the range, and the bunkhouse turning out for the day's work.

"Stick your hands over your head," Jimmy ordered. "You, Mike, sit up and take notice."

He did not speak very loudly, but Mike groaned, and I saw the hands of Champ raised unquestioningly. I didn't wonder that that voice of Jimmy's cut through sleep and a sleep-numbed mind. There was an undertone of pure devilishness in it.

"It's Mister Winslow, ain't it?" said Mike.

"Put up your hands," Jimmy repeated.

Mike and Champ raised them. They looked half foolish and half terrified.

"Hold this light," Geraldi said to me.

I took it, and he directed me to keep it focused on the chair between the beds. In that way, there was a certain amount of illumination for the figures on either side of the room. I began to feel ashamed.

"Don't go too far. Be sure," I warned Jimmy.

He jerked the blanket from Mike. Mike was fully dressed. "Is that the way you turn in?" Jimmy asked.

"When I'm plumb fagged . . . ," began Mike.

"You lie!" Geraldi snapped.

I started. It was like a whip stroke. Mike set his teeth and began to watch through narrowed eyes.

"Get out of bed, both of you, and put your faces against the wall," Jimmy commanded. "Mind you, I'm waiting and hungering for a chance to throw a handful of lead into you two."

They got out of bed—Mike clothed except for boots; Champ in a nightgown that looked ridiculous on him.

They stood obediently against the wall, Champ shivering a little in the cold.

"Keep that light on them," Jimmy said to me. "I'll be busy."

He was busy at once. There was a rolled pack under either bed, and these packs he spilled open and went like lightning through the contents. Suddenly he stopped and stood up straight. "The dope is still in my brain," he said. "I'll never find it here." He stood up and barked: "Champ, turn around and face me!"

Champ turned. His face was fairly glowing. "You're lower'n a damned snake," he said, "to turn me out like this. And I dunno that I could've expected you'd stand by and see this thing done, Miss Ingall," he declared to me. "I'm gonna pack and leave today, ma'am."

"Another word," Geraldi stated with a really terrible ferocity, "and I'll put a bullet through your throat. Stand still, and shut up. Put out your hands."

Champ dropped his hands to his sides. "Look here," he said, "if you've got something ag'in' me, step outside, and we'll have it out, but for bullying me behind a gun . . . why, to hell with your gun, and to hell with you, too! I'll make you eat that Colt in another minute and. . . ."

I actually thought he would throw himself at Jimmy. And from the corner of my eye I saw Mike tightening himself, as though ready to whirl away from the wall and join in the attack.

"Jimmy, Jimmy," I muttered. "Be careful."

"I want them to try me," Geraldi said. "I yearn for them to tackle me, Aunt Emmy. You, Champ," he added, "put out your hands!"

Now, how he looked when he said this, I don't know, but I do know that Champ lost his courage in an instant and became like a child before its schoolmaster. He stood gaping, wondering, quiet, while Jimmy examined his hands with the most scrupulous interest.

"Go back and face the wall again," he said. "You, Mike, step out here and let me see your hands."

Champ obeyed; so did Mike. I wondered what on earth it was all about.

Over the hands of Mike, Jimmy bent. Then he straightened with a start, took a knife from his pocket, and opened a blade. He drew an envelope from his pocket and laid it on the table. Then he made Mike lay the tips of the fingers of his right hand on the middle of the paper. After that, he began to scrape around the nails with the point of the knife.

"Go back to face the wall," he said.

"All right," said Mike, and half turned.

But not to go to the wall again and stand beside Champ. Instead, he flung himself at Geraldi before I could cry out the slightest warning—flung himself sidewise, so that I had just a glimpse of a savagely tense face. I was watching with my whole soul, of course. And still I don't know what happened, except that Mike seemed to rush up into the air, was suddenly floundering over Jimmy's shoulder, and then went crashing to the floor.

Champ, as he heard the disturbance, came with a lurching charge, his balled fists ready. Instinctively I raised the little .32, but Jimmy knocked the barrel of the gun up with his left hand. With his right, he struck Champ in the face, and that big, strong man dropped forward and spilled at the feet of Jimmy as loose as a half-filled sack.

Mike began to groan and twist on the floor. Then he pushed himself up on his hands, and at last climbed to his knees. His nostrils were expanded; his face was simply horrible as he stared up to Geraldi.

"Take this box of matches. Light that envelope," Jimmy said to me, "and inhale the fumes."

VIII
"QUEER PORTS"

Then, for the first time, the possible meaning of all this dawned on me. My hand trembled a little, but I lighted the envelope, and, as the flame rose, there was no longer the slightest doubt. That same faint, delicious fragrance ran through the room, and the heady sense of it made the brain sicken.

The fire ate up the paper. I had to drop it. It fluttered to the floor, turned to a thin, white ash, and then rose and fluttered like a ghost in the wind, and all this time no one had spoken. Champ had struggled to his feet and stood swaying, scowling at Jimmy. Mike stood with his arms folded, leaning against the wall, his eyes on the floor.

"Champ," Jimmy said suddenly. "Do you know my name?"

"I know you, Winslow," Champ responded. "You carry a punch with you. I admit that free and easy. But we're gonna meet again. I'm gonna look for a chance to. . . ."

"My name's Geraldi," said Jimmy.

It wilted poor Champ as hot vinegar wilts lettuce. "Geraldi! Hot fire and little Injuns," murmured Champ.

"Pull a blanket around you and get over there out of the way," said Jimmy. "I don't think that you've had a hand in this."

"In what?" Champ asked. He was vastly subdued. There

had been sufficient magic in that name to quite unman him.

"Poison is a size or two outside your methods, Champ," Jimmy replied.

"If I know what you're talkin' about, Geraldi," Champ said, "I'll eat a rope."

"Go sit down," Jimmy recommended, not unkindly.

Champ withdrew. He made no effort to interfere, after that. He merely sat with a blanket huddled around him and watched what followed. It was apparent that he would have raised a hand against a flaming thunderbolt as soon as he would have raised a hand against Geraldi.

And I was not surprised. I had seen those two powerful men turned into battered, helpless things by the mere touch of Geraldi. And yet, as I've said, Jimmy is not a big man. There is nothing bulky about him.

"And now you," Jimmy said to the other.

Mike shrugged his shoulders. He would not look up.

"You've been at sea?" said Jimmy.

"Aye, sir."

"You've touched at Bombay?"

Suddenly Mike looked up. His face was losing its color; his eyes seemed to be sinking into his head. He did not answer this question.

"You've seen them smoke opium," Geraldi posed. "And beyond that, you've seen them use datura?"

Mike moistened his white lips with the tip of his tongue. I've never seen such wretched guilt in the face of any man. I suffered for him.

"And you've watched them handle other poisons there?" asked Jimmy.

There was silence again.

"Answer!"

"I've finished talkin'," said Mike.

"Walk out that door ahead of me," Jimmy hissed in a terrible, quiet voice.

"What for?" groaned Mike.

"I'll tell you when we're outside."

Mike suddenly covered his face with his hands. "Will you send Miss Ingall away, sir?" he said.

"She'll stay here. I need a witness."

"Lord help me, sir," said Mike. He was shaking. It seemed as though his limbs were giving way.

"Sit down on the bed," directed Jimmy.

Mike sat down.

Then Champ said suddenly: "Mike, old feller, I dunno what sort of weather you're makin' of it. But luff, man, luff, and shake the squall out of you. Don't funk it!"

Mike shook his head.

"Show me the price," Jimmy stated.

Mike put his hand inside his coat and drew out a wallet. There was no danger of his drawing a weapon, instead. He was utterly unmanned and subdued now. He unfolded the wallet and took out a sheaf of bills. He counted ten one-hundred-dollar bills in a heap and held them out.

Champ started up. He looked at that money as though he were looking at a snake grasped in the hand of his friend.

"Mike, Mike!" he groaned. "How'd you come by that?"

"Put it back," Jimmy snapped harshly. "Do I want it?"

Mike let the notes shower to the floor and then dropped his face in his hands. I could see that he was swaying a little. I've never felt such horror and such pity for any human creature as I felt for him at that moment.

"It's a long trail, this life of ours," Geraldi said suddenly, and his voice had altered and grown wonderfully gentle. "It takes us to queer ports, and we pick up queer ideas. How long ago did you go wrong, Mike?"

Slowly Mike lifted his face from his horny hands; there was a convulsion of his lips, but no sound came.

"I've knowed him man and boy!" Champ cried, his voice filled with emotion. "I've never knowed a better shipmate, or a truer chum, or a straighter pal! Geraldi, I'd lay down my life for him. He's offered his for me. We been through torture and back. He's white!"

"Thank you," Geraldi said to Champ. "I'm glad to hear you say that. Mike," he addressed the other.

Mike shuddered. He had clutched his face with his hands again.

"I think you'd better go out, Aunt Emmy," Geraldi suggested. "You'd better go downstairs and stay with Mary." Then he added with a return of that frightful, purring malevolence in his voice: "It would have been her turn next, Mike? Would it have been her turn?"

"Who?" Mike asked, startled even out of his misery, his shame, his anguish of soul.

"The girl's turn."

"No, no!" cried Mike. "Lord help me if I'm lyin'. It was you. It was only you!"

I went out, giving Jimmy the light.

But to my surprise, as I slowly closed the door on that strange scene, Geraldi snapped out the light and left the room in total darkness.

I heard his voice say softly: "I believe you, Mike. And I believe that a thousand dollars is a lot of money."

"May I burn," Mike said with savage sorrow, "for ever lookin' it in the face."

I hurried down the stairs to the room where Mary still was sleeping, and I was a little irritated that she should be able to sleep through such a time as this when, as it seemed to me, all sorts of electric impulses must have been jumping through the air. But there she was.

I decided that I would lie down for a few moments to rest until Jimmy should call me. But, to my astonishment, when a tap came at the door, it waked me out of a sound sleep.

I got up and went to the door and called softly through it: "Who is there?"

"It's Jimmy," was the answer.

I opened the door.

"Is Mary still asleep?"

"Yes."

"Then will you step out into the hall?"

I went out; he closed the door behind me and led me into the little living room, where I found Champ and Mike. Mike sat very much as I had last seen him, his head bowed and his eyes fixed on the floor. Behind him stood Champ, his hands folded on the back of Mike's chair, and his whole attitude that of a protector.

"We've talked this whole thing over with a good deal of care," Jimmy began. "It's lucky that Mary Ingall has slept through the whole affair, and so she knows nothing about what has happened tonight. And I've been telling Mike that you, Aunt Emmy, are one of those extraordinary women who actually can keep a secret."

I saw what was wanted, of course, in a moment, and I said: "Of course, I can. To the end of my life."

Jimmy went on: "Now, Mary Ingall knows nothing. Miss Ingall, here with us, promises to forget everything. So far, so good. Now, Aunt Emmy, we come to another point. We've tried Mike and found him failing. Would you be willing to try him again?"

I looked wildly at Jimmy, and he nodded almost imperceptibly.

"Yes," I said in rather a shaken voice, I fear. "Yes . . . of course. If you wish to trust him, Jimmy."

"I don't want to force anything on you," Jimmy said, looking coldly at me.

I saw that I should have to do something to make up for my own lukewarmness, and so I marched straight up to Mike and held out my hand.

"For my part," I said, "I've believed in you from the very first, and I knew that Jimmy Geraldi would come to some reasonable explanation of what you seemed to have been doing this evening."

Mike heaved himself out of his chair when I came close to him. He took my hand and gripped it in his palm—rough as chapped leather—and he looked at me very wildly out of his hollow, bright eyes.

"Now you fellows had better turn in again," said Jimmy.

"I'll . . . I'll take a look around," Mike said, and stalked out through the front door.

Champ went after him, paused at the door as though about to speak, but, instead of speaking, he simply gave to Jimmy a glance of gladness and of gratitude that went to my heart. Then he disappeared after his friend.

IX
"THE POISON WORKS"

Jimmy dropped into a chair near the little fireplace so that just above his head was the clock, which was ticking out the seconds with ridiculous solemnity and slowness. Jimmy was greatly changed. He looked pale, his face was drawn, and his lips trembled a little as though from nervousness or from exhaustion.

"Excuse me for sitting down before you," said Jimmy.

I sat down on the edge of another chair and looked straight at him. "You're about finished, Jimmy," I said.

His face twisted with the uttermost effort into something akin to a smile. "I'm about finished," he agreed.

I made no comment. There was none to make. Only—it sent a chill to my heart, of course.

"And what happened?" I asked him.

"I fried him," said Geraldi. "I toasted him for half an hour. That was all." He spoke of it as of something that had happened long ago—something that he was trying to remember and found it difficult to bring his mind to. He went on, in much the same manner, abstracted, and growing constantly a little paler than before, as it seemed to me. "I thought at first of sending for the sheriff . . . or for neighbors . . . but then I saw that that was all no good," Jimmy explained.

"And why?"

"Because no matter if we got one honest man or two, the

rest would be sure to be the agents of the gang. They've got the neighborhood peppered now, and they're going to make their great trial this very night."

I caught my breath.

He continued with haste, speaking rapidly, but so faintly that I had to lean forward to catch what he was saying. I wondered at him. There did not seem to be any particular need for great secrecy on this occasion. I saw no reason why he should choose little more than to whisper to me. But then I saw that he was speaking softly because he hardly had the strength to do more. He was failing rapidly, before my very eyes, and that while the house, as he himself had pointed out, was surrounded by the most terrible and immediate danger.

Can you imagine being on a sailing ship in the middle of a most terrible storm, working through a narrow passage, with great rocks, say, reaching for you out of the water, and then noticing that the captain—the only one capable of holding the helm—was staggering and drooping at the wheel? But even that could give no idea of what I felt at that moment.

"I saw," Jimmy continued, "that we would have to make our trial with the force in the house. And what force is that? You . . . Mary . . . myself . . . Champ. But if Mike went, Champ would be sure to go with him. That narrowed the garrison down to you, Mary, and me. But even that had to be contracted still more. I knew that I couldn't last out many more minutes. It really left you and Mary alone, in case I sent Mike away, and therefore. . . ."

I could stand it no longer. I started up out of my chair and cried out to him, keeping my voice as soft as I could: "Jimmy, you're ill . . . you're dreadfully ill . . . and you sit there talking . . . no, no! What can I do for you? Something must be done."

"Are you going to disappoint me?" Jimmy asked. "Are you

going to turn out hysterical, like the rest of the ladies when the great pinch comes?"

He could not have struck me in a tenderer place. There my pride was greatest. If I can't have the charm and the grace of a great many women, I've tried to console myself that I have some of the firmness of a man. Well, I stiffened and prepared to endure anything rather than be accused of feminine weakness.

"I saw," Jimmy went on, "that I would have to try to lean on a broken reed that might snap and drive into my hand . . . and be the death of me, in short. The broken reed is Mike, of course. As I made him out, he's a fellow who has mostly gone straight. But he's dropped from grace two or three times, say, and, when he dropped, he fell clear down into the bottom most pit. Mike, Aunt Emmy, is a poisoner."

I nodded, and put my hand behind me to grip the back of the chair and so make myself more perfectly steady.

"Even Champ never guessed the secret sins of Mike, do you see? But Winchelmere has an omniscient eye, and it appears that he was once in India and knew just how Mike had been involved in an important and terrible crime there. When he got in touch with Mike on the range ten days ago, he determined to use his man. You can see that his lordship is a deep-minded fellow. He knew that you and Mary would be likely to look about for protection while I was away from you. And here were two formidable and yet honest-looking men. He half bribed and half threatened Mike to make him come in to San Felice and plant himself wherever he best could, so as to come to your attention if you should want a hired protector. And, of course, the obvious course was the one that Mike followed. He went to the employment agency and hung about there, refusing the jobs that came his way, on one pretext or another, and waiting for the time when he might have a chance at you. Of course, at last you came, and then he was ready with his proffer. He's a handy man. Most sailors are. But Mike, being a criminal, has an extra touch of brains. Therefore, he was able to qualify as a cook."

While Geraldi was talking, it seemed to me that he was slipping lower and lower in the chair, and his shoulders appeared to bow forward, and his chest to grow more hollow. His color grew more and more waxen. At last I could not stand it any longer, and, in spite of the last rebuff I'd received, I exclaimed: "Jimmy, you are dying as you sit there!"

He held up his hand, and I was silenced—not by the gesture so much as by the hand itself, for it was shaking violently, shaking like a leaf in the wind. And this was the hand of Geraldi—the iron hand of Geraldi.

"Bad material as Mike was," Jimmy said, "I saw that I had to try to use him again. So I've done my best to make a new man of him. I didn't have many minutes. In those minutes, as I said, I fried him over a very hot fire, and he's changed, I believe. I've offered to forget the past. You made a grand performance here, a moment ago. He sees that we're in his hands. He knows that I'm at the end of my rope. And I think that, taking everything together, he may stand by the guns and fight like a man." He stopped. "I'll have to ask you for a glass of water," Jimmy muttered.

I flew to get it. When I came back, he tried to take it. It shuddered in his hand. I had to hold it for him and put my hand behind his head. His teeth rattled violently against the rim of the glass, but he managed to drink half the water by a great effort.

"That will do," he said.

I put the glass back on the table. His face was shining with moisture; his lips were twisting in agony; and such eyes can only have looked out of fire.

"I want to obey you like a soldier, Jimmy," I told him. "But for pity's sake let me do something more for you."

He paid no attention to that appeal of mine. He went right on talking in that hurried, faint, terrible voice. "Mike is ready, he says, to do his utmost, and die for us if need be. Champ is in a state of great emotion. Champ most certainly *will* die for us, if he gets half a chance. He's full of battle and self-sacrifice. Champ is a heart of gold!"

He paused and closed his eyes. I thought that it was death, but after a moment the eyelids fluttered and those tortured eyes were looking out at me again.

"Now for the rest of it," he said. "Listen closely. I haven't much time, but I must explain fully. Winchelmere, Seyf Kalam, and Edgar Asprey are somewhere near us. Outside the house as yet, I hope and trust. With them, doubtless, are others. I can't tell about that. In a case of this importance, they may not wish to leave any of the work in less expert hands than their own." He smiled faintly. "Winchelmere has forgotten about the three emeralds . . . and the yellow diamond . . . and the golden box of Horus. You must understand that there were six of them in the beginning. Three of them are now dead. Two of them I killed with my own hand. Another, I was the means of bringing to his death. On Asprey I've put a mark that will last him the rest of his life." A glint of grim satisfaction appeared in his face as he said this.

Then he continued, hurrying more than before, and in a fainter voice: "They've been touched with superstition about this business, Aunt Emmy. They feel that the golden box of Horus is nothing at all compared with me. They want my life, and my life they'll have at the risk of all their own. Now, there's not one of the three that isn't a dangerous fellow. Seyf Kalam is as bad a character as the whole Orient can furnish. Edgar Asprey is a sneak and a scoundrel, but he's also a consummate fighter who understands all that can be known about guns. And as for Winchelmere . . . he is worthy to stand to me by himself." He smiled in faint apology for this egoistical remark. Then he added: "They are going to make a desperate and united effort to get at me in this house before the morning. They hoped, in the first place, to numb my brain with the drug. Or, perhaps, to poison me. And perhaps they've succeeded. I don't know. The poison in this case works in two ways. In the first place, it acts as an opiate and steals away the consciousness. In the second place it acts more slowly as a nerve poison. I never should have wakened out of that sleep I was in if it had not been for you. And . . . I haven't time to thank you."

Even then he could smile at the irony of the event.

"Once with a clear head I was able to act for a little time, as you saw. I was practically myself again. But now I'm being eaten up. The fire has been touched to me, and I'm burning. But before the end, I want to see Mary. Will you waken her and bring her here?"

X

"MIKE GOES OUT"

I fled without a word.

Mary lay face downward, drugged with exhaustion. But when I whispered—"Jimmy wants you."—she was awake and sitting up instantly. She had not taken off her clothes.

I caught her by the arms and said rapidly: "Jimmy is ill."

"Dead!" she gasped, her imagination leaping to the worst at once.

"No, no," I assured her, although I felt that it was death, indeed. "But he's very ill. Winchelmere has managed to use some hideous drug on him. He's growing very weak. He wants you . . . in the living room. . . ."

She was up and past me before I had finished. By the time I reached the room she was on her knees before his chair, holding his hands pressed against her cheeks; and he leaned above her, wavering a little from side to side, his tormented eyes dwelling on her face, consuming it, as a man at the stake might look at distant mountains of snow, or at his own vision of heaven.

He was saying to her: "I want to prepare you. I am going to faint. Blackness is piling up in my brain like clouds on the edge of the sky. When I faint, I may die. But death should come inside the first half hour. After that, if there is the least flicker of life in me, I should recover. I mean to say, I shall have one chance in three of recovering. You will have to defend yourselves. Trust Mike and Champ absolutely, and try to send some sort of a signal to the nearest houses. It might be that you could communicate with them . . . but this place is unluckily hedged in with trees and it's low." He paused.

Mary did not stir or speak.

"If I am about to die," Jimmy continued, "I think I should say one thing before the end. I am a bad fellow, Mary. I've gone the rounds of the world doing harm, breaking laws like glass windows, and suiting my own pleasure. I've sinned and sinned again, Mary. But one good and pure thing has come into my life, and that is my love of you. If I live, I shall live for you . . . if I die . . . heaven bless you."

And then, as though his failing brain had endured just long enough to say what was necessary to him, he collapsed, pitching forward into the arms of Mary.

Between us we managed to carry him into our room and stretch him on Mary's bed. She pressed her ear against his heart, while I opened the window to the full, and brought cold water, and arranged his feet higher than his head. Then I found my own pocket-flask of brandy.

She was beating out the count of his heart. It grew feeble and more feeble every moment—more fluttering—more horribly running and uncertain, like a watch that has been dropped and runs a few hysterical seconds before it stops altogether.

She sat up, at last. "I can't hear it any longer," she said quietly.

Let these democrats say what they will, blood tells—how vastly it tells. She was as steady as rock. There was not a tremor in her when she took the flask from me.

A miracle happened, then. A small miracle, perhaps, but

one that impressed me enormously. When I tried to open his mouth so that we could pour down the brandy, his teeth were rigidly locked. But the instant that Mary tried, she opened his mouth without the slightest trouble, and all the stiff tension relaxed in an instant. She gave him a tablespoon or so of the liquor. I listened for the heart, then, in my turn, while Mary laid towels dipped in cold water on his forehead and face.

And it seemed to me that I could hear the very end of the heart work—the faintest sound, not of beating, but of the fluttering valves. I tried to count the sound. It whirred off into a couple of hundred pulsations a minute. Not real pulsations. Mere sudden, semi-contractions.

Then I heard the front door open softly.

"You go to them," Mary advised. "I think I can do more, here."

There was a lamp burning in the room, with the flame turned down very low, and by that light I could see her face. She was actually more beautiful than ever before, and a strange sort of holy contentment appeared in her eyes, like the light that Da Vinci put in the eyes of a Madonna. And there was her lover dying—or dead.

But it seemed to me, in the hard depths of my old maid's heart, that I could understand what had happened to Mary. And it seemed to me, also, that I actually could understand love itself, which has nothing to do with the flesh at all, but is simply the intermingling of two spirits—a sort of mutual adoration—an opening of gates—a power like spiritual gravitation affecting only two objects in all the world.

I left the room, knowing that, if Geraldi died, our Mary would never marry. And if he lived—she would become the wife of a professional criminal, in due course. Tremendously depressing to me, that thought should have been. But I felt my heart lifted by the idea, for it seemed to me then that the greatest hero in all this world of ours was that same James Geraldi, criminal, and gentleman.

Outside in the hall I found Champ and Mike standing. They were loaded with weapons. Each of them was weighted down with a cartridge belt, and each carried a pair of heavy Colts in hip holsters.

Champ had under his arm a shotgun with short barrels. Sawed-off shotguns, they call them out here, I believe. Their disadvantage is that they are very short in range and quite useless beyond a definite number of paces. But their advantage is that they throw a double handful of shot and that one does not have to be a good marksman in order to strike a target with one of them. Just as the hose throws a spray of water, so a sawed-off shotgun sluices down a considerable space with pellets of lead. At close range, no weapon in the West is so respected, partly because it cannot very well miss; and partly because, if an object is in range, it is blown almost to bits. Even Western desperadoes don't like to die in such a fashion.

That was the equipment of Champ. Mike carried a rifle under his arm—the usual Winchester. And he handled it with a certain air of experience which can't very well be described but which always is apparent in an old hunter.

They were waiting to report, obviously.

When I came out, it was Champ who spoke. "There's nobody right up close to the house," he said, "but I got an idea that they're layin' off in the distance, waiting to dab a rope of lead onto the first gent that tries to leave the place. But Mike, here, he's got a suggestion to make."

I turned to Mike. He flushed, and his eyes went down to the floor and then up to the ceiling in a way I didn't like.

At length he said huskily: "It was sort of arranged that, when everything was fixed and ready, I was to make a signal, and then they was to start for the house. Well . . . suppose I give the signal, and then, when they come, we stand ready for 'em . . . ?" He paused.

"What do you think of that?" I asked Champ.

"I ain't thinkin'," said Champ. "But I'm follering orders, no matter which way they come."

I replied, of course, in the only possible way. But was it the only possible way? Weren't those fellows on the outside more snakes than men? However, I couldn't allow such a mantrap to be set—treasonably set, you know.

I said: "I don't think that either of you really like this trick that you've proposed. But at least, I can't have it."

"You might," said Mike, "ask Mister Geraldi whether he'll have it or not."

"He *won't* have it," Champ interrupted. "Not the kind of a man that he showed himself to be tonight. He wouldn't have you chuck your honor away, Mike."

"My honor," echoed Mike softly, bitterly.

"At any rate," I said, "James Geraldi can't give you your answer. You'll see why for yourselves."

I took them to the bedroom, and opened the door, and we all three looked in on that dull pool of lamplight which enclosed the white, still face of Jimmy, and Mary on her knees beside the bed, with one hand pressed under his shoulders. She heard us and turned her face toward us. There was the beauty of motherhood in her look, and the pain of it.

I closed the door again.

"My honor," said Mike again, whispering to himself.

We all went back into the living room.

"He's dead," Champ mumbled.

"Not yet," I answered, but I hardly knew whether or not I was right.

"Now," said Champ, "it's hard, but plain. Before the

pinch comes, one of us has got to get out of this here house and get to a place for help. It ain't far to go, either. Only. . . ." He paused. "We'll draw straws," he proposed.

To this Mike answered, out of a depth of thought: "Him and her . . . that was one of the things that I didn't even think about. Him and her. . . ." He held out his hand to Champ. "So long, Champ," he stated. "Take care of yourself, will you?"

"So long, Mike," Champ returned, and Mike disappeared into the dining room, moving for the side door. It opened and closed softly. We knew he was gone on his great adventure.

"There wasn't no use arguin' with him, you see," said Champ.

XI
"MIKE GOES DOWN"

It's necessary to leave the house, for a time, so I'll ask you to consider that you've left it with Mike. Partly, I know what he did and felt and thought. Partly, I'll have to guess. But I can make the picture of his excursion fairly complete.

He stood outside in the open, for a time, gathering himself, as a cat gathers itself before it springs. So Mike prepared himself, being reasonably sure that he would not be able to break through the lines without some sort of contact with the enemy. There was one great point in his favor; he was supposed to be a member of the attacking gang. He looked carefully before him. The trees stood up in a solid circle around the house, so that it seemed like the pit of an amphitheater. They were not tall trees, but poplars, and some others—things that shoot up quickly and make a sort of grove.

When Mike had surveyed the trees with a gloomy eye, he stepped a little to the side, and there, beyond the trunks, he saw the glimmer of a light from the nearest house. Very small and far away seemed that light to Mike. But he felt that there was nothing nearer. Although, as a matter of fact, if he had only taken a little more patience and time, he would have found that there was a house not a quarter as far away on just the opposite side of the place.

But Mike was not really in a philosophical humor. He wanted to get at the work before him in very much the humor of a martyr going to a sacrifice. He felt that his life had been given back to him after it was once forfeited, and Mike was not the man to take something for nothing. Savagely and eagerly, he wanted to rush off into danger and offer up the supreme sacrifice. At least, that is the only way that I can interpret what followed. He set off straight for that glimmering light, therefore. Once or twice it disappeared from his view, but he went on again, and crossed the circle of the poplars, with the leaves all making a hushing sound above his head.

Then as he went through, a voice said quietly to his right: "Is that you, Mike?"

He turned about. There was only one man, and that one man was now aiming a gun at him through the darkness. Nevertheless, Mike did not try to shoot and get on, because that one man was no less a person than Lord Winchelmere.

I've always felt that some part of his success in the States was due to the fact that he carried a title, and titles go a tremendous distance in this democracy of ours. And when it was discovered that in addition to being a lord he was actually a man, people didn't know what to make of him, and they exaggerated his importance. I am sure there is a bit of truth in this suggestion, although I know that even James Geraldi himself felt that Winchelmere was a great force.

At any rate, whatever the explanation, Mike wavered for an instant—and could not afterward recover. His best move would have been the brutal one of shooting down Winchelmere on the spot, and after he had allowed that first impulse to weaken in him, half the game was lost for him.

What influence the West and these terrible days have had on me.

"Hello," said Mike to his lordship, "you're the one that I want to see."

"It looked to me," said Winchelmere, "that you were going straight on."

"Why should I be going straight on?" Mike asked. "What good would that do me? Wasn't you to be here?"

"What's up?" asked Winchelmere.

"What do you think?" Mike answered sullenly.

"Look here, my man," said his lordship, "I like you very well and I don't mind a free tongue, but I won't have you impertinent. Tell me what's been done in the house."

"What you wanted done," Mike responded.

Winchelmere caught his arm in great excitement. "What do you mean by that?" he asked.

"He's done up."

"By heaven," said his lordship. "Is that a fact?"

"As sure as I live."

"Where is he, then?"

"Still up in his room."

"Mike . . . is he dead?"

"I dunno. Dead, or pretty near dead."

"Near dead? Confound you, man, couldn't you make sure?"

Mike had to pause a moment to control himself at this cold-blooded suggestion. He could see now the thing that he had attempted to do. He went back in mind to the time when he was placing that fuming, delicate poison outside the window, where the wind would blow it into the chamber.

"You saw him?" insisted his lordship.

"Of course, I seen him."

"Well? Well?"

"He looked pretty white and groggy. But his heart was still beating," Mike stated.

"And a stroke of your hand could have ended the business for us," said Winchelmere.

"Look here," Mike protested. "I promised that I would put the dope where it could have a chance to do its work. I didn't say that I'd do murder. I've done my job. Now I want my pay . . . I want the second thousand."

"You want the second thousand," repeated Winchelmere, "and, of course, you shall have it . . . but first we have to have the proof that you've done the work that we wanted."

"Are you gonna try to dodge me?" asked Mike.

"I'll tell you," his lordship replied, "it strikes me as odd that you haven't brought Champ along with you. Where is he?"

"How should I know?" Mike said unguardedly.

And there he made his fatal mistake, for a man should not be unguarded for a single instant in the presence of such a brain as that of Winchelmere. Mike could see his error an instant later as his lordship went on in a softer voice: "But Champ is your inseparable companion. Champ is your old friend and Bunkie. Whatever else you could answer for, you knew that Champ was in the hollow of your hand. Am I wrong?"

At this, the brain of Mike reeled. He had been hard pressed. And his whole soul had passed through such a shocking test this night that he was far from himself. He stumbled outright at this question. "Champ is all right," he muttered.

"But you couldn't bring him with you?"

"How could I?" Mike asked. "I didn't know that he'd be such a stubborn fool."

"You've had years and years to know him thoroughly," said Winchelmere.

"You never can know a gent that's gonna play the mule on you."

"In what way do you mean that?" said his lordship.

Mike wondered desperately if this were not surely the time when he should strike a blow and escape if he could. "I mean," Mike stammered, "I thought that I could make Champ go as far as I liked. I didn't dream that he'd. . . ."

"What?"

"He balked."

"I don't understand that."

"He wouldn't go through with it," said Mike.

"What was there for him to go through with? He knew nothing of what was to be done, did he?"

"He . . . he smelled the fumes," Mike stuttered. "The breath of it come through the house. He smelled it, and he guessed."

"And then?"

"Why, when he thought that there was murder in the air, he wouldn't do nothin'."

"He knew that you'd tried to kill Geraldi?"

"He knew that."

"And yet you couldn't persuade him to go away with you?"

"I couldn't. He was a mule, he was," Mike insisted. And very feebly he must have said it.

Lord Winchelmere was pressing forward relentlessly. "He preferred to stay there behind and be charged with the murder himself, no doubt."

"I never thought of that," groaned Mike.

Suddenly his lordship said: "You've double-crossed us, Mike. Admit it!"

"Me? I done nothing of the kind," Mike insisted.

A shadow stirred behind him. He dared not turn his head, but he knew that another man was at his back. He was a trapped rat.

"What did you find out, Seyf?" Winchelmere called out.

How the heart of Mike must have beaten when he heard that question.

"I found out," said the Egyptian—because, of course, it was he—"that they're in the big bedroom. The girl and . . . he."

"He's there with her?" snapped Winchelmere.

"Yes."

"How did you find out?"

"By coming near enough to listen to them."

"What did they say?"

"He's sick, feverish, raving. She was doing most of the talking."

"You were near enough to hear that, but still you couldn't strike a blow at him, Seyf?"

"The shutters were drawn. I would have had to open them to get in a fair shot."

"What was she saying?"

"She talked like a mother to a child. She said many words, but they meant only one thing. That she loved him."

"And the other man? Where is he now?"

"I saw his shadow fall on the curtained window of the first room. He had a rifle in his hands."

Winchelmere turned abruptly to Mike. "And what have you to say to that?" he asked.

For answer, Mike flung himself round on his heel and tried to bolt into the darkness. But Winchelmere sprang after him and with the barrel of his revolver felled Mike to the ground.

XII
"A GHOST OF A CHANCE"

It was a stunning blow, and, when Mike recovered a little, he lay flat on his back. His arms were stretched out, and Winchelmere was kneeling on one arm, Seyf Kalam on the other. A light flashed across his opening eyes.

"Now, my friend," Winchelmere hissed at Mike, "you see where treason takes you?"

Mike stared.

"You could have had a comfortable start in the world," Winchelmere said, "and my friendship to back you up, if you fell into trouble. But you preferred to betray me, and the price of that is death, Mike. Seyf!" Winchelmere shouted.

The Egyptian slowly raised his hand. There was enough starlight to slide down the blade of the poised knife like water.

In spite of himself, a groan of terror escaped the lips of Mike.

Winchelmere went on: "I ought to let Seyf strike home," he said. "But you still have a certain value to me, Mike. I want to know exactly how things stand in that house."

Valiantly Mike fought against surrender. But the ground was cold, and the stars were beautiful, and death by sharp steel is not pleasant.

"I'll count to five," Winchelmere said quietly. "If he

hasn't spoken at the fifth count, send the knife into his throat, Seyf."

Seyf murmured a word from another language. What it was, Mike could not say, but he gathered that it was assent. The fifth count was never reached, however. For Mike's nerves, twice tortured on this night now, gave way completely. He surrendered, in short. And although I don't like to think about it, he lay stretched on the ground under the knife and confessed everything he knew—how he had placed the poison and ignited it; how he had waited for a long time for the thing to take effect; how, finally, he had left his room and carefully opened the door of Geraldi's room to make inquiry into his condition; but hearing a noise on the lower floor, he had drawn back and decided to wait. Then Geraldi had entered, searched them both, discovered the incriminating evidence on the hands of Mike, and finally broke down the nerve of the latter by his mercy. He told how the sick man had succumbed gradually to the effects of the drug again, and how he had been taken downstairs and placed in the room with Mary Ingall.

When Mike had finished this recount, Winchelmere said: "And Champ? What about him? Will he fight this thing out?"

"He'll fight till he dies," Mike affirmed. "He's a man. He ain't a yaller dog, like me."

His lordship allowed a brief pause. Then he said: "As you see for the hundredth time, Seyf, we have a wonderful man against us. He can work by gun, knife, or . . . kindness. And here with a touch of kindness, he may have undone all our plans. There is Champ resolutely defending the sick man and the two helpless women. And Champ shoots straight, doesn't he?"

"He does," Mike answered truthfully.

"And you, Mike, to make up for what you had done, were

to break through our line and go for help?"

"Yes. That was my job."

"A complete double-crossing, of course," said his lordship. "However, we've promised to let you go free if you would tell the complete story."

He added two or three unintelligible words to Seyf Kalam, and suddenly the latter struck Mike over the head with a gun butt. That stroke seemed to crush or spring all the bones of his skull; but a moment later a red, lightning stroke of torture recalled him a little to his senses, as Seyf Kalam—or his lordship—drove a knife through his throat.

Winchelmere flashed a light in the face of the fallen man.

"He's wearing the death grin already, Seyf," he said. "Now we must work fast. We haven't much time, but the odds all favor us. Geraldi is prostrate. And if we have the slightest bit of luck, we ought to be able to use the cellar entrance, now."

Mike heard this. He lay paralyzed and prostrate, unable to stir, but as the two strode away into the darkness he made a mighty effort and stumbled to his knees. By clutching his throat with his hand, and then, hanging his head, he could draw in a few more than half strangled breaths. He looked wildly before him and saw a light, or rather, what looked like a whirling streak of fire, for he was sick with the weight of the blow. He could not have hoped for his life then, but he could wish with all his passionate heart to undo the last harm he had worked on Geraldi.

So he started in the direction of that light and stumbled vaguely and blindly along until he came against a tall picket fence. He could not use both hands for climbing. With one of those hands he was holding on to the thin thread of his life. For some time, he leaned against the fence, unable to think. Like a moth, he had been drawn toward the light. He was stopped by an obstacle that his mind could not solve. Then a great wave of faintness ran through his body. He turned and fumbled down the fence, shocked into attention and half-thinking by the sudden weakness.

Poor Mike. He had gone in the wrong direction, and he had to walk all around the back of the house and so to the front before he found the gate. And, when he reached that front gate, he was overcome and sank to the ground. He gritted his teeth and fought back that weakness, that cloud of darkness in his mind.

He struggled up again. His arms were numb beneath the elbows. He felt as though his legs were cut off at the knees. But he managed to get to the steps of the porch, and there he was able to see why there was a light so late in this place.

The door was open, and, looking through into the room that was exposed, he saw five men in their shirt sleeves, seated around a table, playing poker, with their piles of cash stacked before them. When Mike saw this, the commonplace scene made him stare, and as he struggled to take the first upward step to the porch, he heard one of the players begin to curse savagely a losing hand.

An almost uncontrollable mirth took hold upon Mike and shook him as a terrier shakes a rat. Mirth at the knowledge of these men who quietly played poker—or else cursed their luck. He, too, had cursed at a poker game in his day. Now, dying, he could hardly struggle up a short flight of steps to get aid.

But he succeeded in that struggle. He staggered into the open doorway. A bearded man opposite the door saw him first, and started to his feet with a cry of horror. The others recoiled. The table was a litter of money and dropped cards. One would have thought that Mike was the plague incarnate.

He slumped into a chair. He could not speak. He was

growing black in the face for lack of breath. But he brushed the heap of money away and began to write on the surface of the table with his own blood: **Next house . . . men trying to break in to murder. . . .** And as he finished that sentence, he slumped forward, his strength giving away. He pried himself up again, and saw that he had rubbed and blotted out his writing by his fall. And he knew that the last seconds remaining to him would not be sufficient for him to trace out the letters again. For writing was not the strong point of poor Mike.

And then, as he stared in hopeless dismay, and, as the gamblers circled around him, he looked at them, heard their excited voices, and read their faces.

Never in his life had he seen such depravity. They were the scum of the scum—low ruffians and gutter-driftings of the range. Even if he gave them his message clearly, would they raise a hand to help the people in that beleaguered house?

At that moment, there was rapid rattling of shots. He started to his feet, and, pointing wildly in the direction of the fire, he tried to gibber a few words at them. It was too much for his strength, and he pitched forward into a cloud of darkness, with a strange feeling that everyone was rushing away from him, and leaving him to sink helplessly to his death.

Four of those men had, indeed, rushed out from the house, but there was a fifth who stayed behind—the bearded man who first had spied Mike standing, a terrifying figure, in the doorway. He remained, turning to the fallen man on the floor. And the reason he remained was that he had been a doctor in earlier and better days. And he had gone into surgery at one time with success. Interest was greater in him than alarm. He examined Mike's wound carefully, and he saw a chance that was not great—but at least enough to tempt an experimenter. So he stripped off his coat, and managed—for he was a strong fellow—to lay Mike on the couch at the side of the room, where the blood would drain out of his throat, instead of flowing down into his lungs. When he had accomplished that much, he set to work with compressed lips, eagerly struggling with the problem of life and death, and never allowing the chance of defeat to keep him back.

All that night he worked and until the gray of the morning came, and by that time the doctor was a trembling wreck, but for Mike there was a ghost of a chance to live—because he had the vitality of an animal rather than of a man.

XIII
"THE DANGER WITHIN"

I have followed Mike so far because I could not leave him helpless and bleeding on the ground, while I told how things went with us in the house. But now it is time to go back to the moment when he rushed out, so generously bent on giving up his life, if need be, in order to serve us all.

It left me face to face with Champ, staring like a child, because I was being shown such things about heroic manhood as I had thought belonged only to the days of the Romans. Champ was perfectly self-possessed.

He said: "The trouble ain't over, ma'am. I don't think Mike has got more than one chance out of three of getting through for help. But even if he does break through, the gents outside are apt to tackle us any minute. This here house is our fort. It ain't any too airtight. Danger is likely to leak through, and we'll flounder before the pumps can be manned. Now I say, ma'am, that the thing to do is to mount guard, all of us, and perambulate around, and see if we can't keep our eyes on the leaks before they get wide open."

I saw that this was good sense. I said as calmly as I could: "We'd better have a look at Geraldi first."

Champ nodded. "You take a look at him. I'll throw an eye aloft."

I saw him turn and go up the stairs, the shotgun grappled

under his arm. But he went so heavily and noisily that I was filled with fear. His coming could be noticed at a distance—perhaps I would never see him come down again.

I was rather sick at heart as I went into the room where Geraldi lay. His eyes were wide open now. His face was white and drawn, and his feet, his hands, his whole body were visibly and strongly shaken. It was doubly horrible. It was as though he were overwhelmed with hideous fear. It was as though Geraldi had collapsed like a coward. I had to rally myself and force myself to understand that there was not a scruple of fear in him. It all was weakness of body and nerves brought on by the poison.

He stuttered as he told me that he was going to get well. That it was only a matter of time. And that we should at once look to ourselves and the house.

I said to Mary: "Champ thinks we must start going the rounds. Mary, here is your revolver. I'm going to take a rifle. We'll have to keep moving softly from room to room. Champ is upstairs now. And Jimmy should be moved into the center of the house where we can keep an eye on him. Because it's Jimmy that they want."

She was as quiet as you please. That faint smile was never off her lips, and she helped me to get Jimmy off the bed. He was not strong enough to bear his own weight. His legs shuddered and wavered beneath him as we carried him into the hall. He was laid on a folded blanket there, and a pillow put underneath his head. He stammered out a request for a gun, and we gave him one of his Colts. It fairly shook itself out of the hand in which he received it. He grasped it with both hands and smiled desperately to see how they twitched and shook from side to side. Still, it seemed better to see him with some sort of a weapon.

I laid my hand over his heart. It was racing horribly, but

the beat was infinitely stronger than it had been, and seemed momentarily to be growing more powerful and sure. Perhaps in another few moments, his nerves would become steadier. And if he were only a ghost of his old self, he would treble our strength for resistance.

He must have seen that hope in my face, for he whispered with twisting lips: "A few minutes . . . I'm rising fast."

Mary and I agreed that we should go through the rooms one after another, keeping all the doors open and a lamp, with the flame turned low, burning in each. In that way, we might have light enough to see to shoot.

My confidence increased every moment. Mary was perfectly steady. I myself was cold with fear, but I was not shaking.

When Champ came down, at that moment, and announced that he had secured the windows upstairs and felt that we could all turn our attention to guarding the lower floor, I was still more relieved. Time was fighting for us.

And yet, there was Lord Winchelmere on the outside of the house, a man whom Jimmy had declared that he feared—and declared it when he was in full possession of his strength. And Mary and Champ and I—what fraction were we of the strength of Geraldi?

I went into the kitchen first, and took note of everything. The windows were shut and locked, and the inside shades were down. I tried the windows and made sure of the latches being turned in place. Then I looked at the trap door that ran from the kitchen down into the little cellar. There was a small bolt that secured it on one side, and I shuddered when I saw that bolt had not been sent home. I remedied that, and tried the edge of the door. It lifted a fraction of an inch, but I was certain that any attempt to break the door open by force would make a great deal of noise.

Secure of that, I went on into the dining room. The lock of this door was not strong, and a chair had been braced under the knob—by Champ, I think.

As I came out into the hall, I saw Jimmy still striving to master a gun with hands that certainly shook less than before, but that were with equal surety still of but the smallest use. Mary was going up the stairs. It brought my heart into my throat when I thought of her wandering through the dark chambers above. But Champ had been there just before. And surely it must be hard to force a window silently.

I stepped into the front room. It seemed to have a presence in it, so much had happened there. But there was nothing to see—no sight and no sound, and the flame burned upward bravely and steadily in the lamp.

From the front room, I stepped through the second door into the kitchen—and found a wall of darkness. What had happened to the lamp? It had been blown out by a gust of air, of course, for the wind was rising a little, making faint, moaning sounds through the house, and I could feel the cool, damp air circulating. I opened a box of matches that I was carrying. As I scratched one, sure enough, there I found the lamp standing on the floor just where it had been placed. I lighted it again, and the draft was so strong that it fanned the flame out sidewise. I turned up that flame so high that it swayed wildly, and pressed the chimney down into the holders again. And, as I did so, I had the most eerie feeling of being watched by hostile eyes. The draft grew stronger and made the flame leap in the lamp chimney and almost go out. And, twisting myself around in sudden fear, I saw that the cellar door was wide open.

It stopped my heart. For an instant, I could not think; a mist spun before my eyes. And then I told myself: *No! Brave old Champ has gone down those steps to examine the darkness of the cellar and make that sure.* It was vastly reassuring. I leaned over the black pit—but all was silent. There was no sound stirring. And how could Champ examine such a pit without a light?

I turned away in perplexity—and in a corner I saw an odd heap. A man, fallen there like one crushed by a drop from a great height. At that moment, the heap of humanity stirred, and I saw the face of Champ, distorted, empurpled, the eyes staring and sightless like death, and a streak of blood down the side of his face. His movement was very slight, and he collapsed again.

He had been struck down, and those who had struck him had come up through the cellar door. I glanced back to it, but with such an agony of terror that I dared not move a step toward it. I felt as though great hands would reach out for me if I came near it. But he who had struck down Champ so silently—where was he now? What silent fiendishness was he accomplishing?

Jimmy Geraldi! Toward him murderers were undoubtedly creeping—using precious seconds, but making sure with silence while they stole—yonder through the dining room—then to the hall, where they would find him lying helpless.

I started, gripping my rifle hard, praying that I would not fail in my duty, forcing myself stealthily, step by step, toward the dining room door, and then I heard a sudden outbreak of turmoil—a loud rattling of shots which seemed to break through all the house like thunder. I stood frozen in my place, and I remember that the explosions were so violent that at first I thought: *They are blowing up the house.* A little piece of plaster was dislodged from the ceiling and fell at my feet, where it broke into a powder. To this moment I cannot understand how I had an eye for such a detail as that—at such a time.

Then I heard heavy boots striking against something—as though they were striving to batter down a door. I was standing at the entrance to the dining room now, and I saw a man dart in from the hall—a lean, yellow-faced man running rapidly, but making no noise with his footfall. Seyf Kalam, of course! I pulled the trigger of the rifle. He yelled and leaped to the side, and I slammed the door and turned the key.

I whirled about, desperate; something was coming into the other door of the kitchen.

XIV
"FIVE MEN ACCOUNTED FOR"

I knew that it was the end. I had no doubt that it would be murder for me, as well as the rest. And then I saw Mary Ingall come staggering through the doorway, half carrying and half dragging poor Jimmy.

She let him fall on the floor. There was a rending and crashing as the door of the bedroom went down, a yell of triumph from some man's voice, and Mary slammed the door and turned the key.

I was on my knees beside Jimmy. He made a desperate effort and hunched his shoulders up against the wall, holding his revolver in both hands, so that it covered the dining room door. My hand happened to touch the barrel of the gun, and it was hot—so that from his gun some of the bullets had come which had thundered through the house.

A great crunching weight fell against the kitchen/bedroom door as I straightened on my knees, and I fired instinctively straight at the center of the door.

"Good," whispered Geraldi. "Barricade it."

I heard violent cursing beyond the door. I braced a strong chair under the knob of the door and started to drag the heavy kitchen table into place to increase the resistance. Mary had already blocked the dining room door with the second chair.

Then a brief silence followed. No doubt, the scoundrels

were planning their next attack.

I heard Mary whispering: "I came down the stairs. As I reached the bottom step, two men slipped into the doorway from the hall to the dining room. Jimmy fired at them. They sprang back. I caught at him and dragged him into the bedroom. I slammed and locked the door. And they . . . they were breaking it down and shooting through it, as I got him toward the kitchen door . . . ah, ah."

With a sudden crash, they beat at the dining room/kitchen door now. It sprang beneath the blow. Mary and I fired through it. But the battering continued. Apparently they were using the dining room table, standing at a safe distance to either side.

I looked at Jimmy. He was as white as ever. His lips grinned back from his teeth with effort, and he was rising to his knees until he sat back upon his heels, slumped awkwardly against the wall. No man ever made a vaster effort than that, I suppose. He wanted to die on his feet, I think, and this was the nearest he could come to the proper position of a fighting man, the gun shaking crazily in his hands.

The door split suddenly down the center, and through the yawning crack I fired, threw out the empty shell, and leveled the rifle once more. But it was no use. The battering ram swung again, and the door fell in shattered fragments. At the same time voices shouted outside the house, and against the outer kitchen door hands beat. More enemies?

I saw a huge man with a fat, handsome face spring through the entrance where the dining room door had been smashed. Mary and I fired at the same instant—and missed. A gun spoke behind us. Geraldi! And the fat, handsome face of Edgar Asprey wrinkled and crumpled with pain, and he pitched forward. I saw guns spitting behind him as he fell, and the big shoulders of Winchelmere, and the narrow, yellow face of Seyf Kalam, the Egyptian.

I was not more frightened but less, as the moments jumped past us. And then I heard a crash as the kitchen door to the outer yard was cast open and a squad of four men rushed in, guns in hand.

Winchelmere, I remember, leaped high into the air and to one side, strangely like a puppet moved by a string. And Seyf Kalam was nowhere to be seen. Then the strangers charged on through that doorway, tearing the smoke screen apart, and plunging on. But they did not take Lord Winchelmere. It was Seyf Kalam that they finally brought back into the kitchen, hideously wounded.

The kitchen was a dreadful shambles. Edgar Asprey lay dead. Seyf Kalam was bleeding freely. Two of the rescuers who had broken in to face the fire for us had been scraped by bullets. Champ lay in a corner groaning, and slowly coming back to himself; and finally there was Geraldi, growing calmer every moment, and with more color in his face, more intelligence in his eyes.

One of those rough bringers of rescue, going the rounds and taking count of wounds and injuries of all kinds, paused over Jimmy and suddenly shouted: "Boys, here's a fine soger! There ain't anything wrong with him . . . but he's dyin' of blue funk."

I said to that discoverer of strange things: "Do you want to know the name of the coward?"

"I do, ma'am," he said. "I'm gonna make him famous, I am. The skunk that lay in the corner while a brace of females stood up and fought for him. . . ."

"His name is Geraldi," I said.

He grinned stupidly at me for an instant, and then he turned a sad gray-green.

Someone had brought in a doctor. Everything began to be

put in order. Now that the gun firing was ended, some other neighbors ventured in to do what they could. They had stayed away because people never show too much curiosity about gunshots in the West. It isn't considered good form. But when they came in, they were wonderfully cheerful workers and helped to put everything in order. We turned the living room into a sick ward.

There lay Seyf Kalam. The doctor said that he would surely die. Beside him lay poor Mike, who was carried gently over in the dawn because he had signified his desire to come back. There was half a hope for Mike, said the doctor. He was able to breathe with difficulty, and the pain of the constant effort kept him staring fixedly at the ceiling. Champ had been struck by a sandbag—that is to say, a small chamois bag filled with shot or heavy sand. It rarely breaks bones, but it stuns the victim, and apparently it had been used on Champ because a gun would have made enough noise to alarm the house.

Of course, Mary would have spent all her time with Jimmy, but he was able to sit up now, with a face like white iron, and he ordered her to take care of Mike.

So she sat down beside the poor fellow and read aloud to him, and her voice took his mind away from his own sufferings. After a time he fell asleep. He made dreadful choking sounds now and again, but he did not waken; and the doctor, watching critically, said that he would surely have two chances out of three of recovering, once his body was fortified with a little rest.

Then I fell into bed and went to sleep myself, and, when I woke up a few hours later with a feeling that I had been living through a dream, the house was well in order. Two women had scrubbed the kitchen and then cooked a meal for us. The broken doors and chairs had been cleared out. Altogether there were few signs of the terrible battle that had been fought there.

Seyf Kalam was murmuring in a weak delirium. Mike still slept, breathing more easily. Jimmy was asleep, also. He had taken a chair into the open and sat there in the full glare of the sun.

When I paused in front of him, worried, he opened his eyes suddenly, and I saw by their clearness that he was almost himself again. He stood up at once.

"Jimmy," I said, with tears in my eyes, "is it possible that we still have you?"

He took my hands and looked at me with real affection. "When you and Mary put your heads together and decide on a thing, no one can stand against you," he said.

It was the second compliment he had paid me, and I was ridiculously pleased again.

I wanted to know if any report had come in from the men who had been sent out to trace Lord Winchelmere. But he said in an odd voice: "Winchelmere isn't needed, you know."

"Not needed, Jimmy?" I asked him. "But wasn't his lordship the heart and soul of the whole affair?"

"He was. But his portion will probably come later. He isn't needed now," repeated Geraldi.

"I don't understand that," I said. "If I could control things, I would have every officer of the law in the whole country hunting for that evil creature."

"Of course, you would," Jimmy said, "but all the officers in the country never would be able to locate him. He's gone. Probably he's now a yellow-skinned muleteer driving a pack mule up a trail, or a rough-looking prospector steering a burro in front of him. There are a good many identities wrapped up in that one skin, you know."

"Is that why you say that he isn't needed?" I asked.

"Merely because he can't be had by the law?"

"Well," Geraldi said, "suppose you look at the thing in another way. Edgar Asprey doesn't count, to begin with."

"What in the world are you talking about?" I asked.

"I'll try to explain, then. It's a queer idea, but it has a hold on me . . . and this is the thing that's in my mind. In the first place, the golden box of Horus was stolen. There were four great emeralds on it. There was also a great yellow diamond for the head of Horus himself. Robert Ingall was the first to die for taking that box from its rightful place. Then Strozzi died, and then Oñate. That made three. Rompier was the fourth. And the fifth will be Seyf Kalam, according to the doctor's report."

"Jimmy," I exclaimed, "do you really mean to say that you think there is a connection between these deaths and that box with its five jewels?"

"At least," he said, "the numbers agree."

"Edgar Asprey also died," I reminded him. "And he was the sixth man."

"He had nothing to do with it," Jimmy protested. "That was a little private account between him and me. It was long overdue for a settlement."

XV
"TOO HIGH A PRICE"

In the middle of the afternoon, Seyf Kalam opened his eyes. His brain was clear, at last, and he looked earnestly at Mary, who was still patiently sitting between Seyf and the slumbering Mike. But she could not do much for Mike now. Champ, with a great towel in lieu of a bandage wrapped around his cracked head, sat over his friend, smoking pipe after pipe, and watched, and brooded, and smiled at Mike's battered face with such tenderness that it choked me to see him.

But now Seyf Kalam said to Mary: "May I see your lord?"

He said it so solemnly that she was frightened. She came to me about it at once.

"He isn't out of his head," said Mary. "But he's asking to see my lord! What can it mean?"

I was a little staggered, too. But suddenly Mary smiled. "He's very far spent, poor fellow, and he's simply translating Arabic into English. Don't you see? Jimmy is my lord, to him. That's it, of course!"

She went for Geraldi, and, when he came in, Seyf looked eagerly up into his face.

"I am about to die," Seyf said. "And before I die, my lord alone can give me a little happiness."

Geraldi asked him, kindly enough, what he could do for him, and Seyf answered: "I have done enough evil, and particularly to the father of your woman. For all that, I am now going to my reward. But I beg from you a small favor, and I bid you to remember that in the heat of the desert men do not give water to the good before the bad, but to those who are most thirsty. From me, my lord, the blood of my soul has run, and I am thirsty."

"For what?" Geraldi asked.

"For a sight of the golden box, and the jewels, and the prayer to Horus." He waited, lips apart, eyelids fluttering.

Geraldi said to Mary: "This is something for you to answer, Mary. Is it safe to bring the box from the bank and show it to this man?"

"Bring it to him!" Mary exclaimed. "Poor Seyf Kalam. Poor Seyf Kalam."

The Egyptian closed his eyes with a smile of contentment, and he remained with exactly that expression during the half hour when Mary was gone to get the treasure and return with it.

Geraldi himself then fitted the jewels into the empty spaces until all was complete, and Ra, Atum, Kheperi, Osiris, and Horus all wore their priceless disks above their heads. It made a blinding array with the highly shining surface of the enamel, and the glittering gold, freckled with hieroglyphics. This double handful of glory Jimmy carried in and held at the foot of the Egyptian's bed.

Seyf opened his eyes and muttered: "Allah is Allah, and Mohammed is his prophet." He stretched out his lean hands, and Jimmy unhesitatingly placed the box in them. Seyf at once turned the top of it so that he could look at the strange, stiff, high-shouldered form of Horus, with the splendid yellow diamond flaming and flaring upon his head. He smiled, closed his eyes, and opened them again dreamily. Death was not far from Seyf Kalam, but he was dying happy. I could not help a cold-blooded feeling that it was the happiness of the born thief.

"Seyf," Geraldi said, "will you tell us, now, the story of the golden box? Because there's no one else who knows it?"

"I shall tell my lord," Seyf said, his eyes fixed on the yellow diamond. "When Robert Ingall entered the tomb, I carried the light for him. I was at his side when, working in the rubbish that the robbers had left littered on the floor of the rock, he found the golden box. I saw him put it under his cloak and carry it up. I sat beside him while he studied it. Then he went back with me, and we searched with more painful care, trying to find the yellow diamond, but it could not be discovered. I, however, discovered something else. It was written in hieroglyphics on the side of the wall. It said . . . 'It seemed good to me to make a house of gold for all my fathers. I made that house of gold. I made my father Ra who sails by day across the blue waters of the sky, and at night he passes among the gates of Tuat and does not fear the serpents. I made my father Ra and I placed a great green stone above his head. In all the world there was no other stone like that except in my treasury.

" 'Then I placed my father Atum, old and wise, on another side of the box. No one is as old as Atum, and no one is so wise. He gave me wisdom, therefore I honored him. I made my father Atum and I placed above his head a green stone. In all the world there is no other stone like that except in my treasury.

" 'Then on the third side of the house I placed the sacred scarab, I placed my father Kheperi, rolling the sun across the sky. Kheperi is my father, and the sun that he rolled through that golden sky was a great green stone. In all the world there is no other stone like that except in my treasury.

" 'On the fourth side I made my father Osiris stand, like a

mummy, as he stands to rule and to judge the dead. I made my father Osiris, and upon his head I placed a great green stone. In all the world there is no other stone like that except in my treasury.

" 'Those four stones I set in the gold of the box. There are no other stones like them. There are no more in the world.

" 'But then at the end I made my father Horus on the lid of the box, because he is the top of all things. I made my father Horus of the two horizons. He is a greater god, and therefore I made him greater, and I selected a great stone to be his solar disk. But I did not place that stone above his head. I hid it, instead, where no man could find it, but Horus could find it, because his eye looks from both horizons, and he sees all things. I made my father Horus, and I gave him for a sun a yellow stone. There is no other like it in all the world or in the king's treasury. It is a sacred stone. It is the sun of Horus. I hid it so that only his eye could be pleased by it.

" 'All of these things I did to make my fathers happy.' "

Seyf paused here. He had been half whispering and half chanting the words.

Now, gaining a little strength again, he went on: "After reading those hieroglyphics, I thought a great deal. I had looked at the four emeralds and yet in the eyes of the dead king they were nothing compared with the yellow stone. Where could the yellow stone be, then? One thing I decided at once. I would not let my master see the writing on the wall. That same day I found a chance to spoil it so that not one sentence was clear.

"Then, whenever I could, I searched and searched in the tomb. Robert Ingall left Egypt suddenly. I stayed behind to steal into the tomb and search. But I found nothing and no sign of the yellow stone. Where could he have hidden it?"

"At last I met Lord Winchelmere. I was in despair. I knew

that he had a great mind and an eye like the eye of Horus, which looks from both horizons, and sees all things." Seyf Kalam smiled a little as he said this. "The moment I told his lordship he exclaimed at once . . . 'It is the box! It is hidden in the gold of the box, of course!' And I saw that he must be right. I gnashed my teeth. Robert Ingall had taken the box away, and the yellow stone was hidden in it.

"Lord Winchelmere said that he would follow. We crossed from Egypt to France. There he took Strozzi and Rompier. We crossed the ocean. In New York we found Oñate, and we went to Boston. But it was very hard to do anything there. The box was always kept in a great vault in a bank. What could we do?

"Lord Winchelmere has a plan for every occasion. He determined that he would lure Robert Ingall away from Boston, bringing his box with him. He knew that the mind of Robert Ingall was not strong. It was disturbed about the worship of the sun. And his lordship somehow lured him with a very strange bait, talking to him about the sun-worshiping Incas, and a great yellow stone that had been stolen there by thieves. They had it in the West. It was too big to sell to a fence. They would keep it for a fair offer.

"All that his lordship wrote to Robert Ingall I cannot tell, but I know that Robert Ingall came out here. Twice we tried to steal the box from him, and both times we failed. Then we tried to steal his daughter and hold her until he ransomed her with the golden box. But this we failed to do because Geraldi was there." He paused again. His face was like yellow marble, his lips barely moving as he spoke. "All the rest you know, and particularly you alone know, Geraldi, how you stole the golden box from him, and how you gave it back to him again, and how Edgar Asprey betrayed you both and so the emeralds were lost to you for the time. And how you got those stones one by one and were able after the death of Robert Ingall to restore everything to the hands of his daughter. You have done more than any man could do. It was your will, but it was also the will of Allah. For Allah is Allah, and Mohammed is his prophet. I, Seyf Kalam, avow to Allah that I. . . ."

He paused again. He bit at the air like a dog snapping at a bone. As his arm stiffened in his last moment, he seemed to be holding up to heaven the golden box as a sort of peace offering. An instant later he collapsed and was dead. Geraldi took the golden box and placed it in the hands of Mary, but she would not keep it. She set it down on the table and shook her head, with her eyes firmly closed.

"*No one* deserves such a thing," she said. "The price has been too high."

XVI
"BECAUSE HE WAS FAITHFUL"

We went to the burial of Seyf Kalam. We were the only mourners, if mourners we could be called. While we were standing by the grave, a man brought up a great armful of flowers and spilled them down over the mound. There was a card attached to one bouquet, and I leaned over and read, in femininely small printing: **These flowers to my friend, Seyf Kalam, because he was a faithful man**.

The note was not signed. It did not need to be. Because, as Geraldi knew at once and as even I could guess, the flowers had come from Lord Winchelmere, and they made a sure proof that the villain was not far off. I saw an ominous tightening of the lips of Geraldi, but he made no comment.

We went back to the house, but we stopped at the bank on the way, and there Geraldi made all arrangements for shipping the box—not to Boston, but straight back to Egypt—to start on its way east by the evening train.

At that grim little house where so many men had come to their end, we found that Mike was infinitely better and even able to whisper dim curses because of the pain in his throat. Champ had not left him. Champ never would leave him. That we could guess well enough.

I sat out in the garden that evening. Geraldi sat beside me. Mary was at an upper window of the house staring out across the trees, but I did not know why. In fact, my brain was too numbed and tired to wonder at anything, no matter how very strange it might be.

I said: "Jimmy, what is next?"

"I take you East," he said.

"And then?"

"I see you safely and comfortably in your Boston house."

"And then?"

"I slip quietly away, Aunt Emmy, and come back here . . . for black Peter will be lonely without me."

To this I made no answer. It was logical, of course. It was what I myself had urged on him before. He was not the sort of man to marry, not the sort of man to marry an Ingall, above all. However, I could not speak to him now to encourage the idea that I myself had first insisted on.

I merely said: "It isn't Peter you will be wanting to have in your sight again, Jimmy."

He said nothing.

"Be honest, Jimmy," I urged him.

"Ah, well . . . ," he said.

I smiled at him sadly, and he smiled back. He was still a little pale, but that creature of steel springs could not be killed by poison, I think.

"Very well," I said, "you won't be frank with me?"

"About what?" he asked, wickedly avoiding the question.

"You know perfectly well what I mean, and you know that I'm right," I said to him. "Jimmy, you are coming back to the West to forget Mary by jumping into the midst of a great deal of excitement. Isn't that true?"

"Aunt Emmy," he answered, "what sort of excitement should I find here?"

"Hunting, Jimmy."

"Perhaps."

"Manhunting," I persisted.

He looked quickly at me, but said nothing.

"You'll follow Lord Winchelmere," I said, "until. . . ."

"Yes, that's true," he said. "I'll follow him, by heaven, until I've. . . ."

"Hush!" I said.

"Well?"

"You mustn't be so extremely sure of it, Jimmy."

He frowned. "I don't think you understand a man's obligations to himself and . . . his honor," he said.

"Stuff and nonsense," I said. "Don't you try to make a mystery of a man's honor and such folderol. As a matter of fact, I know perfectly well the whole ridiculous thought that's behind your mind. But, Jimmy Geraldi, though you may be ready and willing to break your own heart . . . if you really have one somewhere . . . I'm not going to stand by quietly and see Mary's life ruined."

He frowned at me very darkly.

"You wonder how I can make such a change of front?" I said. "Of course, you wonder. That's because you haven't lived through such hours as I've spent with Mary. I'm ready to retract everything that I've said before. I'm ready to admit that without you Mary won't have an instant of happiness in her life. And, after I've admitted that, are you going to be stubborn and hold on with your man trail?"

He looked at me. He cast a wild glance above him toward Mary at the window, and at that moment she cried out in a cheerful, relieved voice: "It's gone!"

"What's gone?" I snapped at her.

One always feels snappy after having done a really good action. At least, I do.

"You can hear it," Mary said, and began to clap her hands and sing a phrase of some ridiculous song.

"Mary," I said to her, "will you kindly talk sense . . . and begin by telling me why you are hanging out that window?"

"But it's gone!" she cried. "Listen! Listen!" She waved her hand. "The golden box of Horus! May we never see it again. Listen."

I could hear, then, the sound of the engine pulling out from the station and gathering speed with obstinate patience as it struggled with the long grade. The golden box was gone, and with it perhaps the danger was removed from our lives.

Mary, laughing like a child, was still singing and waving her handkerchief and actually kissing her foolish hand toward that vanishing sound.

Geraldi turned back to me. He seemed nervous, anxious. "You know a good deal about me," he said. "And if. . . ."

"I know so much," I said, "that I don't want to know any more. And now I suppose you want to thrust the whole responsibility upon me?"

"Of course, I do," said Geraldi.

"Well," I stated, "I suppose I shall have to do it."

He sped into the house. I looked up at my dear, dear Mary still smiling and waving in the window until she turned with a sudden cry and disappeared into the dark of the room. And then I heard the cry again, and may the memory of it never be far from this withered, dry, and dying soul of mine.

The Return of Geraldi

I
"HOW THE TRAINER FEELS"

As they came up to the brow of the hill, Cullen raised a hand to warn his companion, then dismounted. When Darcy had imitated him, they tethered the horses in a clump of poplars and went forward, scouting carefully until they came to the skyline itself. There, lying flat, Cullen wriggled forward through the grass, with Darcy a length behind him.

Finally they paused, when the dip of the valley descended beneath their eyes to a strip of swift water, ruffled with white by rapids here and there. It was a naked valley floor, beneath the edges of the tall woods that clothed the hillsides, except for one lofty island of silver spruce in the very center. And at the edge of this island there was moored a small shack of logs.

One could see the sawbuck behind the shack, the white streak of sawdust beneath it; the corral, composed of marvelously irregular logs and branches, some running from post to post, and some thrust into the ground as a mere brush entanglement, loosely surrounded by a little lean-to that, apparently, had to serve as shelter for the horse or horses that would serve the master of such a place as this.

There was no horse in the corral at this moment, but they could see the black mark where one's impatient wanderings up and down near the bars had rubbed off the surface grass.

"Whoever this gent is," Darcy said, "he ain't got but one hoss."

"Whatever horse he has," Cullen answered dryly, "one of it will be enough."

Darcy was generally in a position of mental inferiority to his companion, but in this case he felt the point was worth an argument.

"I dunno about one hoss," he said. "You look at the Injuns, which they knew all about travelin' fast. They went sashayin' out with six hosses apiece. I dunno how you can say one hoss can be enough. Neighbors is sort of scarce, out this a ways."

He waved to the mountains behind them, over which they had come during this day's march. They seemed to crowd closer as the two looked back; they seemed to thrust out elbows and knees toward the pair, but both of them knew how many a bitter long mile stretched between.

"I'll tell you," Cullen said, after hesitating as though this argument were hardly worth consideration. "I'll tell you, Darcy. How far can a puma run?"

"Oh, they can run a good pair of miles. They're plumb lightning for a coupla furlongs. And for fifty yards they could run faster than the stone you throwed at 'em. Why, when they're started, a bullet might part their hair, but it'd hardly get to the roots. That's all they need . . . fifty yards of sprinting to kill their colt, say. They certainly are partial to hoss."

"Well," said the other, "look at this point of view, then. All that he needs, this fellow down below, is to have a horse that can sprint fast enough to give him a chance to make a kill. One leap, Darcy, and he finishes his game."

"I've heard tell of such as that," muttered Darcy.

He lay flat on the grass and talked with a contented mumbling, poking at the ground with his oddly bunched fingers, which were always collected as though he were trying to pick up some very small object. He allowed his companion to keep the look-out for the sake of which they had come here.

"I've heard tell of such as that," went on Darcy. "I remember when Champ Logan got out of the pen after he done his stretch. He comes back to Tombstone and walks down the middle of the main drag lookin' ferocious. You know how sometimes a Christmas turkey looks, all lumpy with stuffin'? That was the way with Champ. He's got guns in pairs, beginnin' at his knees and goin' up to his chin. He's so heavy with shootin' irons that it would take two men and a boy to lift him clear of the floor. While he's still around the corner, you can hear him chimin' as he walks. He sounds like a grandfather clock bein' toted to the repair shop. Matter of fact, he'd make the prosperous beginnings of a hardware shop, this here Champ Logan would. Wherever he can't put a gun, he lays up a Bowie knife.

"Well, every time Tombstone hears Champ Logan jingle, it shakes in its boots. It gets indoors and gives him the right of way. Even the mules and the hosses shy when they see him go past. And every day he walks into the saloons and tells the boys how small he's gonna carve the skunks that railroaded him up the river. But one day in comes a little sawed-off runt of a mining engineer from Pennsylvania, and bumps into Champ just when Champ is beginnin' to roar.

" 'Keep your voice down,' says the stranger, 'you ain't talkin' to a crowd.'

"Says Champ . . . 'Young feller, d'you know who you might be talkin' to?'

" 'Take yourself off of my foot,' says this little gent, 'or I'll kick you through the door.'

"And damn me if he didn't do it. While Champ is loadin'

up both hands with Forty-Fives, the stranger steps in between and pastes him on the nose, and that walkin' hardware shop drops both the guns and begins to bleed, and the stranger turns him around and kicks him through the door, and Champ lands on the sidewalk with a crash like a fallin' stove. That same day he disappears, and Tombstone wakes up in time to start laughin' on one side of its face.

"Now, I've heard a lot of these sure-gun boys, but mostly I notice they do best when they got their gang with them. This here fellow . . . you ain't told me his name . . . I bet he's the same kind. You think he's dynamite, but I bet he's more sawdust than soup."

This speech he made with deliberation, and with a good deal of quiet indignation, and his companion listened inattentively, only saying at the end: "Ideas are free in this country, Darcy. You can think what you please. Now lie low, because here he comes."

Out of the distance they heard a song rapidly approaching them, and, peering down through the green screen of the grass, they saw a rider gallop around the shoulder of the hill. He rode a black horse, polished with sweat until it was one flash of light against the westering sun, a stallion with the stride of a leaping cat, a high-headed king of horses that seemed to be running at its own free will, for the rider appeared to give no heed to the way, but his restless head turned a little from side to side toward the rocks, the trees, the bushes that flowed past them; so a hawk rides the upper air and peers down toward the ground. Swiftly he came past them and was gone, with only one verse of his song ringing behind him in the ears of the watchers:

The gold I want is the gold of flowers . . .
Let them wither whenever they will;

The silver of water that sings in the valley;
The wings of the wind on the hill.

So he fled down the slope and wound away for the cabin beside the lofty island of trees.

Cullen looked at his companion with a faint, nervous chuckle. "You're lying pretty low, Darcy," he said.

"Man alive, man alive," muttered Darcy. "Is that him?"

"That's the man," Cullen said.

Darcy raised his head by jerks, as though even now he feared lest the stranger might see him from the house beneath.

"It's Geraldi," he said. "It's him. It's Geraldi." He pushed himself up on his knees.

"It's Geraldi," Cullen admitted, looking as grave as his companion, but more thoughtful.

"I thought he was bigger," Darcy said.

"He seems big enough," said Cullen, "after you've been close to him for a while."

Darcy drew a breath and shook himself, like a dog coming out of cold water. "It give me kind of a chill," he muttered. "Seein' him come ridin' right at us, that way. Like he was gonna go right over us." He laughed shakily. "Ain't more than a strip of a kid, is he?"

"There's enough of him," answered Cullen.

"But if he's a friend of yours," Darcy began, "why, maybe, after all, we got a chance of winning through."

"He's no friend of mine," answered Cullen.

The face of the other fell. Then he shook his head in disbelief. "As if an enemy of Geraldi would come lookin' him up," he suggested.

"Off and on, for about three years, he hunted for me," said Cullen.

Darcy gasped. "Git on our hosses and break for it, then!" he suggested.

Cullen stood up.

"You chump!" Darcy cried. "He'll see you!" And he reached up with one of his deformed hands to draw his companion down.

Cullen, however, stepped back. "Take my guns," he said. "I'm going down to pat his head and call him good dog. Then we'll see what we see." He took a long-barreled Colt from beneath the pit of his left arm. A smaller weapon, short but of large caliber, he took from within his vest on the same side, and then produced a slender knife with a blade as thin as a dripping of light, and supple as thought, and keen as death. He flicked this blade with the tip of his finger and then held it close to his ear to hear the vibrations. However, in that still air even Darcy could hear it, like the faint song of a wasp in the distance.

"Why'd you peel off everything?" asked Darcy in wonder. "Suppose you get cornered . . . just suppose he tackles you?"

"If he tackles me," Cullen replied, "I'm a dead man, anyway. But if I go without my weapons, I'll have an air of conscious virtue, as one might say, and that air will do me a deal of good with Geraldi."

"You're gonna go down and face him?" asked Darcy. "You got your nerve with you," he broke out in involuntary admiration.

"I have my nerve with me." Cullen smiled, although he had lost a good deal of color.

"Aw, I know how you feel," said Darcy.

"How do I feel, then?"

"I remember seein' a animal tamer. He was in a circus that hit Tucson, and the way he went in and kicked the bears in the face and pulled the tails of the lions and booted the tigers out of the way, it was wonderful to watch. He had to have half a dozen of 'em in the ring at once with him, and he made 'em do somersaults, and stand on their heads and mix drinks, and pretty near everything. But after that was all over he put on his biggest stunt. He got a couple of assistants with long iron spears, and he went over with a loaded gun in one hand and a club in the other and went into the cage of the black panther. Why, you couldn't hardly see where it was before that. It was just a pool of shadow on the floor. But that pool untangled itself and turned into a black leopard and didn't say nothin', but only looked. Well, the trainer, he pasted himself ag'in' the bars, right up ag'in' the door, and he talked mighty soft, and then he fired the pistol a couple of times, and after a while the panther, he put up one paw on the stool that he was supposed to get up and set on. He put up one paw and opened his mouth, and you seen his teeth, like icicles, thin and sharp. Still he didn't say nothin', but the trainer, he got out of that cage and called it a day's work. Which everybody agreed to and it was about five minutes before I got my breath again.

"Well, Cullen, I reckon that you feel like the way that trainer did?"

Cullen did not answer. He merely turned and walked rapidly down the hill.

II
"OLD ACQUAINTANCES MEET"

A brisk change increases the courage with the circulation. The heartbeat mounts, and the will to do with it. And that was the reason that Cullen advanced so briskly, with a swinging stride, and even managed to start whistling, although one tune died and another followed it without rhyme or reason, breaking in upon the middle. Yet he found himself, at length, marching straight up to the door of the cabin. The door was open. And from the top of the chimney, which leaned foolishly askew above the roof, the first thick, white smoke of a newly kindled fire was beginning to roll.

It was nearly sunset; the sun itself was behind a western mountain, and, although the sky was bright, yet a pleasantly mellow dusk already had gathered like a mist in the valley. It was so dim, indeed, that Geraldi had lighted a lantern inside the hut, and this twinkled faintly through the door.

Cullen crossed the stream, stepping from stone to stone, each with a furl of swift, glassy water rising on its side, and so came to the farther bank. There his heart suddenly failed him. He had to stop and look about him as though to admire the view, while he set his teeth and raised his courage. He succeeded, noting with a sick eye how the first sunset rose was beginning to fall in an impalpable shower on the face of a pool just above him. He succeeded so far in his effort that he was able to whistle again, and, armed with this music, he approached the house.

At the door he paused and knocked. Nothing but silence answered him. He listened more closely, and was able to make out the murmur and dull roar of the fire that was increasing in the stove. He knocked again, and there was again no answer, so that he peered into the interior. The day struggled against the glow of the lantern, so that the hut seemed as dark as a cave, yet, through that murkiness, he could distinguish the vague outlines of pots hanging on the wall, the gleam of a rifle that leaned in a corner, and one red eye of fire that looked through a crack of the stove.

"Old Harry Cullen!" said a voice behind him. "Jolly Harry Cullen . . . brave Harry Cullen again."

The heart of Cullen stopped; the cold cheerfulness of that voice had iced all the blood in his body. He moistened his dry lips as he turned, and there he saw Geraldi before him. Years had not altered him. There was the same slender body, the same handsome face, the same dark eyes, lighted now and again, the same sense of inward power, inward surety, such as takes men safely through hosts of danger.

"And how are you, Harry?" Geraldi asked.

Cullen moved his right hand slightly, but did not put it forth, for suddenly he realized that Darcy had been totally right. He had stepped into the cage of a panther, and his one wish was to conclude the performance by escaping with his life.

"I'm well enough," said Cullen. He managed to smile. "But I feel as though I might have a sudden attack," he added.

"Of fatigue," Geraldi asked, and his own smile was as cold as that of a comedy actor who is tired of his part. "You're tired of walking, of course. I suppose you've come a long distance, Harry?"

"When a man's on a tight wire," Cullen said, "the distance he has gone doesn't matter so much as his height from the ground. Suppose we go inside the house and sit down?"

"I'm afraid you wouldn't like the inside of the house as well as the outside," replied Geraldi. "It's just a shack, and a little stuffy, now, with the stove going. It's pleasanter out here . . . gives a man and his ideas more elbow-room, eh?"

He gestured toward the brilliant sky and the mountains. Cullen noted that the gesture was with the left hand. Furthermore, the glance of Geraldi did not wander from the face of Cullen for an instant. Like a prize fighter, he looked the other constantly in the eye, thereby keeping his every move in mind.

"And if you're tired," Geraldi said, "there's a good stump for you." He pointed, but Cullen shook his head.

"I'm not too tired to keep on my feet," he said. "What have you done, Jimmy? Turned yourself into a Westerner?"

"I'm a Westerner by nature," Geraldi replied. "It didn't need any turning to make me one in fact."

"You know all their ways, Jimmy?"

"Pretty much. Houses and horses and women are sacred. Those are the three chief tenets of the great Western faith."

"How is that?"

"Horses and women must not be stolen, old fellow . . . and a man never offers you his house until he's ready to offer you his hand."

"Ah?" Cullen said. He nodded and smiled in a casual manner, but he felt that he understood now why Geraldi had not asked him into the shack.

"Grand place here, Jimmy," went on Cullen. "This what you use for a hunting lodge?"

"This is where I'm going to build."

"Family house?"

"Yes. I'm to be married in a month or so. Only out here, Harry, to find the right spot, and this is it."

"Geraldi married?" Cullen said. "Well, well, that's hard to imagine. Offhand, I'd lay you on that. A thousand dollars to a hundred that you're not married inside the year."

"Long distance bets are risky things," answered Geraldi. "Accidents happen before a year is out. Some of us might die at any moment, Cullen."

He said it without emphasis, but Cullen shivered as he listened to the soft, caressing voice; he knew the threat was aimed at his own head.

"We'll drop the bet, then, if you want. D'you think that you'll be happy out here, Jimmy, away from all the excitement?"

"I have enough memory of excitement," Geraldi replied. "My life has been fairly crowded, Harry."

"Yes, of course, it has been. You've been at work from Río to Capetown, old fellow."

"And from Capetown to the River Min," Geraldi added with emphasis.

Cullen stiffened.

"This very moment," Geraldi went on, "I can see a Chinese junk swing down the Min and crash straight through the little boat I was sailing. Do you know, Harry, that when I looked up at the prow of the junk, it seemed to me that I could recognize your face there, leaning over the rail?"

He paused. Cullen, knowing that the fatal moment had come at last, looked swiftly into his mind, and deeply. Then he nodded. "I was there," he confirmed.

"You must have been surprised to see me on the little launch, then. Must have cut you to the heart, Harry, to see me tumbled into the water. But then, you knew perfectly well that I was a good swimmer."

"I did," said Cullen. "That was why I kept shooting at your head every time you came to the surface to breathe. If the captain of the junk hadn't acted like a coward more than a sailor, I would have bagged you that day, Jimmy."

Geraldi smiled; real joy appeared in his face as he remarked: "You're a truth-teller, old man. You go up hundreds of percents in my mind."

"Thanks," Cullen said. "They offered me eight thousand dollars for that job. Four down and four if I finished it off."

"Ah, Harry," Geraldi said. "Am I as cheap as that? Now I've turned a corner, I see, and can look at the truth about myself. That's how they bid for me, is it? Four thousand for a shot at Jimmy . . . eight if they take him."

"You were a lot younger then, Jimmy," said Cullen. "You hadn't become an international institution. You didn't represent the new culture, I may say. Kleinroth hadn't tried himself against you, at that time . . . Durkin was still the diamond king . . . and Lafarge still lived in the Trois Echelles."

"Three rare fellows. Three rare fellows," Geraldi stated. "Of course, one doesn't have company like that out here. But women, horses, and houses never were sacred to any of the lot, I dare say. I heard that Durkin was crippled."

"He was," Cullen said. "He has only one leg . . . he lives in an attic in a little Dutch town, and he's hired the children of the neighborhood to let him know if he is being searched for by a young man with a dark, fine face. . . ."

"I love an optimist," Geraldi said, "but, after all, every chance is a step covered with ice, and sooner or later a fellow may miss his footing . . . and roll all the way to the bottom . . . or all the way to destruction."

"Durkin rolled all the way to destruction," Cullen admitted. "I never saw Kleinroth, but I knew a fellow who knew another, who saw a body taken out of the Seine. Only one mark on him. A very narrow, deep knife wound at the base of the throat."

"D'you mean Kleinroth was that dead body?" asked Geraldi.

"Well, there was no beard on the face of the man who was picked from the river. But about the chin and cheeks the skin was pale, as if he might have been shaved recently. I'm surprised you didn't hear about the affair, because it happened just after you reached Paris from Algiers. I don't suggest you know about Lafarge, either?"

"Charming fellow, Lafarge. No, what happened to him?"

"He's in Bucharest, keeping a pawnshop and building himself up in the world again. He's not like Kleinroth. His spirit was broken, but it's on the mend again, I believe."

"Delighted to hear it," Geraldi commented. "But now to speak of your visit, Harry? It seems that you left your guns behind you . . . to lighten you for the march, perhaps? But that's dangerous. In this wild country, one should be prepared for self-defense. Here's a Colt, Harry. Will you take it?"

With his left hand, from somewhere in his clothes, he produced a revolver and held it out, handle first, toward the other. Cullen, with a blanched face, maintained a smile, nevertheless.

He said at last: "A gun wouldn't help me . . . here. But there's a story waiting up yonder on that hill, Jimmy. I'm the forlorn hope that came on to get your ear. Will you let me call my partner down here?" He tried to meet the blazing eye of Geraldi, but his glance wavered sadly. Suddenly he held out his hands, palms up. "Do you think that I would have got into the same cage with you, Jimmy, if I hadn't had something that's more to your taste than even the revenge that you want from me? Man, man, you're going to settle down and marry the woman you love . . . that'll be the end of your adventures. But before that happens, I want you to step into a story out of the *Arabian Nights*. You're the one man who could do the trick. Will you listen to the yarn? But if that doesn't tempt you, and you want me . . . go on. I'm not fool enough to try to stand up against you."

He closed his eyes, waiting, wavering a little where he stood. It was a long silence that followed. Then the voice of Geraldi, quick and hard: "Call him down, Harry. You win this first trick, but the game's not over until I hear the story."

III
"AN IMPOSSIBLE JOB"

Shadows possessed all the valley, but the afterglow lingered in the sky where three separate towers of cloud burned from foundation to turret, making the stream below run softly golden and rose. In this delightful dusk sat the three men on three low stumps before the cabin, Cullen and Geraldi intent upon one another, Darcy only interested in the story that he was telling.

"You know the Naylors?" asked Darcy.

"No," Geraldi responded.

"You've heard about 'em, though?"

"Yes. What everybody hears. That they have enough beef running on their range to feed the whole nation for a week, and that they run their own affairs without a sheriff, a judge, or a jury."

"That's what they do. They write their own laws in gunsmoke, and the periods is bullets, Geraldi. Anything else you've heard?"

"Why, yes. I've heard that those who go in stay in . . . no one comes out."

"No one comes out," Darcy repeated solemnly. "That's a thing worth remembering, too. No one comes out, unless he's turned into a Naylor that won't change his color."

"That won't talk, d'you mean?"

"I mean that. But me, Geraldi, I went into their land, and I come out, and here I sit to tell you what I seen and heard and did." He said it with an odd commingling of fear and of exultation, making a gesture with both his deformed hands.

"I'll start at the beginning. I'd been taking a pretty good rest in a sanitarium where the grub was free, and the rooms free, too. The name of it is Folsom. Maybe you've heard of it?"

"I've known a couple of the doctors there . . . and several of the patients," Geraldi said pleasantly. "They insist on exercise, I believe?"

"Breakin' rocks is their main hold. Well, I was turned loose at last, and went down Frisco way to look things over and get used to turning any corner I pleased. Got a ferryboat from Oakland Pier, and the first thing I hear is someone singin' a cowboy song. I go aft, and there, in a cleared space with a lot of folks standin' around and laughin' is a 'puncher from Texas way . . . I could tell by his get-up as plain as print. He had a five-gallon hat on his head, and the bulge of his gun was printed ag'in' his coat tails every time he spun around. He was dancin' and singin' and carryin' on in a mighty fool way, but it looked good to me, because I hadn't seen a gent with such a pile aboard him for a long time.

"His feet got faster while his balance got worse, until finally his knees hit the guard chain at the tail end of the deck. He tumbled over, rolled, and flopped into the water of the bay.

" 'Done for,' says I to myself, and takes a header after him.

"Well, when I come up, that Texan was swimmin' fine and easy because the cold water had shocked the booze out of his brain. He laid alongside of me and laughed and thanked me for jumpin' in to help him, and hoped that the sharks wouldn't dine off the pair of us. Because if they didn't, he said that he was gonna give me a bust in Frisco that would make the smoke curl higher than the Call building.

"Pretty soon they got a boat down and picked us up, and cussed out Texas pretty bad, until he stood up in the stern sheets and told that bunch, as they rowed back to the ferryboat, that he was a Texas Naylor, and that if he didn't like a ferryboat, he reserved the right to step off of her, no matter where she was. That quieted down things, and finally we got across the bay and hit Frisco with a bang that pretty soon echoed all over the old hills of the town. We spent about ten days circulating moisture through our systems, and, when we finally got pretty damp, we decided that the town wasn't big enough to hold us, so we started south. Jerry Naylor, which was his name, asked me to come out to his place. He explained things pretty good to me about the people that went in never coming out until old Naylor, that run the place, decided they was right. I said to Jerry that wherever he was, was where I wanted to be.

"So we stepped off the train, finally, and was met by a buckboard and drove two days back of nowhere through desert and hills and mountains, and grazing lands and forest. We touched fire the first day and snow the second, and the third morning we rolled up to the Naylor main ranch house.

"It looked ornery enough, and the paint was all sun-boiled off in patches, and the front garden is planted with hitchin' posts and plowed up by the hosses that have pawed the ground into holes. There is a coupla dozen mangy-lookin' chickens takin' dust baths, and three or four poison-faced bronc's at the racks, droppin' one hip and saggin' the lower lip. Right away I says that this looks like home.

"Inside there's the same sort of a picture that you'd expect in such a frame. The floors was wore to splinters, the chairs was tied up with balin' wire, old clothes was hanging from pegs on the walls of every room, and, take it all the way through, that place was plumb comfortable and easy-goin'.

"We rested a coupla days and then I started to get used to the range. The spring roundup was about due, and I worked into that and had a pretty good time. I got a chance to make myself right with old Naylor, too. That's Pike Naylor. He's a pretty picture of a man. Nature never done a more careless job than his face, and, what with age and hoss kicks, his teeth have been removed without no dentist's help, and his beak of a nose shuts right down on his chin. He looks as though he's always smilin', which he's doin' the opposite.

"But durin' the roundup a batch of greasers sneaked over from across the river and started to run off a bunch of cows. I was the lucky one to spot their back trail, and, when it come to the party, I managed to nail one of 'em.

"After that old Naylor took me in and had a talk with me, and said he figgered Jerry was right about me, after all, that bein' the first time Jerry ever had been right in his life, so he deserved a lot of credit. But old Pike said that I was enough of a man for even Jerry to make me out without raised type, and Pike says that he's gonna fix me good and place me right.

"Well, what he done was put me on the inside guard, which was three gents that never done nothin' but hang around in the cellar of the main house and keep an eye onto Pike's safe. That safe filled up one whole end of the cellar room that it was kept in. Pike kept everything there. He'd hauled in that safe on a special wagon with a whole flock of oxen about fifty year before, and by this time the safe was all full of money and business of all kinds.

"The three of us stand eight-hour watches, and the other two are a hard pair of boys, I can tell you, and I ain't tender enough to fry myself. That is the prize job on the ranch. We get double pay. We get one day a week off. We have a greaser to look after us. We get extra special chow, and a lot of attention from the girls whenever we ride to the town. I mean, Naylor's town.

"I'm sittin' pretty, you might say, but all the same that was a mighty lonely job. And the more I sat there in the cellar, the more I get to wonderin' what's inside of that safe? And the more I wonder about that, the more close I look at the safe itself. It's a cinch. It ain't a job for soap and soup. It's just for a can opener, and for an old hand like me it's nothin' at all.

"Well, once the idea got into my head, I couldn't get it out. I played with the thought day and night, and so one night it happened. I cracked that old safe wide open and stepped inside. There was a lot of drawers filled with papers, but there was a lot filled with other stuff. There was gold. Piles of it! There was silverwork, and such things, too. But all that weighed too much to be worthwhile. The paper money was better. I didn't count, but if I didn't rake out a quarter of a million in yallerbacks, I'm a liar and don't know my business.

"But that wasn't the best. There was family jewels! Partly they'd been bought for the weddings of Pike's daughters and nieces and granddaughters, and they rested there in the safe, because what chance is there to show off sparklers on Naylor's range? Partly they wasn't family stuff. There was jeweled crosses and jeweled robes which, if they didn't come from the lootin' of churches, I'm blind, and don't know what I see. But there was drawers and drawers filled with loose diamonds and rubies and emeralds and sapphires, so's you could dip your hands down into 'em. The fact is that old Pike is sold on jewels. Or maybe he figgers that someday he'll have to make a quick start and leave for a better country.

"Well, sir, when I seen this, I didn't stop to think. I loaded up and carried goodness knows how much in the sack when I left. A million . . . two million . . . I dunno. Enough to make you choke, only thinkin' about it." He closed his eyes with a soft groan.

"I get on my best hoss, a buckskin son of the north wind, and I streak for the outside. Maybe I would've done it, with luck, but they must've spotted me the minute I started. I looked back, and I see the signal fires burning from the hill behind the house, and I see the answers from the hills. Well, I went on, because there is no turnin' back. I ride straight on, all that night and all the next day, and just in the twilight I run into rifle bullets that roll the buckskin, and throw me half dead into the gully.

"When I come to, they're all around me, and Jerry is pleadin' for my life.

" 'Sure,' says one of 'em. 'We ain't gonna kill him.'

"They didn't, either. But they found a handy tree where two branches went away from the trunk, and they ties my legs to the trunk with a rawhide lariat, and they drive a pair of big spikes through the palms of my mitts. . . ." He stopped, and raised his hands a little, with the fingers puckered together as though they were making ready to pick up something small. "There I hang," Darcy continued, "until I go blind with pain and bleedin'. And it was there that a pair of greasers found me. Cattle rustlers, but they had a heart. They had time to put me down, after pullin' the spike through my hands. They took me outside. And here I sit and tell you about it."

"And why tell me?" asked Geraldi.

"Because it's a one-man job," Darcy said. "It's a job for one man that can make himself mighty important and get into the guard job, the way that I did. And then open the safe . . . and get away."

"It sounds simple. Am I the one man?" Geraldi asked dryly.

"Mind you, there'd be help," Darcy assured Geraldi.

"There'd be Jerry, that's tired of the inside and wants to go outside. He's got a girl, I guess. He'll play the game with you, no matter how you want it played, if he can be sure enough of a split to make it worth his while. He's been turned loose once, but he never will be ag'in, because the old man won't never trust him ag'in. He thinks Jerry had a hand in my job."

Geraldi shook his head. "I've never heard of such a plant," he said. "A guarded safe, surrounded by a country two days' ride in diameter, and filled with armed men under one head. That's an impossible job, Cullen!"

"Of course, it is," said Cullen, "and that's why I brought it to you, because I knew that anything smaller never would tempt you."

IV
"A LADY IN A DILEMMA"

The night was still and hot. Under the arcades of the old patio, smoky lanterns burned, but in the central portion, where most of the little tables had been placed, the moonlight was brilliant, striking on a smile, a flash of eyes, or the gleam of a lifted glass. Chiefly these were Mexican or half-breed girls of the village, *peónes,* Mexican and American cowpunchers in from the neighboring ranches, and a few people of better station.

"Think that such bad beer has brought so many people out?" Cullen asked.

"Not the beer, Harry," answered Geraldi, "but the moon. See how the incense goes up to it from every table."

"You mean the cigarette smoke?"

"Cigarette smoke by day, but incense on a night like this, worship of the great goddess, religious devotion. . . ."

"Oh, rot," broke in Cullen. "I'm half stifled!"

"You have the thick Northern blood," Geraldi said. "This air is delightful to your true Southerner. It kisses the face, it makes clothes unnecessary armor to the true habitué, while the Northerner distills in drops, and sticks to his chair."

Cullen stirred uneasily. "Speaking of clothes, you have enough of 'em for a fancy dress party."

Geraldi looked down complacently on his tight Mexican jacket on which the metal lacing flashed. "I'm in a country where I don't wish to be known. Beyond my bounds, but, still, some eye might recognize me."

"So you put a spotlight on yourself with all those childish trimmings."

"There's nothing like a spotlight to dissolve the features," Geraldi advised. "Dress me up soberly, and I'll wager two or three people would recognize me, but now I look like a Mexican dandy, and I can speak enough Spanish to fill the part."

"You look like . . . ," Cullen began irritably, and then checked himself. "But what are you going to do? When are you going to make up your mind? In the meantime, we've ridden on, day after day, until we're on the edge of the Naylor place. This little town, I'll wager, is under their thumb, for that matter. What are you going to do? When are you going to reach a decision?"

"There's always time for the man who expects to jump off the bridge," Geraldi began. "In the first place, I need a good excuse for riding into the Naylor place."

"If you ride into the Naylor place without being invited, you'll simply be stopped by a bullet."

"What do you suggest?"

"Wait till you're invited. You can do something that'll make them see you're an expert rider and a fine shot. That's all they want. In a week, you'll be invited in as a member of the gang."

"That's what I don't want," Geraldi stated flatly.

"You don't want it? Then you don't intend to go at all?"

Geraldi tapped his lean fingers rapidly on the top of the table and raised his eyes thoughtfully toward the upper line of the hotel, where a great squat adobe tower bulked back against the moonlit sky.

"I don't want to sneak into the place as a friend. I want to go boldly, as I please, with just a sufficient excuse to keep from being shot as a spy. I don't want to sneak into the confidence of old Naylor, as our friend Darcy did. If possible . . . if I go at all on the job . . . I want to be an honorable thief. What are they whispering about so much?" He said this to the waiter, who was passing by.

The waiter was a dapper little Mexican, who now paused at their table.

"They are all grinning and whispering at the tower," Geraldi said in Spanish, "as if they expected the tower to laugh back at them. What's wrong with it?"

"A girl," said the waiter.

"That's a complaint," Geraldi agreed, "but I didn't know that it bothered adobe bricks."

"There's a girl inside," said the waiter. "Locked up, with a man outside her door to see that she stays there. There's her father now, who came down and caught her here this evening. . . ." He nodded his head toward a lumbering man with all the aspect of a rancher who had just entered the patio, hat in hand, mopping his face with a bandanna.

"She's a runaway?"

"*Señor,* I know nothing, except that she has been here for three days, and gone to the post office five times every day. Some say that *Señor* Jerry Naylor . . . but I know nothing. That is always the best way." He chuckled and went on.

"This moon," Geraldi said to his companion, "breeds such affairs. That's why the incense. . . ."

"Bah!" Cullen said, and fell into a study.

"Why are you so worried?" said Geraldi. "Are you figuring up your percentage already?"

"My percentage? I have my percentage." Cullen smiled. "I've learned that I can sit down with the panther and pat his head without having my hand taken off. That's enough profit for me. I'm able to sleep at night now, without a picture of

Jimmy Geraldi climbing through the window with a knife between his teeth."

"Yes," Geraldi said frankly, "that's an advantage. Hello, sir. Here's an extra chair, if you want to sit down."

The father of the delinquent girl had been wandering here and there in the crowded patio, looking for a seat. Now he paused, peered hard at the two, and accepted the proffered place with a grunt of satisfaction.

He turned away from them as he waited for his beer, as though he did not wish to break into or overhear the conversation of the two, from time to time mopping a fat, handsome face that glistened with continual perspiration. But after he had drained half his beaker of beer and sighed contentedly, he broke out: "It's a cold drink, anyway. If they got nothing else, they got ice."

"They have ice," Cullen agreed politely.

"But it takes more than ice to cool down the girls in this part of the world, I guess. Cool 'em off to good sense, and keep 'em from bein' as flighty as birds. You know about what's happened. Everybody does here, I reckon, so you don't have to look polite and blank."

"About your daughter, you mean?" Cullen asked.

"The little minx!" said the other. "Not eighteen . . . and this! But I got her, and she ain't gonna get away. Not eighteen, and I still got the law on my side. Another month, and she could've snapped her fingers in my face. Would've, most likely. For a Naylor, too. For that wo'thless Jerry Naylor, of the whole lot." He fumed at the thought, and drained off the rest of his beer at a draft.

"Dances and magazines," said the rancher. "As sure as my name is Ben Thomas, dances and magazines . . . the fool dances and the fool stories they do. Their heads get full of men. Plumb disgustin'. But I got her now. Unless young

Naylor is a bird that can fly as high as that tower."

"He might climb, though," Geraldi suggested suddenly.

Mr. Thomas looked at the speaker with a sneer. "D'you think you could climb it?" he asked.

Geraldi considered.

"Here's twenty dollars," Thomas stated, "that says you couldn't." He slid the golden coin out on the table, adding cheerfully: "Don't let that hold you back, if you hanker to make the try."

A second twenty-dollar gold piece appeared as if by magic from under the hand of Geraldi.

"What shall I say to her when I get up there?" he asked, pointing to the narrow window of the tower.

"Give her my love," the rancher replied, grinning, "and tell her I hope she sleeps well because she's gonna take a long ride tomorrow."

Geraldi nodded. He stood up from the chair, removed his hat, and slicked back his hair, while he noted the features of the wall before him.

"I'll tell her that," he said, "and then we'll have an extra twenty for beer."

"Hold on," said Cullen. "You're not going to break your neck, Jimmy?"

"Cats always fall on their feet," Geraldi responded, his teeth flashing in a smile that was grimly familiar to Cullen. Then he crossed the patio and stood beneath the tower.

There were no climbing vines to help him, but only the surface irregularities of the adobe wall, the edges of some bricks projecting well beyond their neighbors. He tugged the boots from his feet, took off his tight jacket, and suddenly leaped high up and caught a projecting ridge. And, to use his own metaphor, as a cat jumps and clings to a tree trunk, so he seemed to jump and cling. After that, smoothly, rapidly, he went up the wall.

It was not half so hard as it had seemed from the ground, for the old tower had settled to the farther side, letting the weight of his body have an excellent support as he climbed. There were two windows, also, to help him, and presently he had reached the upper embrasure. There he paused and looked back to the patio beneath.

They were all on their feet, laughing, clapping, applauding. The moon was so bright that it showed him the fat mouth of Ben Thomas, agape as he stood beside his chair.

He turned back toward the window itself. It was closed. The old glass panes were set crookedly in their frames. Dust and the dissolving adobe itself, perhaps, had formed a little coil here, and out of it grew a sparse amount of grass and little weeds. He reached in and tapped at the panes.

Then he waited. No light showed on the inside of the room, only faint reflections of the moon gleamed dull and faint upon the windowpanes. He began to have an odd feeling that the girl already had left the place, but he knocked again.

Then he thought he heard a stealthy footfall; eventually the windows were drawn open with a jerk that set the frames trembling and shuddering. A faint breeze blew upon the neck and shoulders of Geraldi as the draft set in from behind him, and he heard the fluttering of paper inside the chamber.

But these things—oh, fickle heart of man!—were not what interested Geraldi. Instead, he was straining his eyes to see more clearly the pretty face of the girl before him, and he was breathing deep of a certain delicate fragrance of perfume that tinged the air with delight.

But all was shadow and dimness, until she spoke and seemed thereby to throw a light upon herself.

V

"BOTH HANDS AT TWELVE"

She was perfectly careless and assured.

"Hello, handsome," she said. "What threw you up here?"

"A twenty-dollar bet," Geraldi answered. "And a lot of pity for a poor girl locked up in a tower."

"That sounds like a pretty fairy story to me," said the girl. "Even if they built towers of brass, and hired a flock of dragons to guard the roads, still, along would come a knight and break up everything and ride her away on the wind. I hear them laughing downstairs. Is this a show?"

"Fools," Geraldi said, "laugh for the lack of occupation. Now that I'm up here, your father asked me to say good night to you and to tell you that he expects you'll sleep well."

"Sure, I'll sleep," she said. "But what a monkey I was to stay here and let him catch up. Who are you, partner?"

"I'm a man out of a job," Geraldi replied diplomatically, "and wondering who will hire me?"

"The ranches are always looking for good men."

"I'm lazy," Geraldi said. "That idea doesn't appeal to me at all."

"What do you want to do?"

"A long ride would suit me. But with company, Miss Thomas. I'm a lonesome fellow, you see."

"Lazy and lonely." The girl smiled—faintly he could see

the flash of that smile. "But who are you?"

"A man with a fast horse," he said, "and a great fancy for riding at night."

"At night?"

"Also, I'm a friend."

"Jerry," she burst out in whispering exultation. "Jerry sent you?"

"Not Jerry, but luck put me here . . . and a twenty-dollar bet, as I told you before."

"Speak soft, soft," she said. "There's a rat at the door."

"He may grow sleepy tonight."

"What d'you mean?"

"That I'm coming after you, after midnight. Will you be awake?"

"Wide awake. You really will come?"

"I've promised."

"And then what?"

"We'll ride for the Naylor place, if that's where you want to go."

"But Jerry . . . he didn't send you?"

"Lazy men are always bored," he told her. "This will give us a chance for action. Suppose I climb up here tonight and bring a rope. Could you lower yourself down it?"

"I can handle my weight on my hands," she assured him. "But horses. We'll need fast horses."

"What did you bring with you?"

"A little two-stepping pinto, not worth a cent."

"I'll have a fast horse for you. Remember, it will be after midnight."

"Man, man," she said, "as though I could sleep after this."

He began the descent, but to climb down a steep place is always far more difficult than to mount. Halfway to the bottom his left hand lost its hold, the jerk knocked his feet loose, and he dangled loosely by one hand.

A yell went up from the patio, but in another moment he had secured grips again, and swarmed rapidly down the rest of the way. He passed through a small ovation of cheers, clapping hands, smiling faces, back to the table where he had left Cullen and Ben Thomas.

"Young feller," said Thomas, "you're about as much monkey as man, or you couldn't've done that. Here's the twenty and welcome. Did you see Elsa up there?"

"I saw Elsa . . . gave her your message, and then listened a while. She's a little excited, Mister Thomas."

"Sure she is," the father said complacently. "She's been excited her whole life. Hosses . . . men . . . dances . . . riding . . . anything'll excite her. I aim to expect that she's namin' her opinion of me free and liberal, just about now."

"She has her ideas," Geraldi said. "Sit down. There's more beer somewhere about."

"Not me," replied Ben Thomas. "If that wall has been climbed once, it can be climbed ag'in. I'm gonna set myself here and keep a clear head. If I close one eye before the mornin' comes, my name ain't Ben Thomas. That's all."

Geraldi bit his lip, but shortly after he withdrew from the patio. Cullen went with him, to walk up and down in the greater coolness outside the building.

"Why did you do it, Jimmy?" asked Cullen. "Risked your neck, made everyone look at you, and put our whole game in danger."

"I needed a passport for the Naylor place," replied Geraldi, "and that girl will be one."

"Are you going to steal her?"

"Of course, I am. And your horse for her to ride on. There'll be a pinto left behind for you."

Cullen clasped his hands behind his back. "You're going to

do it, then, Jimmy? You're going to tackle the Naylor outfit?"

Geraldi laughed and nodded. "It's my duty," he said.

"Duty?"

"You see how the matter stands, Harry? I used to be one of the fellows who lived outside the law, but now I'm to be married and settle down. . . ."

Cullen coughed sarcastically.

". . . I have to enforce the laws, you see."

"By going to rob a safe?"

"That's a rough way of putting it, Harry. Looked at from another angle, I can't sit quietly when there are people about who crucify living men who are no worse than other thieves. They need a lesson, and I ought to give them one."

"Of course, you should." Cullen grinned. "A rare lesson that they won't forget. But tell me, how am I to help?"

"You are to raise a row because your horse has been stolen. Tell the people about here that you don't know who I am. I'm only a Mexican rascal you met on the road and took on for company's sake. You think I'm probably a professional thief and cattle rustler. In the meantime, look about for a horse to take the place of the one you've lost. Get more than one. Get three or four, while you're about it."

"And why three or four, Jimmy?"

"Because one of these days you may see some puffs of smoke ride up into the air from the hills toward the Naylor place. If we come out at all, we'll be coming on tired horses, and a change will be useful. Three puffs, we come down the river. Four puffs, we keep to the hills north of this town."

"What about one or two puffs?"

"City eyes like yours wouldn't see them, probably. Besides, puffs of smoke are apt to go up from newly lighted campfires, you know."

"And if it's at night?"

"A fire built strong and high on one of the hills will show you. You can catch a fire signal more easily than a smoke signal. A blanket will make the fire wink clearly enough."

Cullen muttered something to himself.

"What's that?" asked Geraldi.

"Tell me, Jimmy. D'you really want the money out of this affair, or is it only a game?"

"Money?" Geraldi repeated lightly. "I never robbed for money in my life. Good night, Harry, because I'm getting up betimes, as the good old books say." So he left Cullen, went up to his room in the hotel, and hung his watch from the cross rod at the foot of the bed. Then he flung himself down, crossed his hands behind his head, and straightway was asleep.

There were many noises in the old building. There was singing in the halls as the other guests went to bed late, and there were slammings of doors and creakings of floors and screeching of chairs, hastily moved back from tables. But through all this commotion, Jimmy Geraldi slept like a child.

The hotel, in fact, was utterly still when he wakened with a start, and sat up in bed. He scratched a match, and the spurt of the flame showed the hands of the watch joined at twelve. At this he smiled a little, satisfied with that guard that had kept watch during his subconsciousness.

After that he rose, made up his pack swiftly, and, carrying his boots in his hand, went down the stairs and into the stable. There he saddled the black stallion, and the tall, strong bay horse that Cullen had been using on the trip. He made the stirrups short for the girl, and then left the two horses standing loose in their stalls. It was possible that they might get into trouble with the other animals in the barn, but this chance had to be taken.

When he left the barn, there was a clear sky above him,

powdered with white stars; all lights were out in the hotel. The windows on the western side of it were gleaming black and silver against the face of the moon. He went to the entrance of the patio, but in the farthest corner, as he peeked in, he saw the stalwart form of Ben Thomas, who kept vigil there, true to his promise, and with a riot gun in his lap, to give point to his presence.

Geraldi did not disturb him, but, fading back into the hotel, he slipped up the stairs in his noiseless, stockinged feet until he reached the winding steps of the tower. Here he went almost as slowly as the minute hand of a clock, giving the pressure of his weight only by infinite slow degrees to each of the wooden steps. They gave out noise in every instance, but the noises were so widely separated, so soft, so irregular in recurrence, that it was rather like the noises made when a rising wind begins to press against a house. So he came up until his head was on a level with the floor of the top hall.

Fumes of tobacco smoke already had warned him that the guard probably was wide-awake, and so he found him. He sat with his chair tilted back against the wall, a lantern hanging from a peg beside his head, a cigarette between his lips, and a magazine folded on his lap. The story he perused must have interested the tow-headed youth greatly, for he bit his lips and scowled with excitement as he turned the page—then suddenly lifted his head and looked straight at the face of Geraldi.

But the shadows were too thick to be penetrated, and immediately the guard dropped his head again.

VI
"AWAY!"

The guard had seen nothing in the shadows; in reality, he had been looking straight into the face of death, for Geraldi's hand was filled, not with a gun, but with a small knife, whose handle was weighted to drive home the blow when the weapon was flung. For an instant the blade trembled on the flat of Geraldi's hand, but the tremor passed, and presently the knife returned to its sheath as the guard resumed his reading.

Geraldi renewed his advance. He moved in no haste, but rather drifted soundlessly forward without a perceptible variation from slow to fast or from fast to slow. He did not even halt when the guard raised his head suddenly and came on the alert. Geraldi could see the neck harden and swell; he could see the shudder of cold and mortal apprehension that ran over the body of the man. A cruel little smile appeared upon the lips of the hunter, the shadow of whose coming had fallen so visibly upon the soul of the victim.

But the instinctive warning that was working upon the mind of the guard now at last made him start up violently. The magazine fluttered down from his hand, the leaves catching at the air like a hundred rattling little wings, and Geraldi saw the startled face turned toward him. A young face, and handsome, although rather heavy about the jaws, and with the brows strongly marked. Beneath the arch of them, frightened eyes glared out at Geraldi with terror, but with the determination to fight that whipped a hand back to the holster on the thigh.

Geraldi, in response, flicked a hand downward; the elastic of a band about his wrist permitted a small bag of shot, cased in soft chamois, to fall down to his fingertips. There it was clasped, and with it Geraldi slapped the guard without violence on the side of the head. He had gauged the distance, the time limit, the necessary degree of violence, with such accuracy that he was able to pick the drawn gun from the relaxing fingers of the guard, then receive the weight of the toppling body and stretch it gently upon the floor. In that act, he felt the slow throbbing of the heart, which assured him that his victim was not seriously damaged, and he was free to secure the man at once. A few twists of twine trussed the guard helplessly, foot and hand. His own bandanna, rolled and knotted with expert skill, then made a perfect gag.

Geraldi stood up, dusting his hands lightly and nodding with satisfaction at the sight of the man upon the floor. The latter had recovered consciousness some seconds before, and now he lay straining against his bonds with the hopelessness and the patient fury of a tied bulldog. Red and purple swelled his face; his eyes misted over with his extreme rage. So Geraldi smiled down at him in the most genial fashion.

Then he stepped to the door and tapped lightly on it. "Are you ready?" He heard a soft, swift scurry of feet.

"Oh, ready . . . yes. Is Dick there? Will he let me go?"

"I think he will. Has he the key?"

"I don't know."

Geraldi shrugged his shoulders. "The mind of a good old steady-going lock like this could be read with no trouble, I suppose. I'll try it, at least."

He took a bright bit of steel, a mere sliver of it, from a little case in a vest pocket, and, after he had worked in the lock with this for some moments, he felt the bolt give. The door opened an instant later, and the girl came running out to him with her pack slung over one shoulder. She came through a wave of shadow and through a wave of light as the flame jumped in the throat of the lantern. She was far from beautiful, for her nose was what the poet called "tip-tilted," and there were several delicate blotches of freckles across the bridge of it, but she had very bright eyes and a charming mouth, continually smiling or laughing. So she came out to Geraldi, smiling and gay, as though this were a childish game, and not something on which a man might have lost his life.

She gave her hand to Geraldi, coming close to him and smiling with a lifted face, so that suddenly no words of gratitude were necessary, but all was said by that single gesture. Then she glanced down at the bound and gagged man on the floor.

"Poor Dick Orville," she said. "What a lump on the side of his head. Poor old Dick."

"Come," Geraldi said. "Because a half second now may mean more than a half mile later on."

She followed him at once, only pausing, he noted, to throw a kiss toward the empurpled face of Dick, as the latter twisted wildly back and forth, struggling against this bonds. Swiftly they went down the stairs, through the side door, and out into the freshness of the open night.

The house slept behind them, a tall, blank face, staring with deep, dark eyes at the nothingness of the world. Even Geraldi felt solemn and small and useless in such a presence. He led straight on to the stable, where they found the horses and took them out through the rear door of the barn. He gave her a foot up into the saddle, then swung onto the back of the black stallion, which he drew closer to her.

"Look at the hotel," he said.

"Horrible brute of a place," said the girl. "I've seen enough of it."

"It's more than a hotel, just now," Geraldi said softly. "Mind you . . . if you leave this town and ride on with me to the Naylor place, you're leaving one half of your whole life behind. You understand that, Elsa?"

"I've had a good look at that side of the coin," she told him. "Now I want to see the other. Oh, I've made up my mind."

She let her horse lurch ahead a long step, then reined him back as Geraldi held up a warning hand.

"I wish I'd had a chance to talk this all over with you beforehand," he said. "But you know one thing . . . that once in the Naylor place, there's no coming out?"

"I know all about it. I been in prison most of my days."

"What do you mean by that?"

"Stuck on a one-horse ranch, milking cows, making butter and cottage cheese to sell in town, looking after the chickens . . . about the only fun was hunting for new nests in the mow of the barn. All the parties that we had were mostly in the summer, on Saturday nights, when you're tired from the week's work, and you go, dressed up in calico, and sit along the wall of the schoolhouse room, and dance with gents that've lightened up their feet as much as they can with red-eye. I've been in jail, I tell you, and whatever the Naylor place is, it's a bigger jail than the one that I come out of."

"I'd like to do this straight and right," said Geraldi. "And before we start, tell me if you think this fellow you're headed for wants to marry you?"

"Of course, he does," she said. "Once he rode seven days to get to me. Well, I guess that means something."

"You think he's straight?"

"Of course, I do. What do you think?"

"I don't think anything. It's up to you, but I don't wish to take you in if you'll begin to beg to have the door opened the instant that you're inside."

She chuckled as she was about to answer, but that answer was not completed, for out of an upper window of the hotel rang a loud, piercing cry, and a babble of curses to terminate it.

"Dick," said the girl. "He's from out California way, and I recognize the way that he swears. Dick's loose, and that means trouble. Partner, if you want me to win this game, it's your lead, and I'll try to follow suit."

For answer Geraldi loosed the black horse at the low fence straight before them. He glanced back over his shoulder to see the girl flinging her mount well and bravely into the air on the same jump, and then they were plunging through the dark of the trees, then ranging out into the dazzling white of the moonshine.

They heard many voices behind them, but these were of little importance, and all that mattered was that they were ranging farther and farther away from the disturbance at the hotel; fences darted away on either side. Then all fences ceased together; the hills swayed up and down through the moon mist; the loftier mountaintops loomed larger, darker, walking slowly toward them in variegated garments of many colors.

A wind cut at their faces with the acrid smell of alkali in its breath. But now all sound had ceased behind them. They were alone in the desert, and by unspoken, mutual consent they drew up their horses and let them blow. It was not for the sake of the animals that they did this; it was rather for the purpose of taking stock of their new surroundings, for during that last long burst each of them knew that they had ridden across the undrawn boundary and passed into the realm of the Naylors. They stood on forbidden ground.

After a little time they could hear the sounds of the desert at night. These, as a rule, are so dim that only the most practiced senses can catch them as they float dissolved along the horizon, but Geraldi made out the quavering, mocking yell of a coyote somewhat nearer at hand. Somewhere, also—far closer than the other two—a calf was bawling. And the sound, like the insistent squeaking of a shutter blown to and fro in an upstairs room, was the barking of a dog. All of these sounds appeared to the two riders both dolorous and dangerous, as though the very earth was giving out its creatures in order to threaten those who invaded the precincts of the Naylor family.

This thought made Geraldi smile as he dismissed it. "We'd better start on!" he said.

"Listen to me," said the girl. "You've brought me far enough. Why should you go on with this, when it doesn't mean anything to you? Go back. I thank you a million times. Some way I can blunder along and reach him. The Naylors, even, wouldn't do harm to a girl, I guess."

She laughed a little as she said the last, but there was something about her manner of speaking that made Geraldi doubt her security of mind. *Even* the Naylors would be kind to a woman. It was most patent that she wrote them down very low in the scale. Except, doubtless, that she considered young Jerry Naylor a brilliant exception to the family rule.

But he said: "Leave you here in the middle of the night? I'm going to take you right on into sight of the central place. I'll leave you there, if you wish. Let's get on. I've an idea that old Ben Thomas is pretty wild to get you back right now."

VII
"A TALKATIVE GENT"

Dawn came over the mountains in waves of gray, of mauve, of rose, and then of golden fire that flooded through the trees that grew densely along the sides of the watercourse down which the two were riding; and the noontide, furnace-hot, found them in a narrow defile scattered with boulders that yet threw shadows too small to shelter horsemen.

The girl was the guide. She had mapped the estate with care, using many reports that she had pieced together, chiefly from the talk of Jerry Naylor. The reason that Darcy had taken so long to get away was that he had failed to travel in the straightest, easiest line. They themselves should reach the central ranch house, she declared, by the dusk of that same day.

So they endured the heat, focused on them now as though by a burning glass from the glistening face of one cañon wall. Many times the sweat of the horses had been coated over by dust through which the streams of perspiration were breaking again; and all was heat, misery, while the very rocks had a dream-like seeming from the transparent waves that rose shimmering above them in endless succession.

Even in that iron pass, however, there was some life, for cacti had found sparse rooting here and there, and in the midst of the gulch they found a meager trickle of water that ran by as a miracle among the stones.

They dismounted to water the horses here, and, going up the diminutive creek a few steps, the girl and Geraldi kneeled to fill their canteens at a little pool.

It was while they were crouched here that Geraldi whispered to her: "Now steady, Elsa. Just behind that brown rock back of me there's a rider and a rifle. He's coming out to get us. He has us covered already."

"I hear you," said the girl. She did not start, merely stiffening a little as she dipped her hand into the slow current and let the lukewarm water trickle across her wrist. "What shall we do?" she added. "I can shoot straight."

She carried a .32 belted on her hip, but Geraldi merely smiled, and, without looking up, she was able to see that smile dimly in the face of the water beneath them.

"We don't want shooting," he said. "This is a Naylor, of course. He'll be apt to make no trouble if I give myself up to him. Probably take us in to the ranch and let his chief make the decision about us. That's what you want, isn't it?"

She did not answer. There was a slight grating sound of a heel grinding against small stones, and then a gruff voice called: "You picnickers, there . . . where you think you might be?"

Geraldi looked over his shoulder.

It was a bull of a man who stood behind him with a leveled rifle, a thick-chested, huge-armed fellow with a red face, made still more scarlet by the reflection from a violently crimson shirt that he was wearing. He had the flannel sleeves of it rolled up sun-blackened forearms to the elbow. A prickly stubble of beard seemed to be irritating the raw red of his face, and that, perhaps, inspired the glare of his little pig eyes and the scowl that twisted his mouth.

"No harm, sir," Geraldi tried to assure him, rising, canteen in hand, and he smiled brightly at the man of the red shirt.

"Oh, no! We don't mean anything wrong," said Elsa.

"No harm. No wrong," grunted the big man in disgust and in contempt. "Why, you talk like a pair of yearlin' fools. D'you know where you are?"

"We're on the Naylor place, I suppose," Geraldi responded.

"You knew it, then?" said the other, his scowl growing, if possible, yet more ugly. "You knew it, but you come right on in?"

"This," said Geraldi, "is Elsa Thomas. You may know her name. She's a great friend of Jerry Nay. . . ."

He could not finish the word, for the other burst in: "There ain't any friends of anybody in this place, except them that old Pike Naylor has passed on. If she's one of Jerry's women friends, what's that to me or anybody else around here?"

At the last sentence the eyes of Geraldi narrowed ever so slightly, although he maintained his smile steadfastly.

"Unbuckle your gun belt, you," the guard said to Elsa. "Unbuckle it and let that gun drop. Woman or man, I'm a fool if I ain't old enough to take no chances."

Obediently she loosened the buckle, and the belt with the small holster which it supported fell to the ground, thudding softly on the stones.

"You, there," the rifleman said to Geraldi. "You don't wear no guns outside. What you got inside?"

"Guns?" Geraldi said, raising his brows. "My dear fellow, what use would I have for guns when I can't use the things?" He laughed a little as he said it and, turning toward the girl, made a little gesture of helplessness.

She nodded in turn. "Don't you be afraid," she comforted

Geraldi. "It'll turn out all right."

"Will it?" growled the guard. "I'm gonna tell the pair of you. I'll do this for you . . . I'll take you back to the boundary and turn you loose. I'll keep your hosses to keep you from dodgin' back in. You'll have a chance for a fine little stroll. If that's all right, keep right on smilin'. . . ."

"My dear friend!" exclaimed Geraldi. "My dear friend, you don't mean to say . . . a young girl and I . . . unused to travel . . . this rough ground . . . the rocks . . . we'd have blistered feet. . . ."

"It sure makes my heart bleed to hear you yap," said the other, keeping a steady eye down the barrel of his rifle. "Now hoist your hands, you tenderfoot loon, and I'll see if you're as clean of poison as you say. If you're lyin' to me, heaven help you. Hoist up those hands at once and reach as far as you kin . . . reach, I said, reach!"

Geraldi jerked his hands toward the sky. "How extraordinary," he complained to the girl. "I've never been treated in such a manner before, Elsa."

"If I'm treatin' you like you might be a man," said the ruffian, "it don't mean nothin' except that I work careful. You can't tell the poison in a snake by the color of its skin. Stand still, you skinny rat, and, if you budge those hands, I'll let you have it!" He tucked his rifle under his right arm as he said this, holding the weapon balanced with ease in his huge hand, and keeping the forefinger upon the trigger. He approached Geraldi with caution in his step, but with an open sneer upon his face.

"This here," he said as he drew closer, "is gonna be a lesson that some of the gents outside might remember. You rambled right in to make a call, did you? You're gonna write a letter the next time, or I'm a liar. Keep them arms stiff!"

He barked the latter injunction, and Geraldi, apparently

paralyzed with fear, stretched tiptoe toward the sky.

"Yaller-livered as a rabbit!" sneered the guard, and laid his grasp upon the breast of Geraldi's coat. He threw the coat open, seeing in the first glimpse the butt of a revolver neatly secured by a clip beneath the left armpit of the stranger. But that, for an instant, was all that he could see, for the right arm of Geraldi jerked down, and the elbow glanced on the temple of this outpost with such an impact that he staggered back, the rifle exploding harmlessly as he did so.

Geraldi followed him with a gliding step. The Colt whose butt the guard had seen the instant before now flashed in his hand as though brought to his fingers by a mere wish. Straight at the heart of the big man the muzzle steadied. Then, changing his mind at the last instant, Geraldi cracked the barrel across the right hand of his enemy. That stroke loosened every nerve and muscle of the strong hand. Down went the rifle, clanging and clattering on the rocks, and, as the victim gasped out a curse, Geraldi closed with him.

It looked to the girl as though her companion would be swallowed by the vast embrace of the giant. She, desperate with apprehension, scooped her revolver from its holster upon the ground, for she had been raised to act like a man in times of need, but as she straightened, she saw a strange thing.

For the red-shirted monster was strained back, his body bent in a bow, one hand beating at the thin air to recover his balance, and the other reaching blindly toward the throat of her slender friend. Then he fell. It was such a shock that the big frame remained still without a quiver for an instant, and in that instant the practiced hand of Geraldi had removed the gun belt, a hidden Derringer, a heavy hunting knife, from the prostrate Naylor.

Then he stepped back, smiling and nodding reassurance to the girl. She, however, looked no more at the fallen man, but at Geraldi himself, with a frown rather of wonder than of admiration. For it had been like the working of a miracle. Vaguely she had seen the flash of hands working faster than the eye could follow; vaguely she had comprehended a craft of wrestling that had made the very hand power and bulk of the big man fight against himself. But still she could not comprehend the fall of their enemy. And it seemed to her almost horrible that a man should have been rendered helpless and beaten by one hardly half his size. It was like seeing a child master an adult.

The fallen hero, gradually recovering from the shock of the fall, raised himself to his elbows. His face was still loosened; his mouth sagged open, but reason and understanding now suddenly blazed in his eyes again. His huge mouth wrestled with the word, but it came like the gasp of a beast from his throat: "Geraldi!"

"Geraldi!" echoed the girl. Comprehension rushed into her face. "Geraldi!" she repeated, as though that one word could have explained the greatest of miracles.

"Sit up," Geraldi said gravely, "or you'll have a sunstroke. Put on your hat. Now, my friend, what's your name?"

"Lambert Naylor," answered the other, dragging himself slowly to his feet. He stood inert, one big hand propped against a boulder's top, his head sagging.

"The very luck of the lucky has come my way," Geraldi muttered. "How should you know me, Naylor?"

"I was up in Chicago," Naylor began, slowly raising his big head, as though the muscles of his neck were barely strong enough to support it. "I was there that time that Red McIntyre and Scotty Morgan tried for you. I seen you there. . . ."

"You were the third man," Geraldi said, comprehension dawning.

The chin of Lambert Naylor dropped, and a foolish smile made his mouth gape. "Have I been talkin' again?" he asked himself aloud. "I have, and I've talked myself into a Forty-Four caliber slug through the brain."

VIII
"WHEN GERALDI SMILES"

After this, a silence fell over them, Geraldi staring thoughtfully at Lambert Naylor, and the latter looking back with dull, resigned eyes at the slender youth before him. At last Elsa, glancing from one to the other, said quietly: "I don't know what it means, Mister Geraldi. Are you James Geraldi?"

"I'm afraid I am."

"I should've known," she said. "The climb up that wall . . . and taking me out for the sake of the fun of it . . . and riding through all these chances . . . and then handling him as if he was a ten-year-old kid . . . I should've known. But the Mexican outfit beat me a little. And . . . and you never expect that lightning will strike so close to home. But what'll you do with him?"

"He knows me," Geraldi argued slowly. "I can't let him go loose in this place without having trouble jump on my back like a panther out of a tree. Besides, there's Chicago against him. There's Chicago against him," he repeated slowly, with infinite cold venom.

The girl gasped, but Naylor, gathering himself, set his teeth to face the inevitable.

"I could introduce you to a pretty scene, Elsa," Geraldi said. "A wet October night . . . the wind off Lake Michigan with the rain like teeth in it . . . and poor Jimmy Geraldi walking into that wind around a corner where a street lamp seemed to sputter like a candle through the rain . . . around that corner and straight into the arms of three men."

He paused, looking at Naylor with the faintest of smiles, yet that smile turned the blood of the girl cold. And all the old stories of Geraldi leaped into her mind: Geraldi the thief; Geraldi, whose touch, like poison, dissolved the strength of the strongest; Geraldi, for whom locks flew open, and the doors of ponderous safes swung back softly; Geraldi. whose dead men lay from Singapore to Buenos Aires, from Java to misty London; Geraldi, without mercy—as men said—without scruple, without remorse, the cunning of a leopard in his hand, the savagery of a jungle cat in his heart; Geraldi, who loved danger for its own fair face, and battle for the sake of blood.

Now, as she looked at him, she strove to read the legends in his face. She felt she saw one who was neither man nor boy—not boy, because time had flowed richly over him, not man, because no marking of pain, or sorrow, or regret, or of unaccomplished ambition, or of unachieved malice, or of envy, or of hate, appeared in lines about the eyes or the mouth. He possessed—although the girl could not so analyze it—the beauty of sculptured stone, not massive and grave in the Phidian style, but delicately worked, as Praxiteles would have done a fawn.

Suddenly it came to her that he was neither good nor bad, neither evil nor virtuous, but himself an unmoral, untrammeled creature divorced from the ways and from the laws of other men, and therefore strong with a strength which others could not possess.

She had been amazed that any man could have risked for a stranger what he had risked for her, but now, vividly, she saw the truth—that the very danger he encountered was the bribe that forced him forward. Perhaps she was to him a creature with whom he could have some small sympathy, one whose well-being he could wish, but certainly he was not as other men.

They, almost from her childhood, had been aware of her, had looked for her smiles, had dreaded her frowns, had been shy in the presence of her as children are shy before strangers. But Geraldi had ridden with her through the night like a brother or, rather, like something that she never had conceived before—courteous, but totally indifferent. There was another legend, talked of here and there, that somewhere in the world was a woman who had captured him by force of beauty, of purity, of grace, one woman at whose feet his devotion lay. But the girl, looking again at the calm face of Geraldi, denied that legend to herself. For, whatever else he might be, he must ever be free.

These things went through her mind as she watched Geraldi. What would he do now?

"Three men," he was saying, "and I ran into them around that corner. As the wind let go of me, I staggered, and they were at me as I lost my balance. Why, Elsa, we rolled like children on the pavement. Rolled like children fighting after school in the street."

He paused and laughed, a pleasant, gentle laughter, with a brooding holding of the notes. It was like a song, and she knew the quality that sustained it. It was the battle that he remembered, joyed in, tasted again against the palate of his soul and yearned for once more.

"And here is one of the three again," he murmured, and smiled terribly on Naylor.

"But what happened?" she asked.

"Ah, what happened?" Geraldi repeated. "The fact is that one of them was hurt with a bullet and dragged himself off, howling like a dog. And one of them fell down, got up, and ran away, limping." He pointed toward Naylor, and the latter passed a hand across his face, as though to shut out the memory of a nightmare.

"The third man," Geraldi went on, "stayed with me for quite a while. We were busy, in fact, with our hands. . . ." He paused, and looked with question at Naylor.

"He died the next day," Naylor said huskily.

"Died?" Geraldi said.

"It wasn't what you did to him . . . except that he was scared to death. He woke up in the hospital in the middle of the night, with a screaming fit, and died in the middle of it, calling out and. . . ." Naylor paused. "Well," he said in a brisk, matter-of-fact voice, "what's going to happen now, Geraldi?"

"What do you expect?" Geraldi asked coldly.

The girl grew stiff with apprehension. She had no impulse to call out, to intercede, for suddenly she felt as helpless in arresting the course of this man as she would have been under the rushing front of an avalanche that plunges down a mountainside, rolling up the forest as it goes.

Geraldi snapped his quick, lean fingers. "If you shuffle off this mortal coil at this point," he said, "it looks like murder. Murder I detest. The brutality . . . the hopeless stupidity. . . ." His voice trailed away, and, watching him closely, the girl knew that he meant what he said. She could understand, furthermore; it was not to slay that he fought; it was for the sake of the battle. Never would she forget the wild joy that had been in his face as he had struggled with Lambert Naylor on this day.

Naylor himself said nothing, but he blinked as he strove to meet the scrutiny of Geraldi.

The latter continued: "On the other hand, if I let you live,

Naylor, you'll spread the news of my coming, and then there'll be no chance for me at the house. Even as an unknown stranger there'll be enough danger to fill my hands, but certainly poor Jimmy Geraldi would be a dead man if he were discovered there." He shrugged his shoulders. "There's another alternative. Tie you to a tree. But men tied to trees generally escape, or else they're discovered by someone else. Sometimes a hungry grizzly." He laughed musically at the last thought. Then, with another snap of his fingers, he said: "The tree, I take it, is the only thing that I can manage. We'll try to find a safe one."

Neither Naylor nor the girl made any comment, but Naylor looked fixedly at her as this decision was reached, as though he wondered if she might not have been of some favorable agency in bringing about that lucky termination of Geraldi's ponderings.

They took Naylor through the pass, driving him ahead of Geraldi's drawn revolver. Dipping down the farther side of the range, he found what he wanted, a gully with a stream running through it, a dense growth of low, squat trees, and a place where no trail would lead close to the prisoner.

There Geraldi fastened his prisoner to a small sapling, not with rope, but with the twine, which takes a closer hold, which tightens when one struggles against it, and cuts the flesh if one struggles too hard. In a comfortable sitting posture he tied Lambert Naylor and, stepping back from him, regarded him with satisfaction.

"There's at least one chance in two," Geraldi decided aloud, "that you'll stay where you've been put. You see that I don't gag you, Naylor. Otherwise, I'd be haunted by the thought of your struggles to shout if some wolf or any other beast came near you . . . strangling in the effort to frighten them away."

He shuddered as he spoke, and the girl watched him, amazed at such emotion.

It was not actual pity for the victim, she decided, so much as a fastidious disgust at such a prospect. An odd delicacy of sentiment was joined to the love of combat in this man of action. She knew perfectly that Geraldi would have preferred to kill the man offhand, except that the same fastidious sense deterred him rather than passion for justice, any overmastering love of a fellow man.

"Geraldi," said the prisoner huskily, "heaven knows that if I was in your boots, I'd never give the other gent such a chance for his life as you're givin' me. That's all I got to say."

"Tush," Geraldi said, "I'll even give you a hope, as well. When I come back, as I expect to do, I intend to stop by this way and to set you free. You can keep that in mind, old man, as you sit here and watch the day go by. In twenty-four hours, I trust that I'll be back here, and you'll then become a free man."

The other started, the bonds gripped him, and he relaxed with a nod of his massive head.

"Geraldi," he said, "I got one thing to say to you. There was nothin' for me to gain in Chicago. I was taken in, because I was a chump, and was half drunk, and they told me that you were a bluffer, and no man at all. Geraldi, I'd give a lot to undo that day."

"Ah, yes," said Geraldi, "there are days in my life which I would be glad to undo, also, but that can't be managed. We live, Naylor, in such a world that each one of our actions becomes as eternal as bronze. The least word is fixed forever in the air, as you might say. So what's happened can't be undone, Naylor. Forgiven, of course, by a few random saints. But I'm not among the saintly, Naylor. You may even have heard that before, although I trust that I'm not the opposite extreme. I do heartily trust that."

He laughed again as he spoke, and the girl saw Naylor blanch under that laughter. She herself was frightened. It would almost have been better, she felt, to have seen Naylor dead at her feet than to witness the mild, cold, deathless malice of Geraldi.

But now he waved her away. They went to their horses, and pursued their way rapidly down the cañon, through the trees, and out upon a shoulder of the mountain, where all the great central valley lay beneath their eyes.

IX

"HE UNDERSTOOD BIRD LANGUAGE"

It was no mild and beautiful Garden of Eden into which they rode from the mountains, but rather a great and rugged sweep of grasslands, scattered with wild acreages of rocks that glimmered in the light of the western sun. The grass was already turning yellow, so hot was even this early season, and there were only scattering streaks of trees here and there where water ran in the hollow or stood in dwindling tanks after the spring sun had sent down torrents of snow water.

In the center of the valley appeared the ranch house, surrounded by a screen of trees, set back at a little distance on every side.

"They've chopped the nearest wood for the fire," said the girl, smiling as she looked at the place. "Lazy, shiftless lot of men. But men are always that way. They've cut away their own shade, and let the sun come down on their heads."

She laughed as she spoke, and Geraldi gave her a flick of his eye. She glowed from the long ride, from the heat, from the hope of success that was now before her.

"A golden girl," Geraldi said aloud.

She flushed at this, partly pleased, partly irritated by the impersonal condescension of his manner. He spoke as he might have spoken about a child, and a stranger, and this made her ill at ease.

"You'll like this?" Geraldi asked, waving his hand.

"I'll like it," she said. "Why not?"

"For my part," he answered, "I never like to stay in a room unless I have the key to the door. But you'll have a husband here."

He watched critically as she blushed.

"Well," she said defiantly, "why shouldn't I go to him if they wouldn't let him come to me?"

"Wouldn't let him?"

"Of course not. Old Pike Naylor doesn't like to have his people married to outside girls, for fear they might bring in some new ideas. But mostly they do marry strangers, and Jerry is going to be another one on that side of the list."

"Yes," said Geraldi, adding absently: "I hope that Jerry hasn't changed his mind."

"He'd better not," she declared. "The big shambling faker. He'd better not!"

The laughter of Geraldi poured musically forth, and the girl herself soon was smiling and at ease. So they rode down the canon, and drifted toward their goal.

The sun was down when they came through the trees that fenced the house about on every side, but the afterglow would last for a long time. In that clear light they saw the ranch house exactly as Darcy had described it—not a house, to be sure, but rather a collection of shacks resting shoulder against shoulder, obviously built on bit by bit as the needs of the clan increased, and all leaning toward the center for mutual support. Never was there a more jagged skyline than this building presented. Everything about it showed haste and carelessness. The doors sagged on their hinges. The windows fitted crookedly, with half their panes knocked out by violence from within or from without, and replaced by sides of cracker boxes, with oiled paper, or with strips of sacking.

This, at close hand, was the face of Naylor Castle. Behind it, on the side from which the two had ridden up, appeared a cluttering of corral fences, of sheds for horses and cattle, and all in the worst state of disrepair. On the top of the nearest fence a man sat whittling aimlessly at a stick with a great-bladed knife—an old man from whose body age had dried the sap. His head drooped between his shoulders on a long neck, like the head and neck of a buzzard. That bald poll, on which there was no hat, was red and wrinkled, and, when he looked up, Geraldi saw the long nose resting on the peaked chin, as Darcy had described Pike Naylor, the head of all the clan, the founder of their wealth.

"Why, howdy!" Pike Naylor called. "You-all drop in for a call, maybe?"

"We just dropped in," said the girl, with a significant glance at Geraldi.

"You've fetched a long ride, ain't you?" suggested Pike.

Geraldi swung down to the ground and stretched himself, the girl following his example.

"I'll put up the horses," Geraldi said, adding: "A pretty long ride. You could learn more about it if the horses could talk." He started to lead the animals toward the nearest corral gate, but Pike Naylor stopped him with a word.

"You better wait, son," he said. "My boy Alf keeps his string in that corral."

"I'll try for the next one, then," Geraldi said, and started for the adjoining gate.

"That's Harry's hoss shed," Pike advised him. "I dunno what he'd say if you put your nags in there. He's mighty close-fisted with his oats and hay, I can tell you."

"Where can I take them, then?"

"Now, sir, there's a question," Pike said, scratching his red head. "I'd make you mighty free of everything, if I had my way.

But now that I'm wore out, I don't have much influence around here. They've shoved the old man off into the corner, these big boys of mine. They do what they please, and don't reckon on me at all, which is kind of a sad thing, as you might say."

"I'll take a chance with Harry, then," Geraldi suggested, and straightway led the pair through the gate and on toward the interdicted shed.

Pike looked after him with a shake of his head and said in admiration: "Now there's a brave young feller. If I was him, I wouldn't be free with Harry Naylor. Not me! A mighty wild, cantankerous boy is Harry, and bound to have his own way. Is you two married?"

He shot the last question suddenly at the girl, and she shook her head.

"I see," Pike Naylor stated. "Had to run away together because the old folks didn't approve. Your ma and pa didn't like him, eh? Too slick and smart and handsome, eh? Talks too good and smooth, maybe, to suit them? But that's the way with some folks. They don't cotton to anybody that's got soft hands . . . they'd rather take to a cowpuncher that can dash a rope on a cow. They don't appreciate college education and that kind of thing. Was that what was the matter?"

She shrugged her shoulders, uncertain what she could say, and Pike Naylor rambled on in his strange, husky, rattling voice: "But every girl, she wants to foller her own heart. A girl is as sure of her heart as a cow is of her calf. You can cut calves away from cows, but you can't cut a girl away from her fancy. She'll swim rivers and walk across the mountains on her way to what she wants. Here he comes again, singin'. Now, I'd say that young man never fell without landin' on his feet. He could make himself at home in the desert with a rattlesnake and a dried-up jack rabbit for company. Got a good voice, ain't he?"

Geraldi reached the fence, laid a hand on the top rail, and floated lightly over the topmost bar.

"Light as a dancer, he is," commented Pike Naylor. "Mighty slick and easy, he is."

"Yes," the girl said, because she could say nothing else. "I suppose he is."

"What?" said Pike. "You suppose? Ain't you never danced with him at all? No, you ain't knowed him long, I see. But it don't take any time for a girl to understand what her heart is sayin' to her. She listens, and right away she knows. Well, sir, you get your hoss all fixed up?"

"Fixed up fine," Geraldi answered, ceasing his song. "Very good hay, but crushed barley is hardly oats."

"There, there," responded the old man. "My mind is sure goin'. Barley is it that Harry keeps for his hosses? Well, barley ain't bad for a hoss that does a lot of work. That one of yours could step out a mite, couldn't he?"

"He goes rather well," admitted Geraldi.

"There ain't anything more needed," declared the veteran, "than a hoss that can get a man to town in time, or kick dust in the face of trouble, though they's some that would rather have a fine cuttin' hoss than any of these high-headed racers that don't know a cow from a string of Mexican peppers. Hello! There goes old Father Time, and I ain't got a gun, confound him."

A great owl had slid out of the copse of trees, which now was blended in one mass of shadow in the deepening dusk. Swiftly it came toward them, flying low.

"Dog-gone his wise old heart," said the old man, "he knows when the light ain't fit for shootin'. We've used up a hundred rounds on him and never budged a feather and still he won't get scared, no matter how much we blaze away."

"I'll make you a present of him, if you want his skin,"

Geraldi said politely. His gun was in his hand as he spoke, and the last word of his sentence was brought to a period by the explosion of the Colt as he glanced upward.

The owl, however, sailed on, with only a flit of the powerful wings to acknowledge the noise beneath him.

"Missed!" Pike Naylor said grimly. "Dog-gone me if everybody don't always miss. He's got a charmed life, and some of the greasers says that we'll have to use silver bullets before we ever get him. You shot a mite to the right . . . pulled it a little, I reckon."

"I shot him straight through the body," Geraldi corrected. "He'll fall in a moment." The gun had disappeared from his hand, and, leaning against a fence post, he idly watched the flight of the big bird.

As though it had heard the speech of the man, the owl suddenly dipped over and dropped toward the ground. With struggling wings it strove to right itself, worked up again into the air a short distance, and actually sailed back toward the group of people. But, losing height with every yard it flew, it finally struck the ground and rolled in a red-stained heap at the very feet of Pike Naylor.

The latter gave it one look, then with his big knife drew from the stick a sliver of transparent thinness. "Looks like he knows the language of the birds," Pike Naylor said slowly. He raised a hand to his mouth, and raised a screeching whistle through the fingers. Doors banged. Four men hurried from the house toward them, one dragging out a revolver, the others carrying rifles, all obviously answering a danger signal. Pike waved toward Geraldi. "You can take care of this here stranger, boys," he said. "He's one of them quick-shootin' experts with a sign language that even an Injun ain't got a fast-enough eye to read. Maybe he's come out here to look inside the safe."

X
"JERRY COMES ACROSS"

The girl looked in haste at Geraldi, and saw that he had not stirred from his position, leaning casually against the post of the corral fence. He glanced at Pike, at the dead body of the owl, at the four young men who were gathering about him, weapons in their hands, and one might have thought that these things were happenings in another man's dream, so little heed did he pay to them all.

The four, grimly intent upon him, narrowed their eyes and drew closer, while Pike Naylor went on: "It ain't my habit to go around tellin' you boys nothin'. I'm a pretty old man, boys. You can pick up and carry on, but my main job is just to watch and learn over again how to do things."

"Go on, Dad," said one of the younger men. "You tell us what you want done. Is this a job that needs a little neck stretchin'?"

"Why, Hank," the old man stated with a deprecatory air, "you know that I always hate mean ways of doin' things, though they's some knots that're too hard to untie and have got to be cut. You take this here stranger by name of. . . ."

"Crawford," Geraldi put in pleasantly.

"This here Crawford sashays up and puts up his hosses in Harry's own private shed, though I was tellin' him that was dangerous. . . ."

"I'll show him that it's dangerous," one of the group inserted.

He, apparently, was Harry. Big, raw-boned, aggressive, he strode to Geraldi and towered above him, fists clenched. Geraldi looked at him with interest from head to foot, as one might look at a distant mountain or a great tree.

"You know your own business, Harry," Pike Naylor said, "but maybe I could suggest that Mister Crawford here has shot Father Time at fifty yards with a Colt . . . and then called him back to fall at his feet, because he can talk bird language, it looks like."

Harry flushed with impatience and anger. "D'you own this section of the world, young feller?" he asked Geraldi.

"I beg your pardon," Geraldi said, "but I thought that strangers were always welcome in this section of the world. If they're not, why not put up signs on the trails leading in?"

"Where'd you come through?" asked Harry.

Geraldi pointed to a place where the heads of the mountains parted and sloped away from a narrow pass.

"If you come in that way, how come you didn't meet up with The Lamb? I don't understand that, Dad."

"Lambert is a good boy," Pike Naylor admitted, "but maybe he was havin' a *siesta*. Everybody over two hundred pounds finds this here range a mite too hot for him. The Lamb wouldn't want to sleep, he wouldn't figger on doin' it, but yet he might. The question ain't so much how these two came through as what you're gonna do with them, now that they're here?"

"Tie the girl on a hoss and start her back for the boundary," Harry suggested, turning fiercely on Elsa Thomas.

"Tut, tut," Pike Naylor murmured. "And her so young and pretty, and mighty tired already? It'd pretty nigh be the death of her, wouldn't it?"

"What for did she come in here, then?" asked Harry. "Take her out the quickest way, and the roughest. It'll be a lesson to them on the outside."

"And him?" asked Pike Naylor, pressing the point with what the girl could see was truly fiendish malignity.

"He's come for trouble. Why not give it to him? If he's found a way of dodgin' in over the hills, why not shut up the book so's he can't go back and tell other folks about it?"

"Well," said Pike, "that's a mighty sad way of lookin' at it, but sometimes the saddest way is the only way. I wouldn't say that Harry is wrong. Harry's always had a head on his shoulders. But whatever you boys want to do with him, I'd suggest that you do it quick. There ain't any use settin' down to rest because the fox is surrounded. He may find an earth while you're takin' a nap!"

The girl had listened to this judgment as it gradually formulated, and in the meantime was working close and closer to Geraldi, until now she stood at his side. She had not planned to do the thing, but instinct directed her, and now she caught his hand, and, standing between him and the others, she faced them with a high head.

"Will one of you tell Jerry that Elsa Thomas is here?" she asked.

The four looked at one another in surprise.

"That's right," Pike Naylor said. "Run along, one of you, and tell Jerry that they's a lady out here that wants to talk to him. Don't make up your minds for yourselves, but let Jerry come out and do your thinkin' for you, because he has a better head, maybe."

"Dad's right," Harry said, who was the ringleader in all suggestions of violence, since he had heard the quarreling of horses in his shed. "We can think for ourselves, I guess. Boys, we'll finish off this Crawford, as he calls himself, and then start the girl back for the border. If Jerry wants her, he can damn' well go and get her!"

"Murder? Murder?" cried Elsa. "What do you mean to do?"

"Murder it will be," said one of the four with a sudden conviction.

"Shut up, Bill. D'you know more than Harry and Dad put together?"

"I know what I think. I'm gonna get Jerry."

"Do!" said Pike Naylor. "Go ahead. That would make you and Crawford and Jerry against the rest of us, maybe, and a fine chance for a shootin' scrape, and brother lined up ag'in' brother for the sake of a stranger that has sneaked into the valley, we dunno how. And with a woman, too! Why, if two can come through this, so can two hundred, and one of these nights we'll wake up with a coupla hundred greasers runnin' through the house, and tappin' at our bedroom doors and askin' if they can come in."

His voice rose and roared as he came to the end of this speech. But the man named Bill resolutely turned his back upon such argument and strode away toward the house.

The rest stood ill at ease.

"Well," Pike Naylor said, "wait for Jerry to come out and settle this here. Just stand around and wait for him."

Bill was heard calling in the distance. It was thick dusk. Faces became blurred, the mountain receded slowly toward the horizon or else seemed to dissolve and hang suspended in the air above them.

"We won't wait," declared Harry. "We got our reasons. Partly I seen them . . . partly Dad has showed you. Boys, let's finish off this here sneakin' spy, because I'll lay that he ain't nothin' else."

"Why not?" muttered one of the others.

At this Elsa gripped the hand of Geraldi hard, but he did not return the pressure. She could swear, also, that his pulse had not jumped, that his breathing was steady, that not a tremor passed through his slender body.

"Jim, if you'll take him on that side," said Harry.

"I won't fight you, boys," Geraldi said. "I won't have to, for here comes Jerry, and I think that he'll take my part."

For Bill was now seen coming rapidly back toward them, a second man at his side. They walked across the yellow beam of light that struck out through the kitchen window, and so came up to the corral fence and the group that had gathered there.

"Here's Jerry," Pike Naylor said in an odd voice. "Now, it's pretty lucky that we have him here to settle the thing for us. I guess that you'll all agree to that, eh?"

"Leave me be," growled Jerry. "You've hounded me enough lately. What's the talk about a girl askin' for me out here? What kind of a joke is that to talk around here when . . . ?"

He had come striding through the group until he confronted the girl and Geraldi. She did not speak, she did not stir, but waited in silence, although Geraldi could feel the pounding of her heart shaking through her body continually.

Through that silence Jerry leaned above her, and Geraldi saw a tall man with a suggestion of strength in the upper part of his face and perhaps of weakness in the lower, but all was indistinctly seen in this light.

"Elsa!" Jerry said in an incredulous voice. "Elsa, by gum!"

Still she did not move, but suddenly relaxed, so that all her weight pressed back against Geraldi; he thought that she was about to faint.

"Is it you, honey?" asked Jerry, stepping still closer. "Why don't you speak to me?" Then he added, his voice rising into a great cry of joy: "You don't have to speak! I've found you, and I've got you to keep!" He took her, limp, from the arms of Geraldi, and held her lightly, laughing, staggering drunkenly, partly from the burden, and partly from the laughter that unsteadied him, and broke the voice in which he spoke.

"Why, I told you, Dad, what would happen. There ain't any way to keep a man apart from the girl that he loves, or her apart from him. She's come here. She's come over the mountains. She's busted through your guards. She's laughed at everything. And why? Because she loves me! And if you was to multiply your ranch by ten and offer me the whole thing as a bribe, I wouldn't under any circumstances trade it in for Elsa Thomas here!"

"Then take her," Pike Naylor said dryly. "Don't stand around here and get us all tired out, talkin' poetry at us. Write them things down, Jerry, so's you can tear it up afterward, but don't let the world hear you're crazy from your own lips."

Elsa, one arm around the neck of her lover, whispered rapidly in his ear. At once he released her and strode to Geraldi.

Whatever that passive and patient young man might have thought about Elsa's lover before this moment, he was ready to change his opinion on the instant, for Jerry ranged himself resolutely at the side of Geraldi.

And this, in spite of the snarling voice of Pike Naylor, which was saying: "A fine woman you've brought up here . . . one that travels day and night across the mountains with a man she never seen before. . . ."

"Shut your lyin' face," Jerry admonished sternly. "He's done this here for the sake of a girl that he never seen before. He's done it because he's white, because he's on the square. And before you get at him, you'll have to cut through me."

At this there was a breath of silence such as that which precedes violent battle, and then Pike was heard muttering: "I dunno how I ever was the true father to a lump like Jerry."

After this Bill cried out loudly: "I'm with Jerry and Crawford in this here! We'll have no lynchin' this day anyhow!"

And Geraldi knew that he was safe for the moment, though surrounded by fire.

XI
"AN AGREEABLE FAMILY"

Geraldi dined at the family table. There were half a dozen other kitchen fires smoking in the rambling collection of shacks, for there were half a dozen married members of the clan, and these lived apart, but a dozen men were gathered about the long table over which Pike Naylor ruled, leaning with age in his chair, and supporting himself with gaunt elbows that pressed on the edge of the table.

He ate nothing. He remained with his chin pressed into the gaunt hollows of his right hand, and in place of turning his head, his eyes twisted from side to side, watching every one in turn with that hideous grin of toothless age that seemed more ominous than curses and loud-voiced rage.

At the foot of the table, Jerry and Elsa Thomas were placed opposite one another, oblivious of the rest, misty-eyed with happiness. Geraldi himself had been placed halfway down one side, and behind his chair was another in which a man lounged with a gun across his knees.

It was the single concession to the suspicions of Pike Naylor. He had said: "If I was you boys, I'd strip him to the skin and burn his clothes to find what's in 'em. Then dress him up ag'in as fine as you please. You can give him my best suit, if you want to. I won't mind."

He had cackled as he said this, and Geraldi could see

reason for the laughter if the "best" suit were not infinitely better than what Pike now wore, for the elbows of his coat were actually in tatters.

"Leave him alone," Jerry said. "I'll go bail for him."

"Then put a gun behind him, and let him be as free as he likes," suggested Pike Naylor.

So that was done, and the presence of the gun put a damper upon conversation at the table.

They made an odd appearance, these scions of wealth. Half of them unshaven, half as ragged as old Pike himself, one might have thought that this was a collection of beggars picked up at the first crossroads had it not been for touches here and there. Just opposite to Geraldi was Harry, for instance, with a great diamond pin on his breast, flaring and flickering in the lamplight. Geraldi watched it with the eye of his mind. There were other jewels, as well, and Bill Naylor was earnestly discussing with one of his brothers the advisability of buying two or three Thoroughbred stallions to improve the stock on the ranch.

"Hossflesh is hossflesh," Pike Naylor put in harshly, "and a thousand-dollar leg busts as easy in a hole as a fifty-dollar mustang. Fine hosses mean fine barns, boys to take care of 'em, mashes, sours, clean oats, and a mighty pile of trouble. Take the horses that nature sowed in this ground and use 'em, and, when they're used up, they make extra-fine dog feed."

This was considered good common sense, until Bill broke out: "Use the mustangs, the rest of you. I'll go buy me the Thoroughbreds. I'm gonna go down to N' Orleans and get me what fills my eye."

"Go and get 'em," Pike Naylor stated. "It's better to spend young than to spend old. The other boys'll always see that you got a bunk and blankets on it. You, Jerry, you stand bail for Crawford, here?"

"Sure I do," Jerry replied, when the question had been retailed to him by the bawling voice of a cousin, and so roused him from his trance of happiness.

"Just a moment, gentlemen," Geraldi announced.

"Just a minute, he says," remarked Pike Naylor. "He's got some other ideas. What are they, stranger?"

"I came here to take Miss Thomas to the ranch house," Geraldi said, "and then I hoped to get back again, but, in the meantime, I've heard about a safe that has a lining that's worth seeing. It's made me so curious that I don't think I'll accept bail."

Eating stopped. All eyes flashed at his face, and found it smiling and genial.

"He won't take bail," Pike Naylor growled, his whole head jerking up and down as he spoke, because the hand remained beneath his chin. "He's got an idea that he don't want Jerry to take on more than he can pay. He wants the safe, the way that Darcy wanted it. Maybe he's a friend of Darcy, eh?"

Geraldi smiled calmly back at the old man, but, for all his smiling, he was a little startled. For Pike had come perilously close to the truth too many times.

"I think," Geraldi said, "that you ought to take Pike's advice. Rope me down and put a couple of guards over me, and watch me all night, and then tie me onto a horse and send me back for the border. Because, otherwise, I might get at that safe."

Harry, across the table, sneered openly. "He wants to make a name for himself," he said. "He wants to show that the whole gang of Naylors was so scared of him and what he could do that they was stood on their heads. Why, I can see through him dead easy. This here Crawford is a faker and a bluffer, or I'm a liar." With this ugly speech he pushed back his chair a trifle, and seemed ready to rise and fight for his opinion.

"Tut, tut," Geraldi said in his gentle way, looking down at the table. "You're nervous, Harry, or you wouldn't call a guest names."

"You're right," Bill broke in, an ugly-faced boy with a fine, brave eye. "You got no sense of what's right, or you wouldn't hound him like this, Harry."

"Am I gonna take lessons in manners from a skinny runt like you?" demanded Harry fiercely.

"Go on!" Pike Naylor said ironically. "Keep at one another. Cut a few of your own throats, because that'll please Mister Crawford. Maybe he kind of finds things dull. He'd like a little action, and that's why he suggests he wants to open up the safe tonight."

"What with?" asked Harry gloomily, as he saw the folly of his quarrel with Bill. "He ain't got the tools that Darcy brought here. Is he gonna open that safe with his bare hands?"

"Don't laugh at my hands," Geraldi pleaded. "They're quite capable of making a great deal of trouble. You're a bright fellow, Harry, but there are things done in the world that even you can't see and understand. For instance, which. . . ." As he spoke he flicked two heavy Colts into the air. They had come into his hands, Harry knew not how; they rose lightly, spun high, close to the ceiling, and descended, spatting softly into the waiting hands of Geraldi, who spoke as he juggled the guns.

"For instance, which gun is which, and when have I changed them? And now . . . the butcher knife to keep them company. See how the three dance in the air at the same time, and keep going up and down like the red ball on the stream of water in the target shop. You see I have reason to ask you not to despise my hands."

Harry watched sullenly, biting his lips. For the insult that he had just thrown at the head of the stranger now appeared totally foolish and futile. This conjurer could have killed him with lead in repayment of that remark, before Harry had half begun to fill his hand.

"They's a lot of fast hands in the world," Harry said, "but they ain't so many of the fast boys that can hit their target."

"Ask the owl, you young talker," Pike interjected. "What're you gonna do with those hands tonight, Harry? Gonna leave them free?"

"Don't do it," Geraldi declared earnestly. "Remember the safe. Remember how sad you'd be if anything happened to what is inside of it."

This suggestion made Harry almost choke with rage. He broke out: "I know the kind of a bluff that you're throwin' at us. You wanna make a name, about how the whole gang of the Naylors was so dead set on puttin' you in irons. . . ."

"Ah," said Geraldi, "have you irons here, also?"

"We got a coupla full sets," said Harry, "in case that you wanna use 'em."

"Thanks," said Geraldi. "I'd call that a good sporting proposition, wouldn't you?" He leaned forward to take the eye of the whole table. "A pair of guards on me, another guard to watch the safe, and irons on my arms . . . I'd call that a fairly good sporting proposition, eh? Irons on my legs, too, if you have them. Because that would make it fairly difficult for me to walk about the place without making a bit of noise. You'd agree to that, Harry?"

"You mean," Harry said, "to keep you from gettin' clear away? Is that what you mean?"

"To keep me from getting away, and taking the best of the insides of your safe with me."

"Bah!" snorted Harry. And then his glance went instinc-

tively upward toward the ceiling, as though he were remembering the manner in which the two guns had darted up and hung there for an instant in dimly spinning wheels of brightness. Yes, as though he half expected that they would appear again. "I dunno . . . ," he began.

"Take good advice even from an enemy," Pike Naylor suggested. "Do exactly what he says. You know why he's sayin' it?"

"Tell me," Harry insisted. "I dunno that I see the point of all of this here."

"You blockhead," broke out the elder man, "the reason is that he wants you to do anything except the thing he suggests. Ain't that clear? He aims to find you too proud to foller his good advice. Ain't that clear?"

"Why . . . I dunno," Harry said, but he scowled darkly upon Geraldi, and the latter smiled back with the clear eye and the cheerful manner of a child.

"You'd better do it," Geraldi said, nodding. "And then, you see, I'll have a perfectly free conscience about getting up in the middle of the night and breaking open the safe."

"It makes me mad to hear him talk," Harry stated sulkily.

"It'll make you and me both a mite sight more mad if he gets away with what we've been savin' up for fifty year," declared Pike Naylor. "You do what he says, if you got sense. I make you responsible for the security of the safe tonight, Harry."

At this Harry started in some apprehension, but Geraldi, for the first time during the meal, was paying no attention whatever to Harry. Instead, he was looking at the door that faced him, beyond the opposite side of the table. For the knob of that door now turned slowly, and gradually the door itself swung open.

The dark of the night lay without, and into the black triangle stepped the form of a big, wide-shouldered man, with a powdering of stars to make a background for his head. He stepped in and closed the door softly, but with a heavy pressure, behind him. Then, as he turned, Geraldi saw the face, and recognized Lambert Naylor, whom the rest of the clan called The Lamb.

XII
"THE IMPOSSIBLE HAPPENS"

The Lamb looked straight across the table at Geraldi, his eyes burning as they dwelt upon the stranger, then down the table, for a single flash at the happy face of Elsa Thomas, only now turning cold with fear as she saw the new arrival.

"Hello, Lambert," Pike Naylor said. "You look as if you'd met this here gent before. Know him, Lamb?"

"Do you know me, my friend?" Geraldi asked in his gay but gentle voice. And he tilted back a little in his chair and smiled up at the glowering face of The Lamb. But for all his graceful carelessness, he was keyed up for instant action, with the handles of his two guns the hundredth part of a second from the tips of his fingers, and the two big lamps with their circular burners as targets before his eyes. Yet he hesitated, waiting until the last moment, the ultimate instant, before he acted. One never can tell. Miracles could happen in the ordinary course of events, and it might be that he would not have to smash a bullet through the brain of this hulking stalwart.

"Do I know you?" Lambert Naylor asked. He shrugged his vast shoulders. "How the dickens could I know you when I never seen you before?" he demanded. "Gimme some coffee and a chunk of meat," he added, and slumped heavily into a chair.

The miracle had happened. Still, Geraldi hardly could

breathe easily with that formidable bulk of manhood in the room with him, until a new thought jumped into his brain. After all, considering the code of the place and the time, his treatment of big Lambert Naylor had been generous in the extreme. And perhaps this was the big fellow's method of repayment.

At any rate, Pike Naylor now was conversing with his sullen giant of a son.

"What's brought you down here?" he asked. "Ain't you still due to ride out there for another week?"

"I'm due to ride there," admitted Lambert Naylor with his usual growl. "But I got tired, and that's why I'm here. Is it a pretty good reason?" He glared at Pike as he spoke, and the latter looked straight back at him, without uttering a word. Eventually The Lamb stirred uneasily in his chair.

"I'll tell you how it is," he said. "I got tired of bein' up there, and it seemed like I'd pretty near choke if I had to eat another meal of my own cookery. Hardtack and bitter coffee and half-fried bacon that's gettin' soft as butter . . . what kind of chuck is that to throw into the stomach of a man-sized man?"

"Give The Lamb another turn at the home plate," said Bill. "Damn me if he ain't worth three men when it comes to bulldoggin' or to cuttin' wood, or any of them things, but why should you starve two men inside of one skin that far away from a kitchen stove? It ain't no ways fair."

"I'll remember you for that," The Lamb declared gratefully. "We got a new friend along with us . . . come in from the outside pretty recent?"

"He came straight through your pass today," Pike Naylor commented.

"He's a liar," The Lamb said with calm conviction. "He's worse'n that. He's the grandpa of all the liars in the world."

"Hold on," said Pike. "You didn't take a nap durin' the day?"

"Well, maybe I did. A gent can't keep awake a thousand hours a day, can he?"

"That's it," Bill said. "He needs more sleep, just the same as he needs more food. You can't blame him for bein' different from the rest of us, and havin' different needs, Dad."

"I don't blame him," Pike responded quietly. "But this here gent is advising us to put him in irons and under a guard tonight, because otherwise he's gonna open the safe for us and clean it out. What would you think about that, Lamb?"

"Open the safe . . . after he's in irons? I'd put him in the irons, anyway," The Lamb said, "because he looks pretty slippery, and a snake can slide where a lion can't crawl, I reckon."

He began to eat the platter of food that was now placed before him, and, lowering his head, he paid little or no heed to what was happening in the rest of the room.

One thing, however, had been definitely decided—that Geraldi was, in fact, to be ironed and guarded as he had himself suggested, and, when the meal was ended, he was taken to a room at the top of the house, in a third-story attic. It was a small, low room, with space for a narrow bunk, on which were rolled down a pair of blankets, and on this bunk he sat down, and there Harry Naylor in person came and snapped the handcuffs over his wrists, and locked the irons upon his legs. To them, attached by a heavy, four-foot chain, was fastened a fifty-pound lump of lead.

"When you start runnin' around in the middle of the night," Harry Naylor advised, "you wanna be careful goin' down the stairs, because the ball will be jumpin' down behind you."

Geraldi looked at him with calm eyes. "Are you to be one of the guards?" he asked.

"And why not?" Harry asked in his ugly manner. "Why let the other boys have all the dirty work to do?"

"No reason at all," Geraldi replied, with that flashing smile of his. "Except I rather hoped that I could have another Naylor, for a change. Besides, I'm a little afraid of you, Harry, you're so rough and bold. One can see that you're a daring fellow."

Harry flushed with instant fury. "You won't always be in irons, Crawford," he said. "And when you're out of 'em, maybe I'll escort you . . . alone . . . to the border!"

"Will you?" Geraldi smiled and looked thoughtfully up to his guard.

It was patent then that Lambert Naylor had kept his secret even after Geraldi had left the room. The latter wondered to what he could attribute that silence—to shame that others should know of the manner in which he had been manhandled, or to a real largeness of heart?

For if the name of Geraldi were revealed, if these people know what others knew, they would hardly trust to irons to hold their prisoner.

Even as it was, Harry Naylor had no mind to keep the watch by himself. A second guard appeared, and the two took up their vigil together, while Geraldi lay comfortably on his side, watching them and chatting. Not easy words to listen to were these of Geraldi, as he praised the vigilance of the pair, and promised to escape through their hands, nevertheless. And at last the two sat in a sour silence, never making a response in spite of the taunts and quiet jibes.

"Thank you, boys, for the pleasant chat," Geraldi said, and, turning his back to them, he instantly fell asleep.

It was not a sham of slumber, but for four hours he slept

like a child and, at the end of that time, wakened to hear the pair talking softly together.

"He's still sleepin'," said a muttering voice just above him.

Geraldi kept his eyes closed, and heard the watcher move cautiously away. The two kept their voices so low that he could barely make out their words by straining his ears.

"I'm pretty far gone," said one. "I been up to three last night, playin' poker with Harvey and Chuck and Miller. I'm about all in."

"Go take a walk, then, will you?" advised Harry Naylor.

"I'd rather take a sleep, a whole lot."

"Sure you would, and after you woke up . . . if you ever did . . . you'd be so numb all through your head. I know. Go take a walk."

"Well, maybe you're right, if you think that we need to have the two of us watchin' him."

"It ain't the question of need. It's makin' dead sure. Dad would cut our throats if anything happened."

"Nothin' is gonna happen. Look at him. He's made fools out of us. Just a joke he's playin' on us, with all his talk. Why, there ain't anything to him, in spite of Dad. . . ."

"Is Dad often wrong about a gent?"

"Well, he's gettin' old."

"You go take your walk and come back here, will you?"

"I'll take a walk, then. The fresh air had oughta do me a lot of good."

"Don't stay away too long."

"I won't be gone more'n half an hour." He opened the door, and his footfalls creaked slowly down the stairs.

At this, when the door had closed, Geraldi began to snore, and Harry Naylor cursed impatiently in a mutter. Then, jerking open the window, he leaned out to refresh himself with better air, or perhaps merely to make the noise of the snoring fainter.

This, by turning his head, Geraldi was barely able to make out, and the riot gun lying on the table, close to the bed. The next instant, furling his hands small, he had slipped them back through the handcuffs, and, fumbling in a vest pocket, he brought out one of those small slivers of steel in the use of which he was such a master. It was easy to reach the lock of the fetters that clasped his legs. Each resisted for an instant. Each presently gave way, and now he lay on the bed, free. He heard big Harry Naylor stir, felt him come toward him, and covered the loosed iron by turning on his face with a groan, as though freshly overwhelmed by sleep.

"A talkin', lyin', fakin' cheat," he heard Naylor mutter, as the latter turned away again. He went toward the window once more, but this time Geraldi rose behind him.

Softly Geraldi took up the gun from the table, saw the hammers were raised, and curled his fingers around the triggers. "Harry," he said.

Harry Naylor caught in his breath and whirled about. He was a fighting man, and he showed his spirit and his training at this critical moment, for although he had been taken utterly by surprise, yet half the length of a revolver was out of its holster on his hip as he faced Geraldi. Then he saw.

The legs and hands of the prisoner were free; the yawning mouths of the sawed-off shotgun gaped at his breast, and his life lay inside the curled forefinger of the stranger. Utter consternation and bewilderment froze the brain of Harry Naylor. He stared like a child at a ghost. But when he spoke, it was to say strangely: "I knew it couldn't happen . . . but all the time I was dead certain that it would."

XIII
"A SAFE PLACE"

Harry Naylor left his room with a revolver's muzzle leaning against the small of his back. At the head of the stairs, he paused, although the gun thrust cruelly into his flesh as he halted.

"Ah, man," he breathed, "have the killin' of me here and now, but don't be shamin' me any further. Damn, I won't take another step!"

The silent laughter of Geraldi was the faintest pulse in the air behind his victim.

"Why, Harry," Geraldi said, "I haven't the least desire to shame you. I wouldn't be guilty of such a thing, I hope and trust. But the fact is that I'm playing a schoolteacher for you, Harry. Trying to drive home one great lesson. Mercy to strangers, charity to the poor and the afflicted, Harry. I don't think that you'll ever forget that part of your duty to humanity after this day. So you see that I'm taking all this trouble for your own good, my friend. Don't be ungrateful, but go lightly down the stairs. Lightly, lightly, Harry. Go as lightly as a feather. Be as soft as if you were all bubbles, for, if one stair creaks under your foot, I'll turn you into an actual spirit, my lad, and you'll float without a sound for the rest of eternity."

Again there was the soft pulse of silent laughter, and Harry Naylor went shuddering down the steps, bracing his hands on both walls, endeavoring to take as much of his weight as possible from his feet. So, without a sound, they worked down to the foot of the stairs. Then down a narrow hallway, slow as crawling worms, but as noiseless.

At length they reached a door where Harry Naylor paused again to make his last appeal. "I've brought you along this far," he said. "It's through this door and down the steps. Another door at the foot. You can open that, and there's one man in there. Tom Wilson is guarding the safe tonight. That's the whole lay of the land. Crawford, will you tie and gag me and leave me here? Otherwise, it's worse than death for me here in the house. I'll have to go to the end of the world to hide my face."

"Tut, tut," whispered Geraldi. "Think, man, how grateful you should be that you have a face at all. Only this evening you were going to turn the poor stranger from your door, Harry. You were even intent on stringing him up to the branch of a tree so that he never would bother you again. Think of that, old fellow, and be glad you have the face to save. Because, with one silent touch of a knife point, that big heart of yours will be stopped forever. But you see, Harry, that I keep you with me, step by step, imparting little lessons in generosity, in gentleness, in the loving touch of kindness."

Again that laughter which froze the very soul of poor Harry, and the latter groaned, ever so faintly.

"No more of that," Geraldi said cheerfully. "Don't give way to weakness, Harry. Open the door, and pass softly down to the bottom of the stairs. Softly, but not too slowly, because time runs on, and your sleepy friend promised to be back in half an hour."

Harry Naylor, without another protest, opened the door, and led the way with his former care down the cellar flight of steps until they came at last to a flooring of rough stones, slippery with moisture that must have seeped through the foundations of the old buildings. Before them was a door sketched in by a broken line of light; behind that door, as Geraldi knew, lay a safe that contained unknown treasure, and guarding the safe was some hired gunman of tested courage, of tested willingness to lay down his life in the execution of his duty. Since the affair of Darcy, beyond question, Pike Naylor must have tried and doubly tried the guard who remained for this secret post.

"And now, Harry," Geraldi hissed in his softest whisper, "invite our friend to open the door. Call to him, Harry, and tell him that you must speak to him. Tell him that Pike Naylor has sent you. That ought to bring even lions out of their dens."

He heard the gritting of Naylor's teeth, then Harry tapped at the door.

There was a stir inside, and then a gruff voice that called: "Who's there?"

Even in this greeting the man spoke softly, as though unwilling to break the charm that surrounded his post of office.

"It's me. It's Harry," said Naylor.

"Louder, old fellow," Geraldi encouraged gently, but with a shrewd thrust of the gun muzzle into the backbone of his victim. "Louder and more cheerfully."

"You? Harry?" said the man inside.

"Yes, it's Harry."

"Well, Harry, whacha want? A hand-out?" And Wilson chuckled at his jest. "Can't ya wait till the old man dies?"

"Look here, Wilson," Naylor said, urged by the insistent gun of Geraldi, "are you gonna open the door?"

"What for?" snarled Wilson. "I got my orders from the old man. He's my boss here. You ain't!"

"The old man's sent for him," whispered Geraldi.

Naylor obediently repeated this phrase.

"He'd come and get me, if he wanted me," Wilson replied. "What's your game, Harry?"

"Sprained ankle," Geraldi coached.

"How can the old man come and get you when he's got a sprained ankle?" demanded Harry Naylor, throwing himself into his part with a surprising fervor.

"Him? He never took a wrong step in his life!" exclaimed the guard.

Harry chuckled. "Ain't he? He took one tonight, though, and the language that he's been usin' is fit to use for black paint and red, too. I never heard anybody carry on the way he's been the last half hour."

"What's he want of me?"

"How should I know?"

"I'm to leave the safe?"

"Yes."

"And who's to guard it?"

"You are," Geraldi whispered.

"I am, you square-head," Harry Naylor said.

"Square-head, am I?"

"Aye, you are!"

"I'll see about that," Tom Wilson growled, and, with a sudden jarring back of the bolt, he cast the door open and appeared before them.

He was one of those men who seem to have been born for fighting and made for that purpose. The nose, usually such a vulnerable point, was in him a mere upturned button. The eyes, so susceptible of blinding bruises and painful shocks, were defended and ringed about by heavy projections of bone. They were hardly larger than the eyes of a pig. The jaw, too, was broad and blunt, made to sustain blows that would have stunned the brain of ordinary men. In addition to this,

Geraldi saw a fiery complexion, so that the scowling fellow always seemed flushed with fury.

"Now what the hell got you here to . . . ?" began Wilson. Then he saw the gun that Geraldi leveled with his right hand across the shoulder of Harry Naylor. His left still kept a weapon poked into the back of that unlucky young man.

"Who . . . what . . . ?" asked Wilson.

"Up with 'em," Geraldi coaxed gently. "Up, up, Tommy. I'm hurried, and haven't time to make explanations. Don't make Judge Colt do my talking for me."

Tom Wilson backed slowly away, his hands at the same time struggling slowly upward past his shoulders and pausing at about the height of his ears. It was as though they possessed separate intelligences and wills, and desired above all to be down within fingerhold of the handles of the guns.

Geraldi now drove Harry before him, and, entering the safe room, he pushed the door to behind him with the pressure of his heel.

"The two of you," Tom Wilson gasped. "Crawford . . . and he's brought you in, Harry?" Brute and warrior though he might be, Tom Wilson sneered at such treason.

"He got me when my back was turned," Harry Naylor explained with a groan. "What was I gonna do? Have I got eyes in the back of the head?"

"And him in irons?" Wilson laughed sardonically.

"Well-trained hands can slip the cuffs," Geraldi explained generously. "And a touch of steel in the right place will open fetter locks. Stand back to back, my friends. You, Wilson, if you watch my gun instead of my face, will understand everything better. There you are. Raise your hands high and put your arms together. So, so. Two strong young men, brave young men, imploring the gods for a better chance in life. . . ." As he spoke, with one gun leveled, and with the twine working with snaky speed in the other hand, Geraldi snared the pair, and bound them inextricably together.

There is no more utterly hopeless way of embarrassing a man, no matter how strong, than by hitching him to another human. And presently the two lay on the floor, back to back, painfully gagged, helpless.

Geraldi, standing over them, drew out a handkerchief and wiped his hands, while he nodded and smiled at the pair. "All will be well in the end," he said. "A little trouble at first, and some rough words from Pike, I suppose, but after he has had a chance to reflect . . . unless he has your throats cut in the first moment of discovery . . . Pike will realize that you never would have joined a plot that left you behind in his power after the treasure had been stolen. You understand, boys? You see that all this is done as a lesson to you in patience? I feel not like a thief, but like an upright and wise teacher. I shall feel the better for this the rest of my life. Let's see, now, what the old iron cupboard contains."

A new lock had been welded in to replace the one broken by Darcy with his "can opener," and Geraldi now squatted on his heels to examine it. After that, he laid out a little kit that looked like a leather wallet and contained a closely packed row of little tools of the finest and the brightest steel. From this he extracted several, then drew from the center of the room the little round mat that lay there. On this he kneeled, and instantly was immersed in his labor.

XIV
"KIND AND GOOD"

It was Tom Wilson who lay facing the safe. His face was puffed by the distention of his mouth and by the swelling of blood, so that his eyes were reduced to narrow slits, but these slits glittered with fire as he saw Geraldi at work, whistling the while a tune that was barely audible even in the silence of that place.

But not five minutes had passed before there was a noticeable *click,* and the door opened with a faint sigh of the inrushing air.

Geraldi now replaced the tools in their kit, folded it, and thrust it back into a coat pocket. Next he removed the drawers from the safe, one by one, arranging them in a regular row along the floor. Then he began to go through them, making appropriate comments as he reached one exhibition after another of wealth.

He found the jewels about which Darcy had waxed so eloquently. He found the relics that were evidently the product of church plundering, and from these he picked up a crucifix of gold, set with an incrustation of large emeralds. No consideration of the shortness of the time left to him could induce him to let this go without comment.

He carried it to Harry Naylor and exhibited it before the eyes of that unlucky young man. "Now see, Harry," he said, "how much bad luck comes to people who plunder churches.

The bad luck that's making your venerable father lose this entire treasure is, of course, the result of keeping such stuff as this in his safe. There is bad luck for me, also. Because I have to load myself down with a great deal of stuff that I can't keep, because all of these things I shall have to give back to the church.

"What church, Harry? In the old days, how many times did your father slip across the border with a gang at his back and beat up some village at night? How often did he smash in the door of a church and brain the poor guardians who tried to keep him away? How often did he come back with things like this? Altar cloths, too . . . like this lace one. Why, it would take two wise women both their lives to make such a thing as this. How much, besides the few prizes that he kept for their own sake, did Pike Naylor sell and put the money into cattle? Tell me, Harry, if the whole Naylor fortune wasn't built upon exactly that foundation? No, don't tell me, because I can guess for myself.

"Wickedness, wickedness, Harry, regardless of your particular religious beliefs. These things are all gifts, and whoever steals a gift is taking something beyond the fact. I'd rather steal a horse than steal a gift, Harry. Tell your papa that when you next see him. Tell him, besides, that he should never steal except when stealing is a game as well as a profit." He closed this odd speech by returning for more loot.

He worked rapidly, although his movements did not appear hurried. Yet it was as though there were eyes at the tips of his fingers as he routed out wads of banknotes, separated chamois sacks of the rarest and best jewels. A pair of big saddlebags being conveniently at one side of the room, Geraldi piled the loot in these, not tumbling it in, but placing it in good order and arrangement. He finished, at last, by again dusting his hands on the handkerchief, while he smiled at his two helpless captives.

"There's a moral to be gained from this tale," Geraldi announced. "Do good with all your heart, and there will be a reward for you in this world or the next. Perhaps in both . . . who knows? At any rate, you see that in escorting the young lady to her lover, my reward was heaped up for me at the end of the trail. It had been kept safely for me in a pocket of steel, which, nevertheless, opened at a mere touch." He laughed again. "If Pike Naylor wants desperately to see me, after this, tell him that my address is uncertain, but that a warm greeting always awaits him, wherever I may be. And so, my dear friends, farewell!"

He left the cellar softly, closed the door behind him, and mounted the stairs to the hallway above. Here he passed slowly down to the front door when he thought that he saw something glimmering down toward him from the upper stairway. He shrank back against the wall, but as the form came closer a sufficient amount of starlight sifted through the windows on either side to make him visible, he knew. He was prepared to leap and strike, when the form paused on the stairs and a whisper said: "Is that you, Jimmy?"

He sighed with a vast relief and straightened at once. "Elsa. I thought it was a ghost."

"It almost turned into a ghost when it saw a man there between the windows," she said. "But then I remembered that Jimmy Geraldi was not likely to make such a long ride for nothing. I mean, I can guess what's in the two bags."

"What is it, Elsa?"

"A little present from a steel safe," she said.

"Some of this probably out of Jerry's pocket," Geraldi suggested.

"You're welcome to his share," she assured him.

"What brought you down here? Did you hear anything?"

"Not a thing except my own heart, and it's been thundering and racing so that I couldn't stay in bed. I had to get up."

"Happiness, Elsa?"

"The minister comes tomorrow, Jimmy. Of course, it's happiness."

"And after that?"

"I know what you mean. They're a rough lot. So's Jerry. But so am I. I never wanted to live in silks and such. I want horses and a place to ride 'em, and that's what I'll have here. Oh, I'll be happy as a queen."

"Good night," Geraldi said. "I won't say good bye, because I think that we'll find one another some place."

"I haven't thanked you," she said. "But I know that on account of me, you've made Ben Thomas your enemy. Ben Thomas on one side, and the Naylors on the other . . . you'd better move out of this part of the country at once, Jimmy."

"I don't need thanks," he said, "when I'm carrying away two sacks full of . . . what shall I say . . . unconscious gratitude?" He laughed softly in the darkness. "You and Jerry be as happy as you can," he added. "It may be that the others will be hating you for a time, after this. They'll be sure to blame at least some of this bad luck on you. But you stick to Jerry and everything will be all right. When is the marriage?"

"As soon as the minister can come over the hills. Tomorrow night, perhaps."

"*Adiós,* Elsa. I'd give you a handful of wedding presents, but I'm sure Pike would recognize them and conclude that you'd been bribed."

"*Adiós,* Jimmy. Wherever kind men and good men go, there'll be room for you."

"Kind? Good?" Geraldi chuckled.

"You're a thousand times better than you think," she assured him, and then she had a last view of Geraldi in the open doorway with the stars clustering about his head and shoulders, kissing his hand to her. The closing of the door shut out the picture, and Geraldi was gone.

XV
"A DEVOTED FOLLOWER"

Outside, Geraldi paused and looked back at the dark side of the house. All was still, except for a feeble and irregular pounding that seemed to come from the earth beneath his feet, but he could guess that it was the captured pair, beating their feet as well as the cords permitted them against the cellar door. How long would it be before these sounds were heard, or until the second guard came to relieve the first in the natural course of duty?

He went on, unhurried. Straight toward Harry Naylor's shed he took his way. With the black horse once under him, then let them look to their pursuit, for he would give them a chase worthy of a poem. So he thought as he passed through the gate of the corral, when it seemed to Geraldi that under the shadow of the shed, close against its wall, he saw horses and mounted men. The saddlebags were slung over his shoulder, leaving his right hand and arm free, and that hand instantly possessed itself of a gun.

He stared into the shadows, and now he was sure that he saw a rider, but only one, keeping his horse perfectly still. Three other animals were with him. For another moment Geraldi hesitated. He would not turn back, having gone this far, but, as he prepared to shoot, a low voice, a deep, and husky bass voice called to him: "Friend, Geraldi!"

A friend, and in that house? However, he went straight on until he was beside the mounted man. Then he recognized big Lambert Naylor, who could have caused his destruction on this evening, but had held his tongue. He was mounted on a capable-looking animal, two others were unsaddled behind him, and one of the two was undoubtedly the black stallion. The fourth horse wore a saddle, also. It was as if Lambert were waiting for a companion, and about to start out with a relay of horses.

In fact, he said at once: "I been waitin' pretty near a half hour. We better start on."

"We?" Geraldi echoed, amazed.

"You and me," The Lamb said. "I been ready a long while. You got the stuff?"

"What d'you know about this stuff?" Geraldi asked, more amazed than before.

"What would Geraldi be out here for except the stuff that Darcy bungled so mighty bad?" The Lamb asked. "I know what you was after, and that you'd get it."

"Lambert, you have me bewildered. How could you know that I'd get it?"

"Well, didn't even a fool like Darcy get it? Then how could you mess it up? But I got two pairs of hosses ready. When we've used up the first pair, the second will take us over the line. We better start, though."

There might well be treachery behind this, but, for some reason, Geraldi could not doubt what the big man had said. He mounted without another word; they left the corral, and soon they were through the screen of trees and heading out on the home trail.

They went at the lope with which the Western pony eats up the miles of a day-long journey, and, as they rode, they still talked.

"Lambert," Geraldi said, "I can't understand you or what you're doing. D'you mind explaining? You know that, if Pike Naylor suspects you of helping me away from the place, you never can come back?"

"I know that," Lambert answered.

"But you've got as big a share in the place and the future of it as any other Naylor, haven't you?"

"Why, I suppose I have."

"But that means that you're giving up wealth, man."

"What's money," said the other. "You can't eat it. What's hosses? You can't use more'n six or eight for riding."

"But they'll think that you've helped me to steal the money and the jewels from the safe, I tell you!"

"Let them think what they want."

"And in that case, they'll never rest until they've tried to get at you, just as they'll try to get at me."

"They won't get at you," said the other, "and, if they miss you, they'll miss me. Because I'm gonna stay with you."

"Stay with me?" Geraldi cried, almost exasperated by this time.

"You won't want me," the big man said patiently. "But all the same, I'm gonna stay right along with you. The fact is that I'm never gonna leave you, Jimmy, till I've learned something."

"Man, man," Geraldi said, still baffled, "you're giving up your family, your friends."

"I'll take you in their place," Lambert Naylor said.

"They'll call you a traitor."

"Let 'em call me what they please."

"And everyone in the world will be against you. They'll sneer behind your back. They'll swear that you've sold your own family to a stranger."

"Let 'em sneer behind my back, if they can, but if they

sneer in my face, I'll crack their heads together," The Lamb declared composedly. "I been a man that's been able to handle others tolerable easy. I ain't gonna begin losin' my hold on all the rest because I couldn't keep a grip on you."

He paused here, and Geraldi, keeping quiet, felt that the explanation of the mystery was about to be his.

"When I went anywhere," Lambert said, "they used to keep back from me. If there was a street fight, I could walk right through it, and the side that I took was the winning side. If there was a row in a bar, I fixed it. I've kicked twelve men into the street out of Jim Gresham's bar in Candy Creek. I done it myself, with my own feet and hands. Then I had a drink with the barkeep. He said that he never seen nobody fight like I done that day."

"Aye," Geraldi said. "I wish that I'd seen you."

"Do you?" asked the other eagerly. "Well, maybe you will someday. And any day that you say, where there's a big enough crowd to make it worthwhile. I can handle 'em like sheep, even though I can't handle you."

"Is that what troubles you, my friend?"

"Ain't it enough to trouble me?" the big man asked. "I been all by myself, when it come to a fight. When I laid my hands on anybody, he turned numb and got sick. It was always that way, even when I was a kid. The things that I touched, they got paralyzed. But then you come along, and you treat me like I was a kid . . . or a woman." He threw up a long arm against the sky; then arm and head fell together.

"Is that it?" Geraldi asked. "Is it because you want me to teach you some of the wrestling tricks that I know how to use?"

"Would you do that?"

"Of course, I'd do that. Gladly, too."

"Ah, and it's mighty good to hear you talk," said Lambert.

"Hard tricks . . . I know that they're that, and I never could get as slick as you at them. But what with my size and strength, if I was to learn some of the things that you can do. . . ."

"Why, in that case, you'd kill a man, no matter how big, every time you handled him."

The giant gasped out a laugh that was really choked with joy.

"Kill him, eh?" he said, with a brutal satisfaction. "Yes, an' I reckon that maybe I would. I reckon that I could, anyway. Look at you, not big at all. Like a feather! But I thought that you were pulling my arms out of their sockets. Suppose I was to know that trick, why, I'd be able to fix people the way that kids fix flies and grasshoppers."

He laughed once more, enormously, the bellowing sound flooding out in a really terrifying manner.

Then Geraldi understood. More than honor, more than duty to his family, more than fear of the world's opinion, this fellow valued the ability to rule his fellows by the weight of his hand, and this he hoped to learn from the very man who had caused his own downfall. There was a naïve directness about this method of thinking that appealed hugely to Geraldi.

"Take me willin', or do I have to come along and you not willin'?"

"Would you do that?"

"Whatever I say, I do it, or else I die tryin'," The Lamb said without any real sententiousness.

"I'll take you, then," declared Geraldi. "And very glad to have you with me. You've thrown up your family, your money, your place in the world, all for the sake of a few wrestling tricks. But . . . I don't know that I blame you. You could learn some of these things still better in Japan, though."

"I wouldn't go to Japan," The Lamb replied, "for half a

million dollars in spot cash. I'll learn from *you*. I'm glad that I'm goin'. And I'm glad that I've chucked everything for this. I'd rather do this than be on board a pirate ship."

The comparison made Geraldi laugh heartily. He still was wiping his eyes when he heard The Lamb say: "They've got our line, I guess."

"Who? Your family?" Geraldi demanded.

The other waved his hand ahead, and upon the black slope of the mountain Geraldi saw three fires standing in a row, of which the middle one winked out repeatedly.

"That means they know that we're going to take the middle trail through the mountains. But maybe we won't. It'll cost us a detour, but we can stand that, I think?"

"You know this country, and I don't, partner."

"We'll swing left. We'd better go over that ridge. Confound the moonlight, though. It'll show up everything against the skyline, almost like the day. Now we better ride, Jimmy, ride like the furies were one jump behind you. If they get us, they'll broil us and serve us on toast to the dogs."

He put his horse to full speed, riding with such skill, in spite of his bulk, that Geraldi was hard put to it to keep up.

They entered a narrow defile, with rock walls springing up on either hand, fencing high above them a narrow road like a bright street in heaven. Here, the enormous laughter of The Lamb began again, booming and echoing like the roar of a waterfall, so that the very horses became uneasy.

"But if we come on only a patch of 'em . . . on only four or five . . . won't we make hash of 'em, Jimmy Geraldi?"

XVI
"HE'S ASLEEP!"

In the patio of the hotel, Cullen and Darcy drank bad beer, and practiced the rolling of cigarettes in Mexican style, that is to say, in the form of cornucopias, the big end to be lighted and the small one placed between the lips. They had acquired some skill in this labor, because for several days they had had nothing else to do. They were waiting for the return of Geraldi, and their hopes were dwindling day by day.

Around them, on this evening, was the same well-packed crowd of Mexicans and cowpunchers that had filled the place on the night when Geraldi and Cullen had heard the story of big Ben Thomas. But the crowd did not elbow the two at their corner table. Only, now and again, eyes flashed toward the two, and dwelt cautiously upon them, for it was known that these men were, in some way, connected with that daring fellow who, it was said, had actually raided the ranch of the Naylors, and was at this moment harried somewhere along the border line by all the mounted men the Naylors could put into the field. On the nearer side, big Ben Thomas with his cowpunchers, and with as many hired gunmen as he could afford to raise, was blocking the retreat of the fugitive.

But a sudden murmur of excitement passed through the patio as a large man waded through among the tables, looking here and there for a vacant chair until he came, at last, to the table of Cullen.

"Sit down, Mister Thomas," Cullen invited.

"You again," Ben Thomas said, glowering. He changed his scowl for a grin. "Waitin' for the fox to come home?" he said. "But he ain't never gonna get to earth. What's his name?" Thomas went on, sitting down in the proffered chair.

"Crawford," Cullen answered.

"They's some say that he's Geraldi himself," suggested the rancher. "But whether he is, or whether he ain't, he's a gone goose."

"I suppose that he's close to cornered," Cullen admitted with as much indifference as possible.

"And you ain't out tryin' to help your friend?" challenged Thomas.

"What's the use?" Cullen asked. "I'd help Crawford if I could, but every draw is watched. I don't see where Crawford has been able to hide. And they say that there's another man with him."

"There is," Thomas confirmed. "A Naylor, I've heard. And that's why we'll get him, even if he's really Geraldi. We'll get him, because when foxes travel in pairs, they're always caught."

"I reckon they are," Darcy groaned. He had risked very much, indeed, in returning so close to the land of the Naylors, but irresistible curiosity and the great suspense had drawn him here.

"The smart ones nigh all go that way," Thomas said. "Keen as mustard till they get lonesome, and then they're bagged through a partner."

"You're so sure of the job that you've given up the hunt yourself?" Cullen asked.

The rancher tasted his beer and sighed at the poor quality

of it. Then he removed his sombrero and mopped his forehead. "I ain't give it up, but I've come back and corralled a dozen fresh hosses, and I'm gonna freshen myself up a bit before I go back and swaller some more dust. If only the Naylors get him before I do, I'll be satisfied."

"How come?" asked Darcy, bitten with curiosity.

"Why, I claim to be tolerable white. And you take what he done to me, it ain't so bad. He wanted a pass to the Naylor house, and he used my girl for the job. She wanted to go, and he was willin' to take her. But the Naylors, they're a mitey sight more peeved. If they catch him, Geraldi won't never back a hoss again, and you can lay to that."

"It's not Geraldi," Cullen corrected. "His name is Crawford."

"Maybe," Ben Thomas said indifferently. "Maybe they was two Napoleóns, too, and two Hannibals. But I reckon not. He rides a hoss like Geraldi's hoss, and he slips through like Geraldi does, and he raises the same kind of trouble all around in the same kind of a way. He's got the same looks, too, and so I say if it ain't Geraldi, it's his twin brother, which is just as bad. But whoever he is, he's a goner."

"I suppose he is," Cullen said. "But he's put up a game fight."

"Game?" said the rancher. "Nothin' but game, I'll tell a man. I got a boy with a leg broke . . . fall from a hoss. I got three more in the hospital. One with a rake along the ribs where a bullet plowed. Two with holes in their legs. That was when they tried to get through the Chimney Draw, and we turned 'em. But my boys all like the game, and they're stickin' steady to the guns." He waved his hand toward the crowd about them. "These fellers all want to see the pair of 'em get through and clean away, I reckon?"

"They seem to," admitted Cullen.

"The underdog gets the headlines, always, when his back is to the wall," Thomas declared. "Well, this here Geraldi, I like the ways of him. He shoots safe, for one thing. Nobody tell me that he couldn't've dropped some of my boys for good, if he'd wanted to. But he didn't. He played it safe, and only trimmed 'em. And he's a man fightin' for his life, at that." He finished his beer with one great draft. Then, as he got up, he leaned for a moment across the table. "I'll tell you what, young man, I kind of wish your friend luck in spite of myself." Then he turned and passed slowly out, stepping in and around among the tables.

There was a great outbreak of chattering voices as he disappeared, and Cullen exclaimed irritably, under cover of the noise: "Jimmy should have had better sense than to take one of the Naylors in tow."

"He ain't caught yet," Darcy said hopefully.

"It means a four-way split instead of a three-way split, too," Cullen reminded Darcy.

"If he comes through at all, they's enough for four," answered Darcy. "Leave Geraldi be, till we find out what's happened in the end. A dog ain't dead so long as he's showin' his teeth. How many horse-miles, I wonder, have they used up on this chase of him already?"

But Cullen did not answer, for he had fallen into gloomy thoughts.

At last he rose, and Darcy followed him out from the patio, pursued by soft-voiced murmurs that wished well to their *"amigo."*

"It's no use," Cullen commented at last, as they reached the open in front of the main entrance to the hotel. "We'll never see Geraldi again. You've heard what Thomas said? I've made up my mind. I'm starting east in the morning. You can go part way with me, if you like."

"I'll go," said Darcy, "till I find another set of gents to tackle this job."

"Will you find a better man than Geraldi for it?" Cullen asked dryly.

"I dunno," said the patient Darcy, "but, somehow, I'm pretty sure that the stuff I seen is gonna be taken away from the Naylors. Thieves got no right to keep their loot forever, and a lot of the Naylor treasure is stole, by my way of thinkin'."

"Whatever it is," Cullen said, "we'll never see any part of it. Let's go up."

Up the stairs they went, and at the door of their room suddenly paused in surprise.

"I thought you didn't lock it, Darcy?" Cullen said, trying the knob.

"No more did I," replied Darcy. "Did you turn it to the left?"

"Yes," the other said, and tried again.

"Here," said Darcy. "I'd sure swear that I didn't lock that door."

In fact, it gave at once under his hand, and in the gloom before them appeared a form with monstrous wide shoulders and great hanging arms, like the arms of a gorilla. This huge fellow placed a finger at his lips.

"Steady, partners," he whispered. "The chief is asleep."

"The chief? What chief? And who are you?" Cullen demanded, nevertheless, sinking his voice.

"Jimmy, you blockhead," replied the other in a gruff whisper. "He's pretty well tuckered out. He ain't hardly slept at all for five days and nights. Set up and watch over me while there was danger. Now I reckon that I'll see he gets this first sleep out. Come in if you have to, but step soft. You two can sleep on the floor along with me. They ain't gonna be nobody disturbs the chief on that bed."

On tiptoes, clutching at one another in excitement, Cullen and Darcy entered the room. They hardly dared to breathe, but, with held breath, they stared through the gloom. From the lanterns in the patio, a dim radiance entered the window and was reflected from the ceiling to the floor, so that on the bed they could make out the slender form of a man lying sprawled, face downward.

"It's Jimmy," Cullen confirmed.

"It's Geraldi," Darcy echoed, his voice quivering.

"How . . . did he bring it with him?" asked Cullen.

"The stuff? It's there under the bed. You can see the pair of saddlebags."

"We'll have a look at it, Darcy," Cullen said, tiptoeing forward.

He was taken by the shoulder by a hand that seemed capable of smashing the joint with a slight increase of pressure. "Back up, son," said The Lamb. "No part of that stuff is mine, but, all the same, I ain't gonna see nobody else touch it. If you got any claim on it, let the chief hear what you got to say. Hey," he added with a sudden start, "it's Darcy, eh?" He laughed, the hushed noise of his mirth wheezing softly in the room. "You'll have a share, I reckon," the brutal Naylor assured, when he had caught his breath. "You've fingermarked a lot of that stuff with your blood, ain't you? Now back up, and set down, and we'll wait for him to wake up. Step soft, or I'll crack your heads together if he wakes up. Five days . . . five damn', mortal days of livin' one minute and dyin' the next, and him, he never stopped laughin'. . . ."

He approached the bed, and, taking his stand beside it, he faced toward the two thieves, and remained like a tower on guard.

While Bullets Sang

I

"WISDOM OR HONOR?"

In the entire town, there was but one cool room, and that was the rearmost chamber of an inn, which looked out on the pasture behind, bordered with cottonwood trees, through whose trunks one could see the blare of light thrown up from the desert beyond. Indeed, this room was only warm by comparison. Cullen, who was surveying a tray of Mexican gold and silver work held for him by an old woman, squirmed uneasily in his chair from time to time as the heat touched his nerves. Even the Mexican in the apartment leaned back in his chair with a glistening face. Geraldi alone was at ease, even though he had but lately returned from robbing the Naylors in their almost inaccessible ranch retreat.

"If you'd shut the window," Cullen said, his grumbling and inactive partner in the enterprise, "you'd keep out the hot air. Where's Darcy? We could play a game of poker to kill the time."

"Darcy's in the street looking over some horses. Have you seen him?" responded Geraldi with a faint smile. "And if I shut the window, Harry, I'll still be able to see you obscurely, but you won't be able to see those treasures. For my part, I won't be able to see my best friend."

The Mexican chose this instant to break into the talk. "Is that your best friend?" he said, pointing through the window toward a glorious black stallion.

"That's my best friend," agreed Geraldi. "He's risked his life for me . . . no man ever has done as much."

He beckoned, and, although the horse stood with its back turned, yet it came at once cantering from the farther side of the pasture. At the window it halted with head held high and bright eyes. The Mexican, in the meantime, had fairly trembled with delight as he watched the gallop of the horse, and now his eyes went busily from point to point, estimating bone, length of rein, girth where girth counts for bottom, shoulders, and above all that eye which told of the fearless and enduring heart within.

Wherever he looked, he could find no fault, and he bit his lip with envious pleasure. Geraldi stretched out his hand with a quarter of an apple in the palm. This the stallion nibbled at, or was about to, when it disappeared and came into view in the hollow of the master's elbow; the black horse struck at it angrily, as a snake would fling its head. But it missed. Geraldi was holding the apple at a distance to the side.

The Mexican, however, did not approve of this jesting. "A high-spirited horse like that, *señor,* may be ruined by such play, as, of course, you know?"

"Ruined, my friend?" Geraldi asked, opening his eyes in an innocent way he had.

The stallion chose that moment to catch him by the forearm, and the Mexican blanched with horror as he saw the head of the horse made snaky as with flattened ears and gleaming eyes it kept its hold.

"*¡Dios!*" said the Mexican, and reached inside his coat for a weapon. "Your arm is crushed, *señor!*"

Geraldi, however, now turned up the imprisoned hand with the apple in it. "This is the rule of the game," he explained, as the horse took the bite with accurate teeth from the palm. "But generally he has to work longer."

He rubbed the moist spot from his sleeve with a handkerchief, and smiled on his startled companion, while the stallion frisked to the farther side of the pasture and stood there a moment with his head a trifle turned, as though hoping that there might be another session of play.

The Mexican watched him with hungry admiration. "Such a horse"—he said rather huskily and with a pause—"such a horse makes a king of his rider . . . his saddle is a throne, *señor.* I, also, have some fine animals that give me pride. I would exchange them all for this stallion. There is no price, however?"

"There is no price," Geraldi agreed. "One can't set a money value on a friend."

"True," said the other, "true." But his eyes brooded greedily on the horse.

Here the door opened, and a great-shouldered man came in with a waddlng gait like a sailor's stride. Red and ugly of face, thick-limbed, with great dangling arms, he looked like some primitive monster from which man might have developed, but which was not man. He was, however, only Lambert Naylor, who had left his kith and kin to go off with Geraldi—for Geraldi was a man whom he could admire.

"What's happening to Darcy?" asked Geraldi.

"He's in a kind of a tight fit," said the big man, taking out a thick plug of tobacco and nipping off a corner with a click of his teeth. "He's between a spavined pinto and a cream-colored mare with ringbone. If he was color-blind, he might pick a tolerable hoss, but the colors is all he can see. They's a roan fit to carry the Prince of Wales all week, and the royal king on Sunday . . . that hoss has been danced up and down the street for Darcy to look at, but he can't make up his mind to see it. It ain't got the color. Besides, he says that a Roman-nosed brute ain't fit for a gentleman to sit on."

"Did you give him any good advice?" Geraldi asked.

"I been talkin'," said Lambert Naylor, "till my throat is dry as the pith of a dead Spanish bayonet. But it ain't any good. He won't listen to me. You'd better come and flash on the light for him, Jimmy. He'll listen to you, maybe."

"I doubt it," said Geraldi, "but I'll try it."

With that, he rose and left the room, accompanied by Naylor, while Harry Cullen, at last weary of looking at trinkets, sent out the old woman on their heels.

"*Señor* Cullen?" the Mexican said, lowering his voice. "May I speak five words to you?"

"About what?" asked Cullen, insolent from nervousness and the exhaustion of the heat.

"About stolen goods, *señor*."

Harry Cullen's face turned to stone, then danger came up like a tide in his eye. He rose from his chair and stepped between the stranger and the door, but the latter spread out his hands in the age-old gesture of surrender.

"You have nothing to fear from me, *Señor* Cullen! I am only an ambassador."

"You know what?" Cullen asked bluntly.

"I know," the Mexican told him, "that Darcy, the man with the crippled hands, broke open the safe of the Naylors, was caught when he tried to escape, crucified against a tree, and saved from death by Indians. I know that he found a clever friend, named Cullen, and told him of a treasure in the hands of the Naylors, and that Cullen went with Darcy to a still greater man . . . James Geraldi. I know that Geraldi actually dared to ride into the Naylor Ranch on the pretense of escorting to the house the girl engaged to Jerry Naylor. That he was, nevertheless, caught and bound hand and foot . . . that he escaped, robbed the safe a second time, and actually succeeded in breaking away from the place and rejoining his companions, accompanied by one of the Naylors in person . . . this Lambert, who worships Geraldi like a god. I know, besides, that you still are not safe, that you have stopped here to rest through the heat of this day, feeling that you have distanced pursuit. But, you see, the pursuit already has caught up with you."

Cullen, with a muttered oath, stepped back and glanced apprehensively toward the window.

"Caught up with you in my person alone, perhaps," said the Mexican. "But, nevertheless, here I am to speak for your enemies."

"Talk," Cullen said with a sneer, "never would stop us."

"I have written words, however," answered the other, and, taking a paper from his pocket, he unfolded it and spread it on the table before Cullen. The message ran:

Dear Cullen:

It's a long hunt, and the four of you have ridden well. But I think you'll agree that we are giving you trouble. You are not simple enough to think that our chase will end as soon as you are definitely over the edge of the horizon, even if we should lose touch with you as far as that. I think you know that we'll never stop. We have money to continue the search, and we intend to use it. There's no corner of the world that will hide any of you. If you think this over, you may see some truth in it.

The ones we want are Geraldi, because he robbed and mocked us, Darcy, because he suggested all of this, and above all Lambert Naylor, because he is a traitor to all his blood.

What price will we pay?

That price will consist in the first place of your absolute safety. You may have the assurance that instead of seeking for your life, we shall defend it. Your share of the spoils that Geraldi took will be given to you. And more. We understand that you and Darcy have quarters and that a half remains with Geraldi. We will increase your share to a full third, if you will assist us to capture the other three.

The means of doing this may be discussed and decided between you and our good friend, José Pinas, who is bringing this to you.

I am leaving this unsigned for obvious reasons. I think the contents will assure you that we mean what we write.

Otherwise, we cannot give you any guarantee. You must simply accept our naked word, if this is sufficient for you.

Here the letter ended without a name, but Cullen continued bent over it as though the blank sheet beneath were covered with inscriptions.

José Pinas began to speak softly: "Already the four of you have escaped half a dozen times by the skin of the teeth, as you know, and by the craft in Geraldi. But you cannot continue to escape forever. I see that you consider the message. As a wise man, you must do so. My dear *Señor* Cullen, this is a fortune placed safely in your hands. As for the means, how simple to arrange. If you are camped in the desert hills, a small fire secretly built and made to wink three times through the darkness would be enough. If you were. . . ."

Cullen threw up a hand as though that current of speech were a physical thing that had to be broken off. "I've heard enough," he said. Then anger seemed to grow up in him like the flower of fire. "Do you take me for a traitor to my companions, Pinas? I've heard enough from you. Get out of my sight!"

The Mexican bowed and moved toward the door.

"Who in the name of all that's evil," said hot-faced Cullen, "told the Naylors that I'm not a man of honor?"

His hand on the doorknob, again the other bowed. "Ah, my dear friend," he said, "in this human world, should not wisdom still walk by the side of honor?" And he was gone.

Cullen, as though struck by a second thought, hurried after him, but at the door he paused, shook his head, and turned back slowly into the room.

II
"WHEN THE SUN GOES DOWN"

Under the horse shed in the late afternoon, the four men gathered while the *mozos* saddled the second-string horses; each had two mounts, the best to be kept in reserve for special needs. It was just past the period of greatest heat, but now the air was totally dead, untouched by a breeze that would spring up toward sunset time. The flies buzzed with an intolerably sleepy drone, flies in myriads, small as gnats; they covered the loins of the horses and rose in clouds from the twitching withers.

The four men accepted this condition in different ways. Darcy was simply sleepy; big Lambert Naylor was sullenly silent; Cullen kept his lips nervously compressed and continually brushed his wet face with a handkerchief; but Geraldi was, as ever, cool, rather detached from the circumstances around him, like a general looking from the rear of the course of battle that he hoped to win, while taking nothing for granted and giving away no chances. He wore a wide felt hat, whose brim slouched loosely, a tan flannel shirt, open at the throat, a gun belt—an unusual item with one who preferred his Colts beneath the cover of his coat—and the usual boots and tight trousers. But even these rough clothes could not disguise the dignity and the peculiar authority of Geraldi.

He was looking over the other three at the present moment. "We trim down to essentials," he said. "If there's any waste weight, we leave it behind. You all agree?"

They were silent; Naylor flapped a big hand at his face to keep the flies away.

"That gold and silver junk you are buying weighs seven or eight pounds," said Geraldi to Cullen. "You'd better cache that here. You've bought a pair of fancy guns, Darcy. They stay behind. One rifle and one Colt is our allowance, and a heavy allowance at that. I'm half a mind to keep only one rifle and one revolver in the party."

Cullen could endure no more. His compressed lips parted with an explosion. "Confound it, Jimmy, who made you the tyrant over this party?"

Darcy added: "I've rode desert trails half my life. I know what a hoss can pack as well as any Geraldi that ever stepped."

They looked to Naylor for confirmation of this revolt, but The Lamb, sullen and silent as usual, kept his eyes fixed upon the face of Geraldi and said nothing at all, and made no sign.

The latter replied to the rebels briefly and to the point: "If we travel together," he said, "we travel under my command. Absolute command, mind you, like that of a captain when his ship is at sea, because we're all like voyagers on a dangerous ocean as anything I can imagine. If you don't like that decision, do as you please, and I cut off for myself."

"You're loco if you don't," Naylor said. "You and me, why should we have the pair of 'em on our hands?"

Darcy, with an oath, would have accepted these new conditions, but Cullen capitulated the instant he felt the spur pressed home. With a forced smile, he said: "Come, come, Jimmy, you're not going to jump down my throat at the first word? Of course, we have to stick together. What chance would we have otherwise? Darcy, don't be a chump. We all need each other . . . you still can squeeze a gun butt into those cramped hands of yours."

That speech decided the course of affairs. Darcy and Cullen went back to the inn to leave their unnecessary burdens behind them. The moment they were gone, Naylor turned briskly to Geraldi. "Well, chief," he said, "why don't we start? They're gonna be a dead weight, the pair of 'em. Darcy's broke . . . his spirit's broke. When they drove the spikes through his hands, they drove something through his heart, too, and he's been more'n half dead ever since. Cullen . . . he's got a sneakin' look. We're better rid of the pair of 'em!"

Geraldi nodded. "You have eyes, Lamb," he said, "but I meant what I said about a ship at sea. We're still in the middle of the voyage, man, and we'll have to stay with one another until the whole crew agrees to leave the ship at the same time. I'm the skipper. You can't expect me to drop over the side and make off by myself, can you?"

Lambert Naylor squinted at him, then raised his eyes to the sky and looked for the answer there, but, not finding any, he merely shrugged his massive shoulders. Brainwork was not the specialty of this giant. By the power of his hands, he had wrought his salvation from all dangers in life, and broken the intricate thread of all problems, until the unlucky day he met Geraldi and found that all his might of hand was useless against the scientific craft of the smaller man.

"You got the knowledge of what's best, chief," he said. "You talk . . . I'll try to foller."

So they were waiting in the saddle when the other pair returned, and started off at once.

It was slightly uphill to the cottonwoods, and, after the first passage under the slant but still powerful rays of the sun, they paused again for a moment in this shade. Beyond it lay the treeless dunes of the desert, where they would be naked of defense. The little village—almost as Mexican as Mexico itself—was stretched in a sinuous line along the bank of the river. It was no river now, but a series of greenish pools until the next lucky rainfall in the highlands might send down a stream of fresh though muddy water. A wretched little village, with the dust rising from the children who played in the street, and hanging like a very thin smoke above the houses, but the whitewashed walls looked as comfortable as a fortress to the four, at this moment.

However, they shrugged that suggestion out of their minds, well knowing that what had been a secure resort for them would become a many-handed trap the instant the Naylors arrived.

After that backward look, they went forward again, and, passing down a short slope, they were fairly committed to the desert. Sweat leaped out on the horses; in five minutes they were dripping, their nostrils stretched for more and cooler air, and their heads dropped in resignation to their task. The riders, too, followed the example of the horses and, bowing their heads, crossed their hands upon the pommels of the saddles and gave themselves up to the labored motion of the horses in wading thin surface sand.

The exceptions were the black stallion and Geraldi, for their heads were as high and their eyes as bright as ever. And the horse, jealous at the sight of his dear master on the back of another mount, ever and anon pressed up close beside Geraldi, with a snort of disgust and a toss of his crest. Geraldi, on such occasions, chuckled a little, but always soothed the stallion with a word, or with a touch of the hand.

Then, mercifully, the sun turned red!

Up to that very instant it had remained as hot, well nigh, as noonday, but now its cheeks puffed out. The lower edge dipped to touch the western hills; it climbed slowly down and out of sight.

Now that it had lost its stinging force, they were sorry to see it go. For a long night march across a desert is not the most pleasant of all labors in this world. However, it was gone, and out of the place, where it had sunk, a wind came back to them and blew their bodies cold with the moisture that had been streaming on them the moment before, and turned their damp shirts clammy. The horses, too, felt the change, and every one of them shuddered a little.

"The Injuns got a story about the sunset wind," Darcy commented.

"Let's have it," said Cullen. "It's a ghost story, I'll lay my money."

"You lay right," answered Darcy. "One time . . . this is the way the yarn goes . . . the sun was travelin' through the middle of the sky, and he seen an Injun girl walkin' out of a village and goin' down to a river. He seen her, and she looked pretty good to him. He couldn't drop down out of the sky and chin with her, because the way he was then, he'd've burned her to a crisp, the first word that he spoke. So he waits for the time when he's climbed down into the west and got cooled off a little. But there still was a rag of purple on his coat and a touch of gold in his hair feathers when he jumped up and ran east across the world. As he ran, his robe spread out, and he was chilly, sort of, what with running so fast and being afraid that he would never find the girl again, and the fear run down in trembles along his shoulders and arms, and run out along his robe, and the cold flapped off the edges of the robe and made the air cool.

"And that's the way the night wind is cool . . . it's the sun, runnin' to find the girl he loves, and the fear of not findin' her is what makes the chill in the air."

"Look here," broke in Naylor, with a puzzled air, "what happened? Did he find her?"

"Sure he found her," Darcy said. "But the purple in his robe, mind you, and the gold in his hair feathers was still so dog-gone bright that blame me if she didn't drop dead just as he was reachin' for her."

"It's got a sad endin', then," Naylor said. "And even him bein' the sun god, he could whoop and holler and dance, but he couldn't dance the life back into her body no more?"

"No," Darcy said, "he couldn't."

"But, look here," pursued big Naylor, whose fancy had been caught at last by this subject. "If she's dead, how come that he's still racin' and runnin' back after her every evening?"

"How do I know?" Darcy shouted. "You talk like a child."

"When you say them things to me, son," came the formidable growl of Naylor, "say 'em slow, so's you can swaller the words afterward, one by one, and get the taste of 'em as they go down backward."

This ugly remark reduced the party to silence, until Geraldi began to whistle.

Even that tune presently died. The desert stars, dim behind a dusty atmosphere, burned far away and small, so that the arch of the heavens grew more and more enormous, until the black of the night was complete. And so great was the sweep of them that it seemed as though where they rode the earth was pressing upward, and they were looking down the curve of the world, and over the external barrier of the horizon.

For some time there was not a sound except the creaking of the stirrup leathers, and the cinch straps, or sometimes the jingle of bit chains, like bells rattling far away. These were the only sounds along with the continual swishing of sand about the hoofs of the horses, like water down the side of a boat. So they journeyed into the dimness until The Lamb took up again the subject that had fascinated him.

"Think of him, though, when she dropped, and he picked her up. Still warm, mind you, but nothin' there. Snapped out like the snapper off of a whip . . . gone like the tail of a pollywog . . . or the flash of a shot . . . or the singin' of a bullet. He couldn't get her back. Not even a god. Think of him, how he must've whooped it up and cussed."

III
"THE DESERT MARCH"

The first chill of the night wind on the desert is deceptive, as a rule, although winds there can blow cold enough, to be sure. But chiefly it is the sense of cool produced by the evaporation of the moisture of the day, and, when that is gone, the skin grows dry and burns once more. But on this evening, there was an alteration in the direction of the prevailing air current. It changed from the delightful west—sea-flavored that breeze had seemed —to the arid south, where the air had been soaking up the shimmering heat of the Mexican deserts for two thousand miles of misery.

And the touch of that wind dried them to the core, like bones turned porous on the sands by a hundred years of baking sun and acrid gales. Each man carried two canteens. The first was emptied almost at once, before Geraldi called a halt to the procession and delivered his opinion briefly.

"I'm not a desert rat," he said, "and I've never spent many years on the sand, but I know, whether in Arabia or in Arizona, that the fellow who spends his water is worse than the man who spends all his gold that's in the bank . . . the inheritance as you may call it. Now, then, go slow with the second canteens."

"There ain't any great call," Darcy said. "I'm leadin' you straight to the wells."

"There're sure to have water in 'em?"

"Been there twenty times, every season of the year. Never found 'em dry. Sometimes kind of alkali, but always wet water, and the chiefest main principal thing that water can be on a desert is wet, I always claimed."

"Very well," Geraldi said, "but this wind is like Death Valley, and I intend to take my second canteen a swallow at a time. Naylor, you, at least, had better follow my example."

"Why," Naylor said, "I ain't more'n half finished the first one. Any gent that trusts a desert is loco. I'm here to say so."

"Aye," admitted Darcy, "they's something in that. And it's a funny thing how quick a gent can get dry. I disremember who was tellin' me the yarn about the gent that started walkin' across from the mouth of a mine in Nevada to the other side of the valley, where he could see a spring jumping and sparkling, and the water disppearin' into the ground. Looked like he could step across in no time, he bein' a greenhorn, and he finished up the canteen of water he had with him, and pretty near died of thirst before he got to the other side."

"He was climbin'," Naylor said, "and, besides, he must have been a tenderfoot that let his imagination get hold of him. There ain't anything worse than imaginin' things when you're in the desert. The gent that starts imaginin' is the gent that starts the trouble, pretty nigh always."

After that, all conversation died down, except when someone made a self-conscious, spasmodic effort, for it is well known that of all the terrible things, silence in the desert is the most awful.

But the words would not come. The wind whistled through their clothes, burned their bodies, half blinded their eyes with its stinging dryness. Like a sponge it touched them, and somehow seemed to possess the infernal property of sucking their blood out through the skin.

It was Cullen who finished his second canteen before the others. He was ashamed to confess it, for some time, and finally he had to clear his throat with an effort before he asked: "Those wells, Darcy . . . how far away are they now?"

"Half an hour, maybe."

"Half an hour," Cullen repeated, and was silent, but there had been horror in his voice.

So Geraldi drew over beside him and covertly handed him his canteen. "Take a swallow of this," he said briefly.

Cullen snatched it, and a long swallow it was that he poured down his throat.

"Thanks," he panted, as he handed it back. "We'll soon be there, anyway."

Geraldi made no retort to this, but corked his canteen and hung it against the saddle.

Suddenly Darcy's horse in the lead grunted and broke into a trot of its own accord, and all the other animals followed, the led horses pulling eagerly ahead on their ropes.

The reason was clearly seen in a moment by even the dullest eyes, for in the shallow hollow before them the saw the glitter of stars upon the ground. A handful of the sky, as it were, fallen through and lying very faintly on the earth. Down they swept to the place, every throat open, every mouth instinctively agape, but when Darcy arrived there in the lead, they could hear the hoofs of his horse plodding in and out of the mud.

"Mud!" he yelled savagely over his shoulder. "It ain't nothin' but mud and a film of wet on the top. It's a damn' cheat!"

They reined back their horses and leaned from the saddle in order to see the better.

It was bitterly true. A bit of surface moisture, hardly thicker than dew, had sufficed to reflect the stars as in a tarnished mirror, but all through the brightest places there were now visible small dark lumps and projections of the mud that struck through and had dried at the top.

Darcy was the first to have heart to speak. "This one is no good," he confessed, "but the wells, they couldn't go back on a gent like this. We'll be sure to hit water in one of 'em around here. Scatter out, and the first one that finds it, sing out loud and let us know, will you?"

They scattered. The very horses seemed to know what this was about, for they stepped out eagerly in the chase of the silver glitter of the stars reflected from the earth.

For half an hour they worked, and then the clear voice of Geraldi, pitched high, rang out to them and called them together like the note of a horn.

Silently they gathered. The horses stood about restlessly, biting at their bits, which were hot in the mouth, and starting off sidewise, now and then, as though they wanted to renew the search.

"We've spent long enough here," Geraldi advised. "There's no usable water here."

"Suppose," Cullen said, "that we were to skim off the scum, and boil that down . . . ?"

"Where would we find the wood for fuel or the pans to render it in?" asked Geraldi. "We haven't a distillation plant with us, Cullen, you'll be surprised to learn." His words were acid enough, but his voice was extremely gentle. He went on: "We'll hear advice, now? Who will say something about the next step?"

"They's more wells . . . ," began Darcy.

A general groan stopped him.

"They're a pretty long march away, though," he confessed. "I never heard of these here givin' out before, and I. . . ."

"Let them drop," advised Geraldi. "This is the situation. We're here in the middle of dryness. We can't get across, without the help of water, and there's no water to be had. If we try to complete this march north, I think that not many of us will get through to the farther side. But we can turn to either side and make for the hills."

"Miles and miles away from here!" Cullen exclaimed. "Look yonder! I can see 'em against the stars. . . ."

"He can read distances at night, can he?" growled Naylor. "He's the first I ever seen that could, then."

"Left and right, they're both about the same distances away, I suppose," Geraldi judged. "Which shall we make for? The southern hills are the ones that the Naylors will be most likely to come into, as they march up from that direction. Those over to the east, they're not so likely to take, unless they gamble that we may try to outguess them, and so take the odd chance."

"They'll be in both ranges," The Lamb said shortly.

The others were silent, convinced that this would be the case.

"Or in the desert behind us," Cullen said hopefully, "and starving for water, as we are, I trust."

"They won't be in the desert," said Naylor.

"Why not? In the village, nobody knew that the wells were dry."

"They did know. They must've knowed. They only lied to us."

"They only lied," Geraldi agreed. "And as The Lamb says, it hardly makes any difference to which range we start, except that the eastern ones will be nearer on our way. Shall we head for them?"

They agreed to that procedure.

"A drink, then," Cullen requested, "before we start out. A

drink, don't you think so, Jimmy?"

"By all means," said Geraldi.

But The Lamb broke in harshly: "A drink for the hosses! What kind of desert men are you gents? A drink for the hosses, you square tops! Not a drop for yourselves!"

And Darcy admitted with a reluctant drawl: "A drink for the hosses. He's right."

"It will be the same as shooting ourselves through the head," Cullen stated bitterly. "These great brutes are still puffed up with moisture, but, for my part, I'm on fire from head to foot. I've got to have some water!"

"You've had more than the rest of us," Naylor insisted cruelly. "You've had both of your canteens, and the rest of us have saved part. Jimmy, shut him up, because my hands are beginning to itch to grab hold of him."

Cullen was sufficiently silenced by this, and one by one they forced up the heads of the horses and gave them the little water that remained in the canteens.

There was only one exception—the black stallion did not receive a single drop.

"He's stronger than the others," Geraldi explained curtly, when he was asked. "He'll have to take his chances on using a little more of that surplus energy without water to feed it. Now get into the saddles, and we'll start. And the first man to make a remark about his thirst I'll turn off his horse and let him walk the rest of the distance to the hills on foot!"

That threat had its effect, for, however much their brains tormented them with visions and dreams of paradises of ice, they were silent about their thoughts.

All other ideas seemed to be suppressed at the same time, and in utter silence they marched on toward the hills that never grew before them, but seemed to be receding beneath the dim stars.

And finally Cullen burst out: “They aren’t hills at all! They’re only mists on the skyline.”

No one answered him to agree or disagree. These were the only words spoken on the last stage of that desert march.

IV
"THE CAPTAIN SPEAKS HIS MIND"

"Wherever they's water for us, they's danger for us, too," Darcy announced, when at last they came near to the hills, and the rolling black outlines were drawn across the sky. "We don't know this country half as well as the Naylors do, and they'll be reasonable sure to get every spring and water hole and creek pretty well spotted in the hills on both sides."

"They ain't got an army, though," The Lamb said. "They can't be everywhere at once."

"I guess we'll think so before we're through," said Darcy.

The first of the dawn came as they entered the nearest gully leading northeast through the hills; and now the slope turned gray, and finally soft green. Rain had been here; streams of some sort surely could not be far off.

And it was as they hurried up the valley that, on passing the mouth of a narrow gulch that fed into the larger depression, Naylor lifted his hand and stopped the party. They sat their saddles like statues, listening, while the sides of the horses heaved rapidly, and their whole bodies shook with the trembling of their legs.

"Water," Naylor said, and swung straight into the mouth of the little cañon.

As he spoke, they all could hear it—a soft sound of rushing and gurgling that seemed to freshen their dry throats immediately, as though the water already were being swallowed. And in a rush they followed The Lamb.

The little cañon twisted before them like a snake, as though trying to delay them, but when they found the place, it seemed even to the calm mind of Geraldi one of the most beautiful spots on earth. For from beneath one steep bank, a head of water sprang a foot at least, and, running outward, formed a big pool with the sand sloping down all around it like the sides of a natural basin. There was no exit for this water that could be seen, showing that it was drained off from beneath through the porous soil. Yet perhaps this very stream was the source of the current that wandered far underground and reached at last the wells in the desert. At least, Geraldi thought of this as he saw the horses rush for the water.

The men had to fight them back, for fear that, hot and dry as they were, the animals might be foundered. Geraldi saw Naylor, half to his knees in the flood, striking at the noses of the horses, and with his free hand scooping up mouthfuls of the water.

When the horses had been allowed all that was thought fitting for them, they were drawn aside and tethered, while the men went on with the work of washing out and filling canteens, and of filling themselves to the very lips with this treasure of which they had been dreaming during so many hours. No matter how much they drank, still their dried bodies craved for more, insatiably, and no matter how much lay before them, they could not be satisfied.

Cullen, now that the crisis was over, was seized by an overwhelming laughter, and seemed to feel that the joke was upon the others. He kept pointing at one or another of his companions and actually staggered with his mirth, but they paid him no heed, being ashamed to look at a man who could not hold himself together better than this.

They stretched themselves on the sand around the edge of the pool now, and watched the dawn colors thicken in the sky above them. The coolness of the earth sank into their hot bodies, and they raised their heads and envied the images of the willows about the pond, forever floating in crystal water.

"Hungry?" asked someone.

"Could eat a coupla bear," declared The Lamb.

"We'd better breakfast," Cullen said. "We're all dizzy with hunger."

"We'd better march, and we shall march," answered Geraldi. "Get up, boys, and tighten your cinches."

They scowled at him, one and all, but his voice was also that of their own consciences, so they rose with groans and went to the horses that grunted in turn like pigs when they felt the sudden jerk and gripping of the girths again.

A morning wind had commenced to blow, singing among the crags above them and rustling in the willows nearby, and doubtless it was this noise that allowed disaster to creep up on them unheard. As Darcy swung into his saddle, a rifle clanged from the cliff above, and he pitched on over the back of his horse, cursing like a pirate.

He was not too badly hurt to spring up from his fall and run in under the verge of the rocks where bullets could not be fired down at him. The others had done the same thing, and in this momentary shelter they mounted in grim haste. Geraldi lingered to help the wounded man to the back of his horse. He saw that the left arm of Darcy hung useless. He gave one questioning look to Darcy, but the latter, white-faced, with teeth set hard, made no response except to spur frantically down the ravine.

Geraldi followed, letting the black stallion find his own way, while the master turned in the saddle to watch the rearward rocks, his gun poised for a parting shot.

But no second bullet was fired. Either they were out of range, riding so closely under the high bank, or else it was a single outpost of the Naylors who had found them and dared not show himself enough to get in another round.

So they poured down the cañon, the armed hoofs of the horses raising thunder on either side. Cullen, in the lead, shot down the first opening on the right, and they galloped like mad up a long gully that carried them, eventually, into the open hills. Naked hills they were, over which the eyes could carry for leagues, but there was no need of trees or brush to give shelter to any who were stalking them, for everywhere small draws and cañons ran, splitting the hills into a species of badlands. They had to take a zigzag course, feeling their way down the side of the ravine, then crossing it at the first favorable chance, and climbing up the other bank, only to be stopped again by a similar obstacle a little farther on.

"We've got time," Naylor said suddenly. "They're callin' for help. Look back!"

They looked and saw behind three puffs of smoke rising into the air, the topmost one already dissolving in the wind, the lower two still compacted, looking like white balls of snow. Beneath the three only a scattered haze ascended, showing that the fire had been muzzled thoroughly and beaten out.

"That's the call," said Naylor. "Help . . . riding north. That'll call in every Naylor riding in sight of the smoke, and all of 'em must be in sight of it. Where'll we go now?"

"Straight on north, but faster," urged Cullen.

"Go where they expect us?"

"We'll stop here and talk it over," Geraldi said, dismounting. "Darcy, get down and let me have a look at that."

"I'm all right," Darcy gritted, through his teeth. "Only scratched. I'd rather keep on goin'."

His motive was plain. If he were too badly injured, they were apt to cast him out as a useless burden, and, if the Naylors caught him, a second torturing was the best that he could hope for.

Geraldi did not repeat his suggestion in words; he merely beckoned, and Darcy obediently slipped to the ground. He was ordered to lie flat, and complied at once with a faint groan of despair and relief. In a moment more his shirt had been opened, the blood sponged away with a little water from Geraldi's canteen. The course of the bullet was apparent at once. It had cut down through the shoulder, penetrating the inner, fleshy part, and then ranged across three ribs. When Geraldi manipulated these, two of them were obviously broken; the wounded man turned white under the pressure.

"He's done up," Cullen said critically, who had been standing apart, taking no share in the help of the hurt member, but now ready to speak. "He's used up. Anybody could see that by a look at his face. Geraldi, are you going to waste any more time on him?"

Geraldi looked up for one long second from his work of drawing heavy, tight bandages around the body of Darcy, then he continued his labor in silence. Cullen flushed a little at the unspoken rebuke.

"I mean," he said, "that he could sneak off to the side, and they'd never look for him. It's the rest of us that they want more than they ever do Darcy. They won't even notice. They'll be busy hanging on our trail."

He received no answer. Only the grim eye of Naylor was considering him like a difficult passage out of a strange but obnoxious book, and in another moment he had finished helping Geraldi.

"Are you better, now?" the chief asked the hurt man.

"If I can breathe, I'll be pretty good," said Darcy.

"You can't breathe, against that bandage," Geraldi said. "Not real breaths, or they'll start the wound bleeding again. But you can breathe short and quick. You understand? Short breaths and many of them will keep you going in good style."

"I'll try," Darcy said, looking far off at the mountains, where he longed to be at that moment.

"Try it, and remember that we're with you and won't give you up till the finish."

Darcy nodded. He did not waste time even in thanks, but was heaved into his saddle by the mighty hands of The Lamb, and rode on the trail again.

Naylor had the lead, now, as one best suited to find a passage across such broken territory as this. Cullen dropped back beside Geraldi.

"I wanted to tell you, Jimmy," he said, "that I'm no cold-blooded scoundrel that wants to let a partner go. But I ask you to look this problem in the face. Is there any likelihood that we'll be able to get away when we're loaded down by a half-helpless man like Darcy?"

Geraldi nodded agreement. "He takes away two-thirds of our chances," he said.

"Of course, he does," said the other, happy to find this acquiescence. "And remember that he's at his best now. Every moment he's sure to get worse as the loss of blood tells on him, as the wound grows sore and stiff. And if he's an encumbrance now, what will he be then?"

"Harry," Geraldi said, "I never heard better logic or closer reasoning even from you."

"But. . . ."

"But logic isn't enough, old fellow. We have to have something more. We have to have something out of the way . . . instinct, let's say?"

"You certainly talk just like a woman, Jimmy."

"Thanks," said Geraldi. "You don't hurt me by saying that."

"And you stay with him? You anchor us with him?"

"Not *us*," Geraldi said. "You and Naylor can do as you please. But, as you know, I'm the captain of the ship and have to be the last over the side. I'm in it till she sinks."

V
"A TEST OF MEN"

As a ship labors and strains in a rough sea, so the horses heaved and stumbled and rocked over the ridges of that infernal going. The sun rose and in five minutes was pouring heat over the hills, but still there were shadowy gorges into which they dropped from time to time until high noon came, and then there remained no shelter. Shoulders burned and blistered under flannel shirts. The springing moisture burned dry the instant it appeared, and every face was gray with salt. Gray were the horses, also.

Two of them, far spent, with gaunted bellies and arching backs, no longer could be trusted with saddle and with rider but had to remain on the lead ropes, tugging back at every declivity, at every upward slope.

Nervous anxiety added to the strain, and, above all, when Naylor waved his hand in a broad arch to the rear, and pointed out three columns of smoke that mounted toward the sky.

"There's three gangs of the boys coming after us," he declared. "They've seen the signal, and they're hopping after us."

"There's no law in this part of the country!" exclaimed Cullen. "By heaven, it makes my blood boil when I think of those scoundrels, those known scoundrels, being permitted to ride unscathed through the hills pursuing us. Where's the sheriff? Where are the posses that one reads about? *Bah!*"

"The sheriff," Geraldi replied with his flashing smile, "generally is busied with cases in which at least one side is honest."

Cullen started to answer, but, seeing the point of the remark, he fell gloomily silent. Once or twice his eyes twitched aside and his lips curled over a wicked retort, but he repressed it, and went on without speech. He was in the best condition of any of the others, with the exception of Geraldi. The latter had given up his second-string horse to The Lamb, whose enormous bulk had worn out one animal already; nevertheless, the black stallion seemed to have more in reserve than any other two of the mounts put together. Cullen, however, was equipped with two good nags, and, since he was an excellent rider, he had kept them in fine condition. As for Darcy, he could not help but be a drag on a horse, no matter how excellent and strong it might be, for his horsemanship now was confined to clinging with both hands to the pommel of his saddle.

"You'd better have a drink," suggested Geraldi, as the heat of the day approached its fiery climax and seemed to eat up the very shadows that fell on the sands and on the burning rocks. "You haven't touched water for two hours, I think. One really needs water in this heat."

Darcy rolled bloodshot eyes at him, without a reply, and then Geraldi saw that the strong arms of the man were trembling as he supported himself on them.

Geraldi himself fell back a little with his wounded companion, took his canteen, unscrewed the cap, drew the cork, and put to Darcy's lips. Darcy drank deeply. Afterward, the very effort of raising his head made him sway in the saddle heavily, or perhaps it was the sudden effect of so much liquid.

He recovered himself before the steadying hand of Geraldi could reach his shoulder, and, looking at Geraldi out of those tortured eyes, he said slowly: "I was plannin' to double-cross you, Jimmy."

"We all plan such things," Geraldi answered. "There's no man in the world who hasn't had some confounded weak, vicious moment. But between the planning and the doing, there's a gap. You never would have done it. Go on, Darcy. We'll sit together in some cool room, one day, and talk about this ride, and sniff the fragrance of the drinks in the air, and try to talk foreign languages to waiters who speak English better than we do. We'll walk under the chestnut trees, and watch the fountains blow into a mist, and see the children running through it like butterflies through a rain. We'll have a thousand lazy, easy days until this little affair, old fellow, will be no more than a bad dream. All of it that will remain real to us will be the banknotes and the jewels. I tell you, Darcy, that I know the fellow who will give us eighty percent of their value in the open market, and mighty glad to get them at that. Go on, Darcy, and never say die until you feel the rattle in your throat."

Darcy grinned as he listened—grinned like a wolf in the hungry time of winter when it lifts its head in the cave and hears the pack far off, in hot cry after meat. Then, without a word of spoken answer, he spurred the tired horse forward, and got it into a trot.

The afternoon came, and still they led the pursuit. Once, Cullen, scanning a skyline behind them with a pair of strong glasses that he carried, declared that he had seen horsemen sweep over a ridge and disappear in the next low ground. But, at any rate, this was their only materialization. It frightened the four fugitives, but it did not bring the Naylors closer.

However, it was almost worse to have the pursuit unseen.

For they knew that somewhere in the rear the four parties had joined. Perhaps the best men had been placed upon the finest and greatest-hearted horses to make the final spurt for the capture. These and many other surmises passed through the minds of the hunted. But of only one thing they never spoke—what would happen if the Naylors actually came up with them.

Twice they made brief halts to permit the horses to graze on the grass and swallow some of the water where they crossed runlets. On these occasions, the men swallowed something, as well, and Geraldi saw that Darcy was helped down from his horse and laid on his back. There he lay with arms thrown out crosswise in whatever bit of shadow could be improvised for him. Once, for instance, The Lamb held a blanket between him and the sun, while Geraldi swabbed the caked salt from the face and the throat of the hurt man. Then they would lift him again and place him in the saddle.

Still the Naylors were not in view, and the reason began to be apparent.

Geraldi had insisted on keeping to a straight line of march, no matter what difficulties lay in the way. Over rough and smooth they went, even when long, easy ravines stretched out at only a little angle from the proper point of the compass. Even these he would have none of, but kept strictly to his way.

It had seemed madness to the others, at the beginning. Even The Lamb grew terse and ugly with his idol, but now they were reaping the advantages of his generalship. For certainly all that could have held up the Naylors and their band of horsemen so long was that they were wasting their energies scouring off on side shoots, sweeping away in the probable and sensible directions that fugitives should have taken.

Even so, it would have been foolish to think that the pursuit was far away. But the sun dropped slowly in the west, lingering with a cruel slowness on its downward path, and at length it was on the horizon, showing purple strata of dust streaked in long, wavering lines across its face. The dusk deepened, the color left the sky, the pale desert stars looked down through the dusty air on the four, and then Geraldi mercifully gave the order to halt.

Cullen and Naylor dropped from their horses as though they had been struck with clubs; Geraldi himself was quickly on the ground, stretching, but Darcy rode straight on. Geraldi ran after him and headed him back. The man sat as though glued to his saddle. Naylor came and lifted him from the horse to the ground. There his strength went out of him, and he lay loose as water. When Geraldi lighted a match, the eyes were open, but glazed and fixed as death, horribly bloodshot. So horribly, that it seemed to Geraldi that he could mark the scoring of the individual grains of sand. Actually he advanced the light nearer, until he could see the pupils change in size, but never before had he seen such a dreadful and contorted mask of death in life.

He ventured a fire, on the strength of this. Under cover of a nest of rocks in the hollow, the fire was built, additionally screened with blankets, and the coffee pot made to boil over it. The breath of the aroma of that necessary stimulant lifted every head. Even Darcy groaned with a faint pleasure. Eat he could not, but the coffee gave him enough strength to begin to tremble as he lay, the muscles feebly responding, and in jerks, to the commands of his thoughts and his nerves. He tried continually to prop himself up, and eventually succeeded in doing so, putting his back against a stone.

Geraldi saw him there, his head fallen over to one side, the deformed hands helpless in his lap, and was reminded of seeing a very old woman from whom even the resource of knitting had been stolen by blindness. He went to Darcy and kneeled beside him.

"You'd better lie down, old man," he said. "Then, after a while, you'll be able to eat and sleep a bit."

"I'll stay here," said Darcy. "I feel more like a man, sitting up." He reached out a hand and pawed at Geraldi. "Jimmy, lemme stay here. It's worse than death, to go on."

"You wait till the morning," Geraldi responded, and he laid a hand upon the forehead of his companion.

There was no fever. Instead, the skin was clammy and cold to the touch. It did not seem that life could inhabit so cold a body as this. So Geraldi found a blanket and wrapped it closely around him.

Cullen, in the meantime, had been watching every procedure with a bitter interest. He even said to Naylor: "This night tells the tale. If that useless hulk of a Darcy is dragged along with us, we're all dead men tomorrow . . . dead as Indians would kill us."

But Naylor did not answer. He spoke to no one now except Geraldi. For him, he worked methodically, patiently, fetching and carrying, tending the fire, the horses. The man was indefatigable, and never a word of despair, or a word of advice, passed his lips.

Only, a little later, he stretched out his long arm and pointed.

Geraldi had come back from the invalid, and now a dimly perceived form wobbled away against the stars, and then dipped out of view below the rim of the hill.

"The man's gone crazy at last," Cullen said sharply. "Now be yourself, Jimmy. Take his share. We'll hand it on, of course, to his heirs . . . if the ruffian has any. But now that he's out of his head and wandering, let him go, for mercy's sake."

Neither Naylor nor Geraldi spoke for a moment, and then

the former lurched away into the shadows.

"Go slowly, Lamb," Geraldi called softly. "There's no hurry. I've taken the caps out of his cartridges."

VI

"FALSE FIRE!"

Prejudice and malice had dulled the perceptions of Cullen. "What's that?" he asked sharply. "What's that about the caps?"

"You'll understand if you think for a moment," said Geraldi. "Why do you think Darcy stayed with us all day?"

"To save his worthless hide, of course."

"No, but because he knew I wouldn't let him go. And Naylor wouldn't let him go."

"You leave me out of it, do you?" Cullen snapped. "I'm glad you understand me that well, Jimmy. The fact is there's no stupid sentimentality about me. I like to look the cards in the face and read my hand for what it's worth. When my time comes to go under, I won't cling to straws but throw my head down and swim deeper to end it quickly."

Geraldi replied, after a moment: "Yes, Harry, yes. I believe that of you."

"Thanks," Cullen said, appeased a little. "But seriously, Jimmy, you're making a fool of yourself about a fellow that's not worth saving. Simply low-bred, ignorant, and with a skin that makes the hide of a rhinoceros seem like gauze. There'll be no gratitude in him. I could tell you what he proposed to me the other day when we. . . ."

"Harry," Geraldi interrupted, "I never like reminiscences about what might have been. The facts are generally bitter enough, without the maybes. But just now, poor Darcy has gone out to kill himself and so take a burden off our hands."

"To kill himself? Darcy? You're mad, Jimmy!"

"Hush," said Geraldi. He raised his hand. Out of the distance they heard voices, and one of them the unmistakable growl of The Lamb.

"The Romans were capable of such things," Geraldi said softly. "A few heroes, here and there. But, somehow, I guessed that this poor fellow Darcy had the same mysterious stuff in him. Beyond you and me, Harry. We only peek around the corner at such things, and the world turns unreal when we hear of such men. But they are here about us. Do you know, Harry, that all we appreciate in the people we know is cleverness, hard-headedness, wisdom that can be turned into cash? But the better things, we can't see. Who would have thought that Darcy . . . ?"

"To kill himself!" Cullen repeated. Then he shook his head, and added with great decision: "You're talking through your hat, old fellow. Such things can't be. Not from a Darcy . . . not from any man I've ever known, as a matter of fact."

"Not from self-conscious men," Geraldi said. "You and I, for instance, might conceive of such an act, but then we'd begin to do it in the head instead of with the hand, and, before long, we'd have tears of self-pity in our eyes. The fault, you may say, of a finer organism, more delicate sensibilities . . . but poor Darcy doesn't reach far with his imagination. He's seen his way only a few inches before his nose . . . generally he's seen opportunities for crime. But now he sees a chance for a great act, also. He doesn't know that it's great. But, dimly, vaguely, he wants to relieve us of the burden of himself."

"Jimmy," Cullen said, "your simple confidence in human

nature is touching and amusing . . . astonishing, more than anything else. I, for one, wouldn't have believed that I could find such a thing in you. But here's Naylor come back. We'll ask this ox what the donkey really was about."

However, there was something about The Lamb, as he strode up to the pair that forbade immediate question. He remained with them for a moment, and then made and lighted a cigarette. The end of it flared instantly with a long, yellow-red coal, so violently was The Lamb inhaling the smoke.

At last he said: "I got him when he had the gun at his head. I heard the hammer go down . . . *thud!*"

"Good . . . ," began Cullen.

Naylor turned half toward him. "Aw, shut up," he said. "I'm talkin' to Mister Geraldi." He continued: "I heard him groan. He turned the cylinder, but before he could try again, I got him. He wobbled like a baby when I touched him. He turned all loose . . . like a sick kid that. . . ." The Lamb hurled his cigarette butt far from him, and it fell against the face of a rock with a splashing of bright sparks. "I had to carry him back. He begun to choke. He cried. This here . . . this Darcy, I mean to say . . . he cried." Again he stopped. They could hear him breathing hard.

"I laid him down where he was before. He's pretty comfortable, I guess, now. Maybe he feels better. I been explaining to him about the way you feel . . . I mean, that we're all one gang . . . like one body, you might say . . . and you the head . . . takin' care of us all. Would a man want to lose a leg or an arm? No more you want to lose one of us. I told him he wasn't no burden. We'd bring him through. We all three stood solid on that. All three of us." As he said this, he turned suddenly and fiercely on Cullen.

"Very well," the latter said coldly. "Of course, the majority always rules . . . particularly when it includes the captain general."

He walked off into the night as he said this, and The Lamb stared after him for a moment. Then he added to Geraldi: "Maybe you better not go talk to him, just now. I'm gonna get him to eat, pretty *pronto*."

"I won't go near him. You're much better for him than I possibly could be. I never could have put things so well to him as you've done, Lamb. I'm proud of you."

"Proud of me?" asked Naylor. "Are you?" He laughed, and the laughter had such a foolish sound that it sobered him at once. "I'll get him to eat something, pretty soon. Then maybe he'll sleep. What I mean is, about you going, it would get him pretty excited. He says he knows you know he was no good, but fought for him, anyway. He don't understand. That's what busted him up and made him want to shoot himself . . . to get himself off of our hands. And when he found out that it was you that had taken the caps out of his cartridges, that was what broke him down, and made him like a kid in my arms, carryin' him back. Mind you, Jimmy, he ain't been much before this. But afterwards, hands or no hands, you watch his dust." He concluded, philosophizing: "The things you don't expect. They're what cut the closest to the quick. The punch out of the dark. The hundred dollars from the gent you expect will laugh in your face. The buckin' hoss that one day goes smooth. . . ." He turned away, and disappeared, the darkness soaking him up, as water soaks up a handful of sand.

Then Geraldi sat down and locked his hands about his knees, and looked up at the desert stars, thinking of many a strange sight on land and sea, but none which ever had brought to him a thing as great and as strange as this. He pondered. The Lamb and Darcy, as twisted as a knot in a tree with sin, and as hard with vice. He thought of Cullen, but there he began to frown at the darkness and shake his head.

Harry Cullen had recuperated quickly from the shock of that revelation concerning Darcy. He had looked upon the man as a worm and a tool for so long, however, that he could not learn to readjust himself and look up to a new soul.

He did not understand that transformations are, by the grace of heaven, possible even in sinful man, but what he was himself, he felt all other men to be. Therefore, he dismissed Darcy with the single, sneering word under which he included all actions of generosity, self-sacrifice, noble goodness. "Sentimentality!" Cullen spit, and walked on into the darkness.

He took from his pack a blanket and continued on his way, for he had made up his mind what he must do. His intentions, he assured himself, had been good. He had resisted the first temptation and spurned it from him. He had made the long ride with honest integrity of purpose. He had endured everything until the point came when he made sure that they were about to be ruined by having a lead weight tied about their necks. But this was as far as any man could go, and no further. To endure more would be to place himself in that category which he most scorned and laughed at. A sentimentalist he would not be.

He had chosen the place even when they were pitching camp that night. For two hills behind the hollow where they camped, there arose a taller hill. And to the farther side of this he went. He passed some dead brush, and from this, with as little noise as possible, he picked off some branches that broke easily beneath his hand. Two or three thorns pricked his skin, but he thought nothing of these. He had enough with him for his purpose when he came to the appointed spot.

First he scanned the countryside all around him, making sure that though there were a few hills loftier than the one he stood on, yet over two thirds of the horizon could easily view his signal. Then he arranged his heap of wood and lighted the dead leaves that were to kindle the sticks. Leaves and wood flared up with a strange swiftness, as though they had been soaked with oil, and the suddenness of the flame and the height to which its head rose and stood nodding in the air filled him with terror, for suddenly it seemed to him that the shadow of Geraldi was behind him, that the terrible youth had followed him, well divining his purpose, and now, if he turned, he would see the flashing smile of Geraldi—the last thing he ever would view upon this earth.

The illusion was so strongly persistent that he jerked his head about and gasped with relief when he saw that the hillside was naked about him. Then, with the blanket, he masked the flames three times, and three times let it shine forth again, loosing the brilliance to penetrate far off.

Somewhere among those hills, he could swear, there were eyes watching which would not miss the winking of the light. Yet he would not rest content with signaling once. Again he made the fire blink thrice, then, in feverish, breathless haste, he scattered the small, flaming embers and hastily stamped them out. Still he worked, kicking and stamping, until he was tired. At last he stopped, and breathed deeply with relief, while the chill of the evening wind passed across his face.

VII
"WHAT KIND OF A PROMISE?"

When Cullen came back, he found that Geraldi, in the dimness of the starlight, was busily improvising a horse litter out of two straight boughs that he had cut in the hollows and between which he was weaving a network of ropes. Naylor helped clumsily in the work, but when Cullen offered his assistance, Geraldi pointed out that the thing was nearly completed.

"You could light a match, though," suggested the leader, "and hold it for this last couple of knots."

Cullen obediently dropped to one knee and lighted the match, cupping his hands to shield the weak flame from the hand of the night wind.

"Hello," Naylor said as Geraldi rapidly secured the last rope ends, "you've singed your fine new boots, ain't you, Cullen?"

The match dropped from Cullen's hands. "The boots?" he said, scratching another match. "Yes, I was fool enough to stand in too close to the fire this evening."

When the second match was lighted, he was on both knees, and the boots were out of sight; Geraldi, busily finishing his work, seemed to pay no attention, however, and for this Cullen was profoundly thankful, for he knew that out of small things, Geraldi could draw great conclusions.

"How are the horses?" Geraldi asked, rising to his feet.

"The gray mare is still tucked up pretty bad," Naylor informed him. "I don't think she'll carry more'n her own weight today. The rest of 'em are pretty good. They're eating and that's something."

"Everything," said Geraldi. "As long as a horse will eat, it will run." He whistled, and the pulse of galloping hoofs swept rapidly up to them. The stallion halted at the side of his master, and Geraldi ran his hand along the flank of his horse. "He feels this business," Geraldi said, "but he's still iron. Lamb, go wake up poor Darcy and tell him we're starting. Cullen, will you help me tie this litter between a pair of the horses?"

Cullen did not grumble. His interest in the escape had been lost a little earlier in the evening, so that now he entered no further protest against the waste of time and effort over the wounded man. But when he heard Geraldi singing softly to himself as the horses were saddled, Cullen broke out: "Jimmy, I think, after all, you actually enjoy this business."

"Who wouldn't?" asked Geraldi. "If it hadn't been for Darcy, this would have been a poor show, a hollow show, old fellow. We would have been out of touch with our Naylor friends long ago, and then you'd have nothing but a dull party to remember, Harry. We'd feel like robbers."

"And how do we feel now?" Cullen asked curiously.

"Why, like gentlemen adventurers, buccaneers, at least. Let's get Darcy stretched on this litter, and then off we go."

"Why hurry?" Cullen asked, cautious, but eager to make his point. "You understand, Jimmy . . . the horses fagged, all of us dead tired. Why not risk a few hours' rest? After all, we'll have a better chance of making time, and the Naylors can't smell us out in the dark of this night."

"Distance is the best cure for the Naylor disease," Geraldi replied. "We'll march."

Rapidly they concluded their preparations, the tired horses were gathered, and Naylor and Cullen lifted the sick man onto the litter.

Over the next ridge they climbed, and now for the first time Geraldi varied from his plan of keeping to a straight line of direction from the first to the last. Instead, he slanted the party up a long, gradually rising gorge.

The air freshened as they went, and, when they climbed out of the headlands at the top of the gorge, fresh wind was blowing against them. The stars, too, were more brilliant overhead; a fragrance of the pure pines sifted through the atmosphere. To the right hand they saw what seemed to be a mist rising darkly from the earth.

It was the desert and its enveloping, choking dust, as they could guess, but here the rain had fallen recently. Water was heard trickling nearby.

"Where's Cullen?" Naylor asked, looking back.

"He's fallen behind," said Geraldi.

"A fine time to fall behind. I'll give him a call."

"You have good lungs, Lamb?"

"The best you ever heard. Listen."

"You could shout like thunder, but Harry won't hear you."

"What d'you mean by that, Jimmy?"

"That he's gone on the back trail to find your people."

"Go after him, Jimmy," Naylor said through his teeth. "You can catch him with the black hoss. Go after him, and bring back his scalp, the low skunk! I knew it when I first laid eyes on him. I knew it. I was ready to believe it from the beginning . . . but he was with you, Jimmy. That's why I never let myself think too much."

"He's gone," Geraldi said almost sadly. "There was the weak spot in the rope, but still we're not dropped over the cliff. We'll go on, old-timer. We're not beaten until the last card falls in this game."

The hills through which they traveled now were difficult enough, sown with rocks, steep-sided, but the horses took to their work more kindly, reaching their heads at the grass which their hoofs were crushing, lifting their crests, snorting to clear their noses of the desert dust, shaking themselves like dogs out of water.

"Watch the horses," Geraldi warned. "They know that we have another chance."

The answer came from Darcy, in the form of a heavy groan, then he broke into an excited chattering.

"Out of his head, complete," Naylor commented.

"He'll come back again," replied Geraldi. "He was cold as ice, and I'd rather have the fever than the cold."

"I'll tell you," The Lamb said. "I've seen 'em before like this, and, if we don't get him to cover and quiet before the day's out, my money goes down that he's a dead man for sure."

"Man, man," Geraldi said with his first touch of impatience, "don't you see that that's the chief reason I've pushed forward tonight? That and the burned boots?"

"Burned boots?" asked Lambert Naylor. "I don't foller that."

"He was never close enough to our own fire to singe them. I was sure of that. How were they singed? By another fire. Why another fire? Well, old son, fire light can be seen a long distance, you know, on a night like this."

"Why didn't you smash his head in?" the giant asked. "Why didn't you hand him over to me and let me wring his neck?"

"He's dead, he's dead," Geraldi said. "Forget about him. He's behind us like dust in the wind. Listen!"

They both bent their heads, and heard distinctly, behind them, the neighing of a horse. Almost immediately afterward, they were aware of a distant roaring.

"Hosses comin' through a cañon," diagnosed The Lamb. "We better move, Jimmy, because they're after us. That Cullen has met 'em, and he's turned in news that's worth his board and keep."

They put the horses to a jog. Anything else was impossible, so long as they had the litter suspended between the pair, and, as they rose over a swale of ground, Geraldi heard the roar of many galloping hoofs in the distance.

All the lower hills behind them were black mounds revealing nothing, but he could guess the very faces of the fierce riders.

They pushed forward down the slope, a groan breaking from delirious Darcy every step of the way.

It was The Lamb who called out suddenly and pointed to the right. Geraldi saw the sharp ridge of the roof of a house. He did not hesitate. There was no possibility of keeping on with Darcy and escaping at the pace to which his sufferings confined them. So Geraldi swung to the side and drew up the horses in front of a typical squatter's shack.

He was out of the saddle and had jerked the door open in a trice, when a voice drawled in the darkness: "I got a line on you, friend, and, if you don't back out faster'n you came in, I'm likely to. . . ."

Geraldi did not back out. Instead, he slithered into the darkness of the room.

"Where did you . . . ?" the proprietor began, and then there was the brief sound of a scuffle. Naylor, listening attentively, smiled with grim reminiscence.

But a match now spurted blue fire.

Naylor, looking in, saw that Geraldi held a gun under the

chin of a little, scrawny fellow.

"Murder?" the householder said calmly. "Or might it be just robbery? If it's murder, they ain't enough fight in me to give you no good time, and, if it's robbery, I gotta confess that I feel a tolerable lot of sympathy for you poor gents. You mean well. You wanna make a large job out of this here, but you can't carve a man-sized statue out of a hickory nut, and you can't pick up money where they ain't more than a handful of loose change. Right trousers pocket, if you want that."

"Do you hear me?" Geraldi asked.

"As keen as though I had owls' ears," said the other. "Sure, I hear you, partner."

"I have this gun under your chin not to squeeze money out of your hide, but to get a promise from you."

"Hey," the other said. "Promise? Promise? What kind of a promise? I'd rather give away a gold watch than a promise."

"Bring in Darcy," Geraldi said, and Naylor carried the wounded man into the room.

The rancher looked at the wound with an indifferent eye. "He's feelin' kind of flabby," he said, and that was all.

"Now," Geraldi began, biting his lip as he saw that his stern measures were accepted by the man without the slightest show of emotion. "Now, my friend, you. . . ."

"Gleason is the name, partner. What's yours?"

"Geraldi," the other responded, at a venture, in striving to impress his host. He saw the shoulders of Gleason twitch back, as his eyebrows raised.

But he merely said: "Geraldi? Seems like I may've heard it somewheres, but I ain't sure. Was you playin' the leadin' parts for the stock company that was over to Rawhide last winter?"

Geraldi chuckled. "Whether you know me or not," he said, "I think I know you, Gleason. That is to say, I'll trust you as far as I can see you, tonight. Now, then, a score or so of armed men are riding this way as fast as galloping horses will bring them. I want your promise that you'll let us hide my friend here . . . say, up that ladder and in the loft?" He pointed to a ladder made of two straight saplings, leading from a corner to a trap door in the ceiling.

"And when they come, not say nothin'?" Gleason asked, with a glint in his eye.

"I'll be outside the rear window, to encourage you with a bullet or two, if you don't do right," Geraldi assured Gleason. "Will you give me your word, however?"

"A word and a gun," Gleason replied, "ought to be enough to hold me. All right, Mister Geraldi. You have my word."

VIII
"DANGER RIDES BY"

"Now up to the loft with him," Geraldi said, turning to big Naylor.

"Suppose he's trapped there, Jimmy?"

"As well be trapped in a room as ridden down in the open air."

So saying, he took the feet of the wounded man, while The Lamb took the shoulders, and together they drew him up the ladder and passed with him into the loft above. Only once did Geraldi stop in the ascent, and this was when Gleason moved as though to leave the room below, but he caught the eye of Geraldi and remained steadfast, with a faint grin.

So Geraldi passed his share of the burden to the capable strength of Naylor and returned down the ladder to the floor below. The Lamb followed almost at once, to report that he had found clean straw above and had stretched Darcy upon it. His very words were interrupted by the clanging of armed hoofs on rocks, a sound that rang sharply from the outer night, although still at a distance.

"Get the horses, Lamb," directed Geraldi. "Take the black and ride him."

"And you?" Naylor asked, frowning.

"I'll stay here, but you get on with the horses, and try to make a detour and come back."

"You stay here?" Naylor said. Then he nodded: "I stay on, too. I don't care any more about 'em than you do. What comes your way can come mine and. . . ."

"Get out!" Geraldi commanded sharply. "Get out, climb on my horse, and ride as if the fiend were after you. Go on, man! They're coming after you like a whirlwind. Ride like mad. Never look behind you. You'll have a horse that can't be caught. If the worst comes to the worst, you can cut the led horses loose and go on safely. But try to keep the whole band together, because that will make our friends behind you think that we're still riding together, all three of us. You'll drag them off on a wild-goose chase, and before they come again on the back trail, I'll have Darcy more than half well and out on the road once more. But circle back if you safely outrun them, as you may do when every horse has an empty saddle except the black. Go on, man. No talk! No talk!"

He headed Naylor to the door, where the giant paused again, his face filled with doubt, but eventually he allowed himself to be persuaded out, and, flinging himself into the saddle, he started off with all the led horses rattling around him over the stones and thudding on the grassy ground as they went.

Gleason, who had lighted a lamp and now held it in a corner, so that no light from it might reach the door, remarked to Geraldi: "Those gents that are after you, what do they want? The blood out of your pocket, or the blood out of your heart?"

"They want both," Geraldi answered. He stepped to the table and from his trousers pocket he brought out a handful of jewels. Green and red and blue, and pure crystals of undiluted light, they spun across the table top. One of them rolled off and dropped to the floor.

Gleason, with a gasp, picked it up and replaced it on the

table, while Geraldi smiled at him. For the little man's ironical composure and faint smile of ridicule had been quite altered by the sight of this burning handful of treasure. He seemed to be holding the lamp so that his own mortification and greed could be read more clearly.

"Look, Gleason," Geraldi said. "There's the board bill in advance for my friend upstairs . . . and for me."

Gleason looked sharply at him, greed overcoming even his wonder as he stared at his companion.

"I mean it," Geraldi said. "We have plenty more of the same," he added frankly, "but that's a good deal more than the Naylors would give you."

"The Naylors?"

"You never heard of them, either, did you?" Geraldi smiled.

Gleason swallowed with difficulty, but while his absent gaze dwelt on Geraldi and on the distance behind that young man, his free right hand gathered in the jewels from the table top. He pocketed them, and then stepped back into a corner of the room with the lamp still held straight before his face. It made him look pale, and his skin somehow seemed to glow with the reflected light.

Geraldi, on the farther side, stood motionless likewise, but taking note of the room in the peculiarly keen way in which one looks on a place where a crisis is about to be reached. For the storming hoofs of the Naylors' horses swept closer each moment. Geraldi saw a small room, with low ceiling that sagged in the center, with tufts of hay sticking down through the big cracks of the attic floor. The floor was merely hard-rolled and stamped earth, a trail several inches deep having been worn from the door to the stove, and again from the stove to the table. About the walls hung some rusted traps, a few cooking utensils near the stove; a bunk was built into a corner, and by the stove appeared a few shelves on which the sacks of cornmeal, together with the bacon, salt, and a few other necessities of the pantry, were supported above the occasional dampness of the floor. This ended the furnishings of the shack, which Geraldi now enumerated one by one, so that he could have drawn a careful description of everything on which his eyes had fallen. And, in the midst of this absorption, his only real interest was in the onrush of the hoof beats that roared and echoed from the outside of the house.

"Go to the door," Geraldi commanded, "stand there, and hold the lamp."

The other started, and then obeyed, standing at the door with his hand screening his eyes, as though he were peering out with great curiosity on the procession.

No voice hailed him, though in a land where men are encountered seldom, and far between. But Geraldi, from the farthest corner of the room, saw the shadowy forms fly past, and then the noise of the riders began to die away, sometimes flinging back more loudly, as though they had changed their minds and were returning, then dipping almost out of hearing behind a hill, and arising again faintly on the farther slope.

So that current of danger flowed away across the hills, and grew fainter and fainter.

At last, the little man turned from the door and came back to the table with his lamp. "I suppose you'll want me to turn my pocket inside out, now, Mister Geraldi?" he said.

"Keep what you have," Geraldi said. "I don't grudge it to you. You'll have more, Gleason, if everything goes well here for Darcy."

"I guess that I've got all of the names, now," said Gleason. "You don't hold nothing back from me, Mister Geraldi. It's almost as though you figgered that I'd be a dead man, before long, and so it didn't matter what I knew."

Geraldi shrugged his shoulders. "Did any of those riders swing in close when they saw you with the lamp standing there?"

"None of 'em," answered Gleason. "And that was a good dodge, too. To make 'em think that I was jus' drawed out of my bed, as you might say, to see the noise that was goin' by. I reckon that they won't puzzle none over me. They won't be likely to wonder if I had something worth seeing behind this door of mine." He laughed contentedly as he said this, and his eyes sharpened so that he had an uncanny resemblance to a fox.

A groan came to them from overhead.

"Start up the fire, will you?" Geraldi requested. "I'll go up and look to him. When you get some water heated, I wish you'd bring it up to me. His wounds ought to be dressed again."

The other nodded, turning toward the stove, and Geraldi straightway climbed the ladder to the attic.

There, by lantern light, he worked for a long hour over Darcy, using the heated water that his host presently brought to him. He found Darcy in a bad condition. The wound along his side had begun to bleed again, owing to the jogging he had received in the horse-litter. The main bandage had to be taken off, the wound washed, and then the bandage replaced, dragging it tightly around the chest. Darcy, conscious again, but tortured beyond endurance as the cloth gripped the inflamed flesh, moaned with agony.

However, once the bandage was in place, its own pressure helped to numb the pain. Food the sufferer could not touch as yet, but a pint of coffee went down his throat, and then he lay clear-eyed for a moment, smoking the cigarette that Geraldi had made for him.

At last he said: "Well?"

"We're lying up for a while," Geraldi told him. "The Lamb has baited the pack and brought it on into the mountains. . . ."

"Him? Naylor? For me?"

"He's done it. He's on the black, so there's no chance that he'll be captured, if that's what worries you."

"He done that?" Darcy wondered aloud, slowly breathing out a great cloud of smoke. "Well, I gotta believe you. He's taken them on?" The wounded man groaned, but it was not physical pain that forced out the sound. It was merely an enormous relief of the spirit. The cigarette fell almost at once from his hand. "I'm gonna be able to sleep then," he said. "I'm gonna be able to sleep."

Geraldi trod on the fuming butt and waited, pulling the lantern away so that it might not trouble the eyes of the tired man. After a moment, when he was almost certain that Darcy was asleep, he heard the other mutter: "Jimmy." At once he leaned over.

"Jimmy . . . nobody else. Nobody else in the world white. Only you, partner."

Geraldi smiled in the dimness, but did not speak.

Once more the eyes of Darcy closed, but when he spoke again, it was to say: "Them fountains under the chestnuts . . . them fountains blowin' into mist . . . where might they be, Jimmy?"

"Across the sea, old-timer."

"Across the sea," Darcy repeated. "You reckon that we're gonna see 'em, Jim?"

"Of course, we are."

"Gosh," murmured Darcy, "how I been dreamin' about that, and thinkin' of it. I'd stand there and let the mist blow into my face, down my throat, into my eyes. I'd . . . I'd. . . ."

His voice failed, and he was presently breathing deeply.

Geraldi, turning from him, climbed down the ladder to the room below, and found Gleason frying bacon and corn pone in the same pan.

IX
"A PHILOSOPHER UNDER A ROOF"

They ate on the scarred table in the center of the room.

"Suppose they was to come back?" Gleason asked as he filled his pipe, at the end, and pushed the tin plate and cup aside to give himself elbow room.

"I take things as they come," Geraldi said.

"Do you?" said the other. He closed his eyes as he lighted his pipe, puffing rapidly so that a dense white fog formed in front of his face. This he at last brushed aside with his hand, or rather, cleaved a way through it, so that he could peer out at Geraldi. Never did he look more like a fox than at this moment.

"Yes," said Geraldi. "There's no use worrying before the dice have stopped rolling."

"There's some men," said the other, "who ain't happy when the dice are still. They always got to see them roll." He broke off, to add immediately: "Suppose you'd come down from up above and found me gone?"

"I'd have looked for you at once," said Geraldi.

"Where?"

"Left the cabin and lain down on the ground to try to spot you against the stars, going over one of the hills."

"And if that missed?"

"I would have run straight back."

"Back where?"

"In the direction from which the riders came. Of course, if you were gone, it would be to get in touch with them . . . signal them in some way . . . with fire, I suppose. You'd know that I would suspect that. So you'd take the back trail first, and then make a detour."

"To which side?"

"I don't know."

"So your chances wouldn't be very good, partner?"

"Two out of three," Geraldi said with his smile. "I'm a lucky man."

The other nodded with rather a grim look. "Lucky?" he said. "And yet I bet you ain't got a thing in the world except the money that you've stole."

"What's money?" answered Geraldi. "I generally have enough to spend, and, as for hoarding it, I'm not interested."

"This here Darcy, he's an old friend of yours, and that's why you stick with him?"

"He's a friend," Geraldi confirmed.

"He don't amount to shucks," replied Gleason in an even tone.

"Doesn't he?"

"He don't. I seen his face before."

"You know him?"

"I know his kind. They ain't more than twenty kinds of faces in the world. There ain't hardly that many. You get to know the types of 'em, after a while. This Darcy . . . he don't amount to shucks."

Geraldi was silent. But at last he asked: "Why am I taking care of him, then?"

The little man shook his head. "I can't quite say. They's some folks got no more heart than a tiger, but they're always tryin' to argue themselves into havin' one. Like the gunmen that always would buy a fine funeral for them they had shot in self-defense. Maybe you're that kind." He went on: "Or maybe it's just an idea stuck in the back of your mind like the lessons kids get out of books, about never slacking on a partner."

"That idea doesn't please you, Gleason?"

"Why, the fact is that you can teach a mule to do a lot of things, like pulling a load, and such. And so can you teach a human to do good things, too. But does the mule love the load that he pulls, or pulls it because he loves you? And what about the human, then?"

At this, Geraldi bit his lip and glanced away.

"I touched you a mite that time," Gleason said with composure. "But, still I don't know you. It would take a mite of time to know you." He rose and gathered up the dishes.

"Are you going to wash these tonight?" Geraldi asked, wearied.

"Sure. They might come back before you expect 'em. They shouldn't find two sets of plates dirty. You set still and rest your feet. I'll do the work. I think better when I got my hands busy."

"Do you expect them back, Gleason?"

"Most certain sure," he replied.

Geraldi stared at the stove. "I think you may be right," he agreed. "I'm practically sure that you're right, in fact."

"Of course, I'm right," said Gleason.

"You'd better hide the jewels I gave you, then. You might be searched."

"What difference? If they do any searching, they ain't gonna overlook the attic upstairs, and, if they find him there, I reckon that they'll leave no more'n a cinder of this here house."

Geraldi nodded, accepting the truth of this statement of probability and wondering more than ever at his host. "How long have you been out here, Gleason?" he asked at last.

"Nigh onto long enough."

"Tired of it?"

"No. I mean nigh onto long enough to get used to it."

"And how long is that?"

"Twelve year."

"And only beginning to grow used to it?"

"Why, the fact is," Gleason said, "that I come out here for adventure and a hard life, and I've had both and told myself that I liked it and was happy. But, of course, I wasn't."

"Why not?"

"Who is happy?" said Gleason. "They ain't much happiness in the world, except for chasin' after the things that you'll never get, and, if you could get 'em, you wouldn't be happy chasin' 'em."

"What about married men, the wives they love, their children, and homes?"

"I kinda laugh when you say that," Gleason said. "Wives and children and homes, they don't make a man happy more'n one minute a week. But a man's like a hoss. He gets used to one place, and, if he ain't happy in it, he's just plain miserable out of it. Married men is like hosses that been worked a long time in the same span. They don't like each other. But they can't get on without each other. And you'll see 'em in the pasture, the off hoss always on the off side, and the nigh hoss always on the nigh side. Same way with men and wives. And yet you ask me a question like that. But you're still tolerable young, even if you are Geraldi."

The latter watched and listened, lounging on the bunk in the corner of the room, and slowly smoking a cigarette. "So you got used to this place at last, Gleason?"

"I got used to it, till you come flingin' in, and make me smell the mountains, as you might say, and the out trail and the smoke of the mornin' over the forests. But after you get along, I'll settle down again, most likely."

Geraldi fell into a half sleep, like the sleep of a wolf. For, as he dozed on the bunk, first one eye and then the other opened and looked at Gleason, and always at him, and at no other thing in the room. Hardly a second passed without that surveillance coming dreamily to bear on his host.

Of this Gleason became aware as he softly wiped the last dish dry. He made a sudden motion with the tin plate that was in his hand. The flash of the pan under the lantern light brought Geraldi like a tiger to his feet, but he dropped the half-drawn revolver back into its holster. Yet he remained erect for an instant, keen, alert, breathing danger.

"You were about fifty-one percent dolt, just then," Geraldi commented.

"Well," said the other, "the rest of me was philosopher, as they say. And even if I come a tenth part of a second from bein' shot, at least I missed that. So we're all even."

Geraldi turned his back on him and stepped to the door. Then he passed outside it and remained gone for a moment.

When he returned, it was to find his host standing in the middle of the floor, with his eyes wide with inquisitiveness.

Geraldi nodded. "They're coming back," he said.

"Shall we take him outside and lay him in the brush?" asked Gleason.

"Exposure might kill him as effectually as bullets," said Geraldi. "And if they remain until the morning, he's a dead man, anyway. No, we'll let him stay where he is." He looked earnestly at his host. "I want to believe in you, Gleason," he said. "I want to think you'll keep the promise that you made to me a little while ago."

The foxy face of Gleason wrinkled with interest and secret

amusement. He merely nodded for an answer.

"But all the while that you're in here with them, I'll be out somewhere on the watch . . . outside the window . . . outside the door . . . somewhere watching and listening. They may come for coffee and leave again. But by the tickling in my spinal column, Gleason, I think that there'll be much more trouble than that."

X
"THE PLAGUE!"

Safely outside the house, Geraldi watched the cavalcade of shadows pour up from the next gully and sweep toward the shack, and never did flight appear to him so logical and tempting as at this moment. Yet he remained close by, until it was too late to flee, for the Naylors were everywhere about the house with their horses. Only they did not think of looking inside the dense bush that sprouted just beside the window of the house, allowing Geraldi to stand there at his ease and look in on all that happened within.

They were all there—Harry Naylor in executive command as it were, but, astonishing to see, old Pike Naylor himself was with the party, his long, hooked nose looking blue with night cold and fatigue. The grin which toothlessness had given to him was broader than ever, more wolfish.

Twenty men packed the little cabin, or tended the horses outside it.

But looking through the brush at the bronchos, it was easy for Geraldi to understand why the clan had given up the pursuit for the time being. For the animals were completely spent. It was not necessary to have full daylight to examine them. The sight of their hanging heads and their tucked-up bellies against the stars was enough.

Inside the shack, moreover, Geraldi was seeing hollow-eyed men, unshaven, dusty, their eyebrows whitened. They demanded coffee loudly. Half a dozen threw themselves down on the floor, exhausted. The others moved restlessly about, cursing, raging.

They had ridden furiously forward, it appeared, with the horses of the fugitives, as they believed, just before them. But in spite of their efforts, they had been hopelessly distanced by the horses led by The Lamb.

"They went as light," one of the crew commented, "as if they didn't have men in the saddles."

Cullen came in at that moment. "One saddle was empty, at any rate," he said.

They looked at him with grave, sour attention. He had from them the reception that a traitor usually receives, but, nevertheless, they had to respect his information. And Cullen carried himself very well, with a haughty indifference to the opinions of the other riders.

"What saddle?" asked Harry Naylor.

"The one that was holding Darcy. He wasn't capable of riding. Remember that Geraldi was making a horse litter to carry him along?"

"Why should Geraldi have done it?" asked someone. "If he's the monster that gents say, why should he have done that?"

"Why," Cullen said, "it isn't that he cares about Darcy, but it's his pride to be able to tell the world that he got away from all the Naylors without losing a man. The Old Nick always has been credited with pride, you know."

Gleason had received his guests with his usual fox-like calm; he had built up the fire and was heating water for coffee in a tin bucket, the only receptacle he owned large enough to make a drink of coffee for so many guests. And now, as Cullen spoke, a heavy groan sounded from the attic above.

It struck all the Naylors silent; it made Geraldi turn his head and mark down a horse that stood with a higher head than the others. Flight was his only resource now, unless Gleason were able to produce a miracle. But the latter was blandly stirring quantities of coffee into the water in the bucket on the stove when Harry Naylor clapped a hand on his shoulder.

"Who's that up the ladder?" he asked.

"That? Brother of mine," Gleason responded.

Geraldi started and listened more closely. He had had his doubts of Gleason until this moment. Now his faith was restored, but he failed to see how the little man possibly could avoid a catastrophe.

"A brother?" Harry said. "Sick?"

"Yeah. Mighty sick."

"You'd better have a look at that sick man," Cullen said. "Bullet wounds make a man groan and a good deal quicker than sickness."

On the heel of his words a louder and heavier groan broke from Darcy, and the blood of Geraldi ran cold. His hands were tied, but he had a fiendish desire to shoot Cullen and Pike Naylor from the window and so gain a double requital for the death that now stared Darcy in the face.

"I'll have a look up there myself," Harry Naylor announced. "Why would you shove a brother of yourself into the attic, like that?"

"Because the flies bother him a lot less up there where it's dark."

Harry Naylor, his foot on the ladder, paused. "Why do the flies bother him?"

"Well, he's sort of broke out," said Gleason.

"Aye, with bruises and wounds," Cullen said. "By Jupiter, I begin to be sure that Darcy is up there. It stands to reason, because I tell you that he couldn't possibly have been taken along at the pace they were going tonight. Darcy's here, and only Geraldi and The Lamb are with the horses."

This accurate diagnosis was received without a word by the Naylors, although several of them lifted their heads and stared earnestly at the dark opening in the ceiling.

"Mighty horrible thing to look at, his face just now," said Gleason. "All kinds of pockety, d'ye see?" He made a grimace as he said it.

"Pockets?" Pike Naylor said, coming out of the evil dream in which he had been lost. "Just what sort of pockets?"

"Why, it'd take your appetites to know what they're like. He come down quick, with a rash and a fever, a few days back. The light down here bothered him a lot. He begun to puff and to swell. Then he busted out with these here sores that I was talkin' about, and mostly he's out of his head. . . ."

There was a faint shout, and then another groan from the man above them.

Harry Naylor went straight up the ladder and reached for the edge of the opening, saying: "We'll have a look and see."

"Hold on!" Pike Naylor called suddenly.

Harry looked down. "What for?"

"It sounds mighty like smallpox."

Harry Naylor did not wait for a second cautioning. He almost fell down the ladder.

"Smallpox!" he shouted. "You sneaking coyote, why didn't you tell me what it was?"

But Gleason stood with mouth agape. "Smallpox?" he said. "And me never having had it? Never bein' vaccinated, either. Smallpox. And me takin' care of him every day." He had a big iron spoon in his hand, with which he had been stirring the coffee into the boiling water, and now the spoon fell from his hand, clattering on the floor.

It was like a drum signal of alarm, the whole crowd rushing for the door of the shack, Gleason among them, his voice shrilling out as if in wildest alarm: "Smallpox!"

When the exodus of cursing, raging men had been completed, only one figure remained, and it was that of Cullen. He remained in the center of the floor, looking up at the trap in the ceiling quizzically.

"Come out of that, Cullen!" Harry Naylor shouted. "The longer you breathe that filthy air, the bigger chance you have of catching the disease, and of spreading it, too. Come out of that, will you? Or else we won't have you along with us."

Cullen shook his head. "This is an odd thing," he said. "I never heard of a man catching smallpox out in the mountains like this . . . I'm going up to look and satisfy my own eyes." He began to climb the ladder, but made only one step, when Geraldi saw him shudder convulsively. Hastily he returned to the floor and went toward the door. The horrible fear of the unknown had pushed him back.

Outside the door, Gleason's voice could be heard raised in complaint: "He's my own brother. What'm I gonna do? I never guessed smallpox. We'll both die, and not a soul. . . ."

"Keep away from me, you poison little skunk. Keep away, or I'll shoot. You been around him . . . you been havin' your hands on him . . . and . . . and you was gonna make us coffee! Get out of my sight . . . it sure makes me sick to look at you."

Here Gleason stumbled through the door as though he had been flung bodily back into the shack. He sank onto an improvised stool and sat there with his face buried in his hands, in full view of the door, while Geraldi heard Harry Naylor giving brisk orders to mount.

They had to get food for the horses, food for the men, and then they would take up the long trail again. Wearily the Naylors trooped back to the saddle. Geraldi heard the stirrup leathers creak, the horses groan as the riders mounted. Some of the horses were so thoroughly exhausted that they staggered to the side drunkenly as the men swayed up to the saddles.

"Feed them the rowel till we get over to the Wilton place," Harry Naylor directed. "We want to be on the trail again before the middle of tomorrow morning. Look alive, boys. You know what hangs on this and. . . ."

His speech was cut into by demoniacal laughter that rang hollow from the attic where Darcy lay.

With no more words, the Naylors rode down the slope and were absorbed among the shadows of the next valley like phantoms riding down into a black sea.

So they were gone, and Geraldi came slowly back into the house. He found Gleason singing softly as he stirred at the bucket of coffee.

"All this," Gleason said, without turning his head, "and only the pair of us to drink it."

"I can use a quart of it," Geraldi said, "a quart, black and strong! Gleason, that was a fine little show you just acted through."

"There is some," said Gleason, "that is nacheral born liars, some make pretty good liars with study and practice, and some never amount to nothin' along those lines. But I was a born liar, and I educated myself along them lines. It ain't surprisin' if I was able to bamboozle that crowd. Besides, I looked too small to be tellin' a lie of the size of that one. You take a look at my brother up the ladder, and I'll have the coffee ready by the time that you get back."

Geraldi slipped up the ladder and found Darcy needing no care whatever. He had fallen into a deep sleep. His breathing was so regular that Geraldi knew it would be a different man who awakened the next morning. So he went back down the ladder to Gleason, and found the little man ladling out big tin cups of his brew with the iron spoon. Steam arose in small wisps from the open faces of the coffee cups, and Gleason was stirring sugar into his portion.

They sat opposite one another at the little table, each busied with his own thoughts.

At length, Gleason took from his pocket the small heap of jewels that Geraldi had given to him, and placed them in front of his guest.

"Why?" asked Geraldi.

"I'll tell you why," Gleason said. "I've had 'em. I've seen 'em. I've watched 'em sparkle. I'm through with 'em."

"You don't understand," Geraldi said. "As a matter of fact, there's a tidy little fortune in those stones, Gleason."

"I know," said Gleason. He looked rather wistfully at his guest. "I was once an expert," he added quietly. "Matter of fact, I used to be a collector, and never paid for what I got." Geraldi smiled, and the little man went on: "If I had these, what would I do with 'em? Think about night lights and the big spending. I come out here to get away from that. I was away from it, when you come over the skyline and dropped in on me. Take that stuff and shove it deep in your pocket, Geraldi. I never want to see the face of it again."

Geraldi, without a word, picked up the scattered jewels, and made them disappear. Then he remained for a time, quietly sipping his coffee and watching the odd, sharp fox-like face of his companion.

"Gleason," he said at last, "it begins to look as though I've been a fool from the moment I came into this place and drew a gun on you to the time that I offered you money. Do you forgive me?"

The little man chuckled. "There you go," he said, "getting sentimental, makin' me into a saint. Matter of fact, I'd've sold you to the Naylors in a minute, most like, if I hadn't been scared that your gun would get me before they got you. Things are even between us, Geraldi. You've had your Darcy saved . . . I've had my fun."

XI
"THE NAYLORS RETURN"

Early each morning, Geraldi went out on the highest of the nearer hills; at noon, and again in the evening, he was at the same post, scanning the skyline in the hope of seeing some sign of Lambert Naylor and the horses returning toward the Gleason cabin.

So at last, on a day when the sun stood bright and hot in the central sky, it was more dream-like than real when he saw a small troop of horses clustering about one horseman, and riding across the hills toward him.

He could tell the gait and the form of the black stallion far off; he could tell the massive shoulders of The Lamb still farther, and, therefore, he was waiting with a smile of gratification as the big man rode up. He was mounting the last slope of the hill when Geraldi heard from behind him what sounded like a gunshot, but the wind blew against the noise, and he could not be sure. It might be, however, that Gleason had gone out to try his hand at a random squirrel or at a rabbit that chanced by.

He gave this sound little notice, so delighted was he to see big Naylor come up, waving a hand and shouting greetings.

Naylor seemed as delighted as he. He sprang out of the saddle as the black horse went to Geraldi like a dog to fawn on its master.

"You're here . . . Darcy's here . . . everything's fixed?" The Lamb asked eagerly.

"Everything's fixed. They came back, but they didn't stay long. Gleason was afraid that his brother upstairs had smallpox, and they didn't wait to help the sick man. They ran, and that was that. But you, Lamb?"

"I run the hosses pretty hard. Maybe I would've got clean off, except that the gray's a soft beast. She couldn't hold up but buckled, and there I was. Then I seen what looked like a valley cuttin' back into the hills, and I ducked the hosses into it, only to find out that it was a box cañon, and I would've had to fit all of the hosses with wings to get 'em over the first cliff. I was about to go and save myself, when all at once I remembered what you thought about the black, and so I didn't run.

"Well, a minute later, the Naylors come by like rockin' hosses past the mouth of that ravine. Not the whole body of 'em, but three split to the side and come galloping into the cañon. I seen 'em come, but somehow I didn't have the sense to take a shot at 'em. I just sat there, while they got closer and closer, and finally I was about to send a slug at the nearest one, when they pulled up rein and waited for a minute. Why, I could hear their hosses breathe, and there wasn't any real way that they could've missed the seein' of me. But somehow they did. They didn't expect to find me there, and so they didn't find me. And after they'd gone, I doubled out of that valley, and into another, and worked back very slow and gradual, until I was pretty well back in the bush.

"While I was out there, I wondered how long they'd go, or if they could give up the trail? But that wouldn't have been likely, I knew. I waited for 'em, until I seen 'em duck out into the open again, and they come along pretty easy and gradual. I studied their hosses, and seen three of 'em stumble in a half an hour, by which I knew that there was a good deal the matter with them. Anyway, they went past my stand, and, when they were gone, I waited a while, and then I come out and backtracked into the hills, and since that time I've never seen 'em again. You wonder why I didn't get back quicker? Because I made a circle through the hills. The gray mare, she held me up pretty bad. She was lame in her right foreleg. I worked on her and rubbed her, and took it easy, because it seemed a shame to drop a right good mare that might come around. And there she is now . . . fine and sassy, and the freest on the lead rope of any hoss in the bunch."

He pointed to her with pride, and she was, indeed, in fine fettle. As for the rest, they were a little lean of rib and high of back, but they had come through sound and strong.

"And after we left, back come the Naylors to you?" The Lamb went on. "I would've liked to see 'em when they heard about the smallpox. You know why that hit 'em so hard?"

"No."

"Back in the old days, there was a sick *hombre* come to the place and jus' got started to work on the ranch, when he busted out with smallpox, and five or six men died before the thing was over. How's Darcy now?"

"Sitting up and walking around and ready to ride, but I've been making him take it easy for a while. The time has come now, old son. Away we go, and the rest of the clan will never catch up with us."

"They been set back," The Lamb said, grinning. "They sure been set back a coupla days. Away we go to the shack."

And back they went at a smart gallop, with the led horses prancing, big Naylor on another mount, and Geraldi once more on the back of the stallion.

When they got back to the house, Naylor took the horses to the closed pasture behind it, stripped off the saddles, and turned them loose, while Geraldi went straight on into the house itself.

He called to Gleason as he went: "We've got them back, and not a head lost, Gleason. This will be about the end of the game." So he said as he crossed the threshold of the hut, and then saw Gleason picking himself off the floor with crimson streaming down his face.

The little man regained his feet unaided, before Geraldi could come to him.

"Hello, Geraldi," he said, staggering. "We counted chickens just a mite before they hatched. They nigh to got me, and they certainly have polished off poor Darcy."

"Darcy! Darcy!" Geraldi cried, startled into one of his rare exhibitions of emotion. "They've got Darcy? But how are you yourself, Gleason? Are you badly hurt?"

"I thought I was dead," Gleason said, dipping a towel into a bucket of water and gingerly washing the stains from his head. "All the thinkin' that I done was that I was dead, leastways. But I seem to come through. I reckon that they could slam me in the head with a bullet, but they couldn't more'n bounce it off my skull, d'ye see?" He laughed as he said it, the laughter stopping on a wry grimace of pain.

Geraldi looked at him with lessening concern, for it was plain that the tough skull of Gleason had received merely a shock, and no serious wound.

"Will you tell me what happened?" Geraldi asked at last. "And Darcy gone? After all this . . . Darcy gone?"

"He was walkin' up and down in front of the house," Gleason began. "I was in here rollin' that dough and kneadin' it, and I sings out and tells him that if he'll wash his hands, I'll trust a real delicate job to him. But he ups and says that he can't be bothered with no jobs, when he's just gettin' the taste of the open air into his lungs. I says to him that he's a loafer and no good, and that I wouldn't have him around the place even to do a boy's chores, and he says that the faster he can leave, the more better pleased he'll be. And while we're passin' the time of day like this, free and easy, I sings out to him and I says to him would he fetch me in some wood from the woodpile, and he don't answer me, but pretty soon I hear a thud, like a man had soaked his heel hard into damp clay.

"It has a funny sound to me, that does, and pretty soon, as I'm pushin' my bread into the oven, I think to myself that I'll go and see what it was. I turned around, and there in the door is Darcy standin', out on his feet, his head wobblin' from side to side, an awful thing to see, and a gent on either side holdin' him up. And in front of Darcy there walks another pair, and one of them says to the other . . . 'Slam this gent!' . . . and the other one ups with his gun, as calm as you please, and whangs away, and I catch it in the head, and that's all that I know." He finished with a gesture of surrender and an accent of disgust.

"So there you are," he said. "They've got Darcy in spite of all our work. But why did they bring him in here, and why did they take him away with 'em, instead of stickin' a knife clean through him?"

"Because they couldn't find the loot, Gleason. That's the only reason. Because they couldn't find the stuff that we'd carried away, and because Darcy couldn't tell them where it was, no matter what they did to him. D'you see? They walked him back into the shack . . . they waited till he was back in his senses, which they had more than half knocked out of him. Then they asked him questions, but he could only say that he didn't know. For I was the only man who knew where the loot was cached. That's the reason they've taken him away with them. He'll be the club over my head with which they'll try to hold me up for his share of the stuff, at least." He then broke into a great, harsh laughter.

"Do you see, Gleason? Cullen is back with them . . . a lucky Cullen, if he gets away with any of the stuff sticking to his fingers. And now they have Darcy, whose share I'll have to pay down to get his freedom, and the only outstanding loss they'll have will be my third of the game." He broke off to help with the bandaging of the head of his friend, and it was so that the Lamb found them, as he returned from caring for the horses.

The latter was not a man of many words. Therefore, he asked no questions, but used his eyes the more. He did not even ask where Darcy might be, but, climbing the ladder to the garret and finding that the other was not there, he descended again, and gave a final thoughtful glance at Geraldi, as the latter finished the bandaging.

After that, Naylor went outside and walked pensively up and down, up and down. He examined the ground, saw certain hoof prints leading off from the house, and even scanned the distant hills in the direction in which they had gone.

As he watched in this manner, out of the nearest gully a horseman arose, weaving his way among the little man-high lodgepole pines. A graceful rider was this stranger, with a five-gallon sombrero high upon his head, and silver *conchos* down his trouser legs.

As he came up, The Lamb recognized that same handsome Mexican who had appeared in the village where they last had rested. He raised his hat in high salutation as he came nearer. "I've come to talk to Mister Geraldi," the Mexican said. "Is he in?"

"You've come to talk to Mister Geraldi, have you?" The Lamb repeated. "I've a mind to wring your neck for you. You're one of those who were here a few minutes ago?"

"Here at this house?"

"Aye, and one of then that fetched away Darcy."

"Of course, I am," said the other, well at ease as he answered. "But because we didn't find everything that we wanted, I've been sent back to talk to Mister Geraldi about getting more."

The sharp voice of Gleason barked at him from the doorway. "You'll get no more! Geraldi has finished paying for the dolts that rode with him. He'll now keep what's left as his own!"

XII
"A LETTER FROM DARCY"

"What's to be gained by hard talk, offensive talk?" asked the other. "But here's the famous Geraldi himself to answer me. Have you heard me, *señor?*"

Geraldi came out through the doorway and into the sun, which burned with such a terrible vigor that the Mexican's horse was twitching its withers and hips as though to shrug away some of the constant shower of fiery flakes.

In that sun, Geraldi stood bareheaded, with his hands dropping from his hips as he faced the messenger. The Lamb could not see Geraldi's expression, but he could read it as in a mirror by the reaction it caused in the face of the other man. First of all, the gay and insouciant air of the messenger disappeared, his face grew longer, his very color faded decidedly under the silent stare of Geraldi.

At last, Geraldi said: "What is it that you want, José?"

José was forced to make an empty gesture, to begin with. Then words came haltingly. "I am only sent, *señor.*"

"Oh, of course," replied Geraldi. "Only sent. No volition of your own. Why, of course not. Poor José, forced to come here by wicked old Pike Naylor. What is it you want, José?"

The Mexican actually slipped out of the saddle, as though the words of Geraldi had been so many blows.

Standing on the ground, he gripped the stirrup leather as though to give himself more courage. "*Señor* Geraldi, I was here with the others, but I did not lay a hand on *Señor* Darcy, nor on *Señor* Gleason. *Señor* Gleason will tell you that is true."

"He didn't have an arm that would reach as long as a bullet out of a gun," Gleason said. "But go on, greaser, and let's hear what you have to say?"

The opprobrious name had no effect upon José; indeed, it was as though nothing existed in the world for him but the coldly concentrated attention of Geraldi.

"Unfortunately," the Mexican said, his uneasy eyes widening and then rolling away from Geraldi toward the horizon, only to return anxiously to the slender youth, "unfortunately, *Señor* Darcy did not have with him the things which we had hoped to find. Therefore, we took him away with us, after inviting him to remember as much as he could. But he said very frankly that he did not know. *Señor* Geraldi alone knew."

"And if I turn over the stuff, you give me Darcy again, in the flesh, living?" Geraldi asked.

There was something in his voice that made the messenger turn a paler color than ever. "*Señor,*" he said, "I am nothing. I am only, as it were, a piece of paper on which a few words are written, but what you have said is true."

"I take the stuff to a certain place. Darcy is produced. I leave the loot. All is well."

"Exactly so, *señor.*"

"You'll be carrying some sort of authorization with you, José?"

"Certainly. I have a letter from Darcy." He took it out at once and tendered it with a low bow.

Geraldi, taking it, ripped the envelope open and took out

the paper which it contained. It read, in a great, scrawling, painful hand:

Dear Jimmy:

They have me again, as you know by this time. They got me where I never can get away, and where even you wouldn't have a chance of getting at me. They want to finish me off, of course, and I think that if there was a little less stuff concerned, they'd prefer nailing me to another tree to taking the money that I have which you took from them.

They only ask for my share of it, Jimmy, and, if you'll ride in toward San Hernandez with my part of the loot and come to the edge of the marshes, just north of the railroad, they'll produce me out of the brush. I'm to leave the bushes and go forward toward you a hundred yards. Then, one man following behind me will take the bag from you, and then I'll be free to go on with you.

If they open on you from the brush, they know that the gent that has walked out with me will be pretty sure to die, and to die *pronto*. That'll be the guarantee, and a pretty good one it ought to make.

This'll take nothing out of your pocket, Jimmy, and it'll turn me loose.

These people keep their word. They've kept it by Cullen, who's still with them and getting along fine with everybody here. Jimmy, I know that I got no right to ask you to do another thing for me, but this is a pick between living or dying pretty hard, and I guess you won't blame me if I ask you this one last favor. I been an anchor for all the time, and held you

up pretty bad, but this will be for the last time.

Thanks for the past, no matter what you do about this.

Yours truly,
Darcy

To this letter a postscript was added in a more rapid, and still more sprawling hand.

P.S. Geraldi, the new wounds have stopped hurting, and it seems to me like all I can feel is the old scars in the middle of my hands.

Geraldi, having finished the letter, then read it aloud to his two companions. The opinion of Gleason was quickly given and sharply to the point.

"Darcy's a chump if he thinks that you'll endanger yourself again for him. He doesn't really think you will. Let him slide, Geraldi, and take what you have, and keep his share for his widow and children, so to speak."

The Mexican did not speak to influence Geraldi in this decision, but merely turned his dark, haunted eyes on the face of the youth and waited.

Geraldi, whiter with anger than the messenger with fear, walked up and down, biting at his lips. At last he said: "Your words are written on paper, José, and I've half a mind to treat you the way one treats worthless paper. But . . . go back to the Naylors. Tell them that I'm going to think about this for a day or so."

"There will be until tomorrow morning," the Mexican said. "After that, we must go away. There are little troubles with the sheriff of the county . . . people say that he doesn't approve of armed men riding through his district as we have done. He is apt to make a great disturbance, and my friends wish to return to their own place. But they will wait for you until tomorrow morning."

Geraldi waved his hand, turned on his heel, and walked quickly into the house, whither Lambert Naylor and Gleason followed him. The Mexican mounted at once, jogged his horse a little distance, and then was seen from the door of the house to fling himself forward along the neck of his mount, and to make it fly down the hillside.

"He's feelin' bullets in the back," Naylor said. "I don't blame him. You looked pretty poison there, chief. Now what?"

"Go down to the marshes," Gleason suggested ironically. "Go down to the swamps for Darcy, and there you'll stand with your money in your hand, and be shot full of holes by the Naylors."

"They wouldn't do it," said Lambert Naylor with heat. "They ain't as low skunks as to. . . ."

Gleason raised a withered, bony hand, and Naylor became suddenly silent in the face of this distasteful gesture, as though he well realized that his protest had no background of real importance.

"I won't go to the marshes," Geraldi answered tersely.

The other two were silent, looking at one another in a species of dismay, as though this were the last answer that they had expected from Geraldi, no matter how much they had argued to win him over to that decision.

"Good!" The Lamb said. "I was half thinkin' that I'd have to go down there with you."

"You'll have to go along with me no place," Geraldi advised him.

"We start ridin', then?" The Lamb asked, still somewhat incredulous. "Where?"

"Toward San Hernandez."

"San Hernandez!"

"Wasn't that the town that José named?"

"But you said that you weren't going to go there, Jimmy."

"Not to the marshes, but near the town. Darcy is somewhere close by, of course. And we'll have to hunt for him."

"Jimmy!" pleaded Naylor. "Ain't it better to pay money than blood for a gent like Darcy?"

Geraldi paused to consider this while he made a cigarette. Then he said at last: "I don't know. Perhaps you're right."

"Then why not send down the stuff? A lot better that way, Jimmy."

"Perhaps. But, no doubt, it's a matter of principle with me. I don't mind paying to an honest man, but I hate like the dickens, Lamb, to pay to a flock of scoundrels such as most of that troop are. Excuse me. I don't mean to step on your own kin."

Neither Naylor nor Gleason spoke again to dissuade Geraldi, seeming to know at once that his mind was irrevocably made up. But, after a time, Naylor went into the corral, where he saddled his own horse and that of Geraldi. These he led out before the shack, and after a time they mounted.

Gleason followed them as far as the door, and there slouched against the jamb.

"If we don't come back," Geraldi said cheerfully to him, "you'll know that we're traveling in another direction, Gleason, and the horses are yours. If we do come back, whatever we have is yours."

Gleason grinned. "If I was a churchman," he said, "I'd take it and build a church, or something. But the way that I am, what could I be usin' money for? I could use some extra socks. Keep that in mind, will you?"

He laughed and waved to them as they started down the

hill. And Geraldi and The Lamb, descending the slope, turned at the bottom before they entered the draw, and waved for the last time to the queer, laughing, foxy face in the door of the shack.

"There," The Lamb declared, as they went on, "is a real man, Jimmy. Eh?"

"I don't know," Geraldi said. "He's like a detective story, and I can't guess how he'll turn out until the last chapter has come along. Stir up your horse, Lamb. We've a good distance to go."

Naylor obeyed. The horses swung into a long canter, and the rocks cracked and rang beneath their striding as they wound through the lower hills, and straight on toward the valley of San Hernandez.

XIII
"NEWS OF THE QUARRY"

In the bottom of an amphitheater to which the hills walked down like converging herds with threatening fronts, for it was a rocky region, lay San Hernandez itself. The railroad, which stretched a thin, often broken thread of silver across the landscape, had utilized that rock by stretching a branch line north of the town to one hill whose face had been deeply eaten away.

The two riders, from the higher land, noted these features, and in the center of their picture the bright streak of the San Hernandez River that ran down close to the town and there spread itself out in a great green marsh in the midst of which appeared stretches of open water, still as a mirror. Even in the distance, they could see the white reflections of clouds in those surfaces, floating deeply.

It was late afternoon; a north wind cooled the air; it was more like February than late spring in that region, and the clouds swept grandly across the sky, sometimes masses of white fire as they came in line with the westerly sun, and again like purest heaps of snow fluff.

"Now where?" asked Naylor.

"Straight toward the town," Geraldi responded, and led the way down the slope.

They reached the neighborhood of the town not long

before sunset, and passed several buckboards jogging out the road toward the country, always with the tail of the wagon heaped with sacks and brown parcels of provisions. Then, out of the brush, scrambled a boy of twelve carrying three small birds by the legs, their wings fallen out, their feathers ruffed. In his other hand was the sling with which he had brought them down, a fork of wood, with two stout pieces of rubber elastic to give the motive power, and a leather cup to hold the pebbles.

"What's the score?" Geraldi asked, as he ranged alongside.

The boy looked with admiration at the stallion, and then more indifferently at the rider. "One in four," he answered shortly.

"Good hunting," Geraldi said. "Come here and I'll give you a ride to town."

"I turn off down here at the crossroads," said the boy. "Thanks. Where you come from, stranger?"

"Up country. It's as bare of work as the palm of your hand, and we're down here to try for a job. What chance about here, son?"

The boy looked him over with a frankly doubting scrutiny from head to foot. "You don't pack a rope," he said. "Cows your line?"

"Anything I can get to do is my line when I'm broke," answered Geraldi.

"Well, I dunno," the boy said. "Things is kind of dull around here, too." He added: "Except the Parsons are falling some timber back in the hills. I guess that wouldn't be your size of job."

"Why not?"

"I don't aim to guess that you like to callus up your hands."

"A man can't work without getting a few calluses," Geraldi said.

"But calluses don't come in handy . . . for cards, say?"

Geraldi merely laughed. "I only gamble when I have to," he said. "Any good games in San Hernandez?"

"They got a coupla crooked roulette wheels. Is that your line?"

"Poker is a better hold for me," replied Geraldi. "That flat looks like rich ground to me."

"That? Sure it does, until it's plowed, and then it don't raise nothin' but alkali. The Hughes crowd tried it. They went bust. That black spot . . . that's where their house used to be. They lost a right smart of money, Dad says."

"San Hernandez doesn't sound very promising," Geraldi admitted. "Perhaps we'd better not stop here?"

"It's kind of rough," said the boy. "It's been rough ever since the railroad come in."

"Why?"

"Well, because of the tramps that always are driftin' along the rails. You can count ten bindle stiffs pretty nigh every day, and the blow-in-the-glass tramps, they're thicker still. The kind that always want a set-down meal. I follered one of them, one day, after Ma had sent him scootin'. He tapped six doors, and dog-gone me if finally he didn't get a set-down meal at Widow Small's place. I sneaked up and looked through the window from the back porch, and there I seen him stirring three lumps of sugar into his coffee, and grinnin' at Missus Small, and her grinnin' back at him, sort of sicky sweet, I tell you. Yeah, we gotta lot of roughs around here now."

"Do they make much trouble?"

"Sure. They's been two shootin' scrapes this last month. And then trouble draws trouble, Dad says. He says that there's been talk about Geraldi comin' through this place lately. You scratch a little more deeper, and you'll sure remember. Geraldi, he's the killer, he's the gunman. They're all scared out of their boots about Geraldi. But they'll get him, one day. These here gunslingers, they're always got, pretty soon."

"What sort of looking man is he?"

"Why, he's young. Rides a black hoss. Like yours, but about a hand bigger, I guess. Geraldi, he's got long black hair, I guess. And they say that his eyes fair shoot fire. He scares people nigh to death before they ever start to fight."

The boy set his teeth and looked into the distance, for all the world as though he were inwardly resolving that he himself never would be so overwhelmed by the reputation of any man.

"I suppose that the sheriff comes along now and then and runs the tramps out of town?"

"Yeah. He runs them out of town, all right, but he can't very well run 'em out of the quarry."

"Is that a vacant quarry?"

"Sure it is. They stopped workin' it nigh onto seven months ago. It's always got a few tramps hangin' around it. They's a new crowd up there now, Bill Durer told me. A mean, hard-lookin' lot, too. One of 'em took after him, and scared him almost to death. He run all the way home. He could scarcely talk for a day afterward."

"Bindle stiff?" Geraldi asked.

"No. Looked like a ornery, low-down 'puncher," said the boy. "I gotta turn off here. So long, mister."

"So long," Geraldi returned. "Thanks."

"Thanks for what?" asked the other, turning sharply around.

"For all the news, son."

They went on, but presently Naylor said: "The kid is thinkin' of something. He's still standing back there. Still lookin' after us, Jimmy."

"He's a shade too much on the bright side," Geraldi said. "He'll make his share of trouble in a few more years. But he had the news, didn't he? A boy of that age with a pair of eyes and a set of ears is worth more than a newspaper any time."

"Why, Jimmy, what did you learn from him?"

"Where the gang is now, Lamb. That's what I learned."

"I heard every word and not a sound about the Naylors!"

"You didn't listen very hard. A new lot are in the quarry. Tramps, the youngster called them, but tramps aren't usually turned out like cowpunchers. One of them took after a boy. Well, tramps don't usually chase boys. Don't you see, Lamb?"

"I don't see nothin'," said Naylor.

"Not a thing?"

"Unless there's a crazy cowpuncher out of work and batchin' up there in the old quarry. A quarry ain't such a bad place to lay up. I been in one for a while myself."

"Have you?"

"Sure, a long time ago, when I was a kid and had finished with a job one summer and left the place and was comin' down from the ranch, I got into a blizzard and drifted into a quarry. Never seen anything that looked so much like home . . . so much better than home."

"Lamb," Geraldi said, breaking in gently, "up there in the old deserted quarry we're going to find something a great deal worse than home, but that's where we're going."

"I don't foller you, Jimmy."

"Yes, but you will follow me, old fellow. I know that much about you. You'll follow me into the quarry, and we'll take out poor Darcy without fail, because that's where the Naylors are, and that's where they're holding him."

The Lamb regarded his companion with awe, then he shook his head. "And chased the kid just to make the quarry mighty unpopular with the boys of the town for a few days?"

"Of course, that's it. You'll go with me, Lamb?"

"To the finish."

"Straight on, then," Geraldi said, "until we're close to the town, and then we'll turn. We mustn't come near the quarry until after dark."

XIV
"THE QUARRY"

With sunset, the wind changed, grew stronger, and stifled the colors of the evening with a heavy blanketing of clouds. Rain began before all the sky was covered, whipping rain that came in brisk volleys, fell away to a chilly misting, and then descended again with a roar. It was impossible to keep dry. The wind plucked up the skirts of the slickers and allowed the water to drench them, but still the two riders kept on their way—Geraldi first, and big Naylor plugging his horse steadily in the rear of his leader.

They climbed to the slope at the left of the quarry as the lightning began. Great electric bolts flashed across half the sky, making all the forests and all the distant hills and mountains rush inward on the eye, only to fade far away the next instant. The brain was stunned by the constant variation. It was as though the countryside were in motion like waves, lunging far forward, and then retreating. One moment they were plodding through a thick surface soil that balled on the hoofs of the horses and made them stumble, while about them was a dim, ghostly procession of trees and of shrubs. The next moment, all flared up brightly with the clearness that was not day but like the light imagined in the inferno itself. The wet rocks gleamed as though they were themselves on fire, and the wet trees glittered with a thousand jewels.

So they came, drenched, cold, but resolute, to the upper lip of the quarry, and there tethered their horses among the trees. Thunder rolled; so great was the vibration from this or some quirk of the wind, that a thick shower descended from the moisture-laden branches above them and freshly wetted them to the skin. They discarded slickers that now simply served to increase the chill and the weight under which they labored.

Lurking at the verge of the shrubs, they waited, scanning all that was before them by the light of the flashes.

A moment later, the form of a man loomed before them. Under the lightning, he was clothed from head to foot with brilliance by the reflections from his slicker that ran with water in the rain. Then, as the thunder rolled, he was lost again in the total darkness.

"The sentry on his beat," Geraldi stated calmly at the ear of his companion. "You have your rope, Lamb?"

"Are we going to rope him, Jimmy?"

"No. He has a gun handy. If they're watching for us as closely as this, and mounting sentinels in spite of this weather, then he has a gun in his hand under that slicker, and one gunshot would be enough to alarm the boys below us. We'll have to pass him. How long will it be before he comes back along his beat?"

Two or three minutes passed, and again the form passed them, distinguishable this time without the lightning, since they knew for what to look. The rain, powdering on his hard-faced slicker, seemed in itself a sufficient light to show him to the watchers.

Then Geraldi said: "It's time, Lamb. We'll have to go out to the edge of the cliff. If I knew the lay of the land here, I might find a way to climb down, in spite of the dark, but I don't know. We'll have to get out there, and you'll have to lower away until I'm at the bottom of the drop."

"D'you mean it, Jimmy?" Naylor asked, overcome with awe. "Go down there among 'em? I'd rather be dropped into a pot of boiling water than into that crowd."

"Well," answered Geraldi, "if there's a better way, I don't know it. Darcy's down there. Darcy has to be reached. Come along. Move fast. We have to clip seconds, now."

They hurried out, Geraldi again leading, and Naylor lumbering at his heels like a great Newfoundland after a terrier.

Then the ground fell suddenly away before them. It seemed to big Naylor that Geraldi had disappeared into nothingness, and for a moment his heart stood in his throat.

"Down. Down," hissed a sudden voice at his feet. "There's a safe ledge here."

So, sitting side by side on their heels, they braced themselves with their hands and looked over the edge into the pit beneath them.

Two red eyes looked back at them. Close together at one side of the quarry floor, the thin rays from fires shone up at them, and in another moment the strangely comforting smell of wood smoke was perceptible in the air.

The thought of the heat and comfort which men were enjoying in the darkness below them, under shelter, made their own cold sufferings seem the greater, and their helplessness against odds the more appalling.

"Throw a couple of knots into that line," directed Geraldi. "Then drop it over and I'll go down. D'you think it will reach to the bottom, Lamb?"

"I don't know. If you can't guess, how could I? It's full forty feet, I know, and a little over. Jimmy, I never tried to argue with you before, but if you'd only think for a minute now, you'd. . . ."

"If I start thinking," Geraldi answered, "I'll be helpless

with fear in no time. Throw in the knots, old fellow, and toss it over."

Without another word, Naylor obeyed; the rope hissed through his hard hands; and then the lightning hung a vast torch in the heavens, so that for one moment Geraldi could see what lay before him.

It was sheer drop for twenty feet, the face of the cliff actually receding somewhat, so that there would be nothing to support him except his bare hands upon the rope. However, below this a narrow ledge appeared, and what lay still farther beneath him, he could not tell.

But the floor of the quarry could be seen by the same flash, and he saw an interlinking network of narrow railroads, a few dump cars still standing about to rot in the weather, and several small lean-tos and shacks scattered around the quarry at either side and toward the entrance. They were doubtless quarters for a watchman, for supplies, and perhaps a hut for explosives. At any rate, from two of these fires were now glowing.

Geraldi reached for big Naylor in the dark, and gripped his hand. "Good bye," he said.

"I'm going with you, man," said Naylor. "I'll never stay behind and let it be said. . . ."

"You talk nonsense," Geraldi interjected as harshly as he could. "What would I do down there, if I didn't know that you were up here manning the rope for me? What could Darcy do? Be a man, old fellow, and stay here. You have the hardest part . . . to squat here in the rain and freeze to death, and keep fishing with that rope for a bite in the dark, down yonder. Stand by me, Lamb. I need you here more than ten of you down yonder."

With that, he gripped the big hand of the giant, and instantly slid over the edge of the rock.

Gripping with knees and hands, he slid slowly down to the ledge. From this he strained his eyes, hoping for another lightning flash to illumine his way, but the lightning refused to come, and he had to venture over into the blind darkness. He found rough, projecting rocks, so that he could fairly walk down them with his toes, keeping only his hands upon the rope. And at last, while he was at the very end of the rope, his feet struck yielding soil and little rocks that had fallen down the face of the cliff, having weathered from the main rock. He knew that he was on the floor of the quarry, and, turning his back to the wall, he looked earnestly about him.

The fires were nearer. And so much light soaked through the many cracks of the huts that, now that the rain-mist blanket was not so thick, he could make out the total dimensions of the little houses. He made at once for the nearest of these, and placed himself at a liberally yawning crack.

He saw a wretched group of half a dozen men, with horse blankets around their shoulders, sitting at an open fire, the smoke of which filled the room to stifling, while the rain still beat in through the hole in the roof that was supposed to do duty as a chimney and leaked through cracks in the wall, and flooded in onto the ground where the group was sitting.

Neither Harry nor Pike Naylor was here, nor any other face of distinction in the clan. He waited until he had been able to scan every one in turn, but Darcy certainly was also not with them. He wondered, with a little sinking of the heart, if Darcy really had been hidden in some other place under a small guard. It would have been like the snaky subtlety of Pike Naylor. But there was still another shack to visit, and toward this he went at once.

It was far better built than the first place. The boards had been laid with weather stripping over the interstices, and this made a sound wall all around, except for a few cracks so small that the light was barely able to issue forth, but his eye could not look in to any advantage. It was not until he had traversed three sides of the house that he was able to find a peephole. This was a broken board, perhaps one cracked by the fall of a big stone from the quarry wall nearby, but, at any rate, the board had been both split and caved in by the force of the blow, so that Geraldi could look in, although with some difficulty, through a pair of small apertures. Even so, he had to move his eye from side to side in order to survey any large portion of the scene within.

What he made out, by degrees, was a far more comfortable picture than the one he had last observed. There was no open fire, but a stove that had been packed with wood and was burning so fiercely that the men inside had been able to take off their coats.

It was a very small chamber, but into it were packed fully a dozen men. The first face that Geraldi saw was the lean caricature of Pike Naylor, looking more like a savage old hawk than ever. The next face was that of Darcy. He sat on a low bench, with his hands behind him—probably because his arms were tied together. His ankles, too, were fastened tightly by a rope. In spite of this and the fact that he was surrounded by enemies, Darcy seemed to maintain a great deal of composed dignity.

He looked about him from time to time, meeting every eye that cared to look upon him, his manner was easy, his head high, and only his extreme pallor might have shown that he understood the seriousness of his situation. Yet some of that pallor was doubtless due to his recent sickness.

Seeing this, Geraldi felt already somewhat repaid for the amount of risk which he had taken, the efforts he was now ready to make to free this man, and he continued his scrutiny of the others. A poker game, as was to be expected was going on at an improvised table, supported on the knees of the players, and, therefore, apt to sag unexpectedly, from time to time. At this table, the only face he recognized was that of Harry Naylor. In a farther corner, sat the Mexican, José.

There was a little disturbance at this moment, for the wind blew up with such sudden violence that it burst the door partly open and allowed such a gust to enter that the stove fumed forth thick white smoke that burst through every crack and made the lantern light by which they were playing very dim. The cards, too, were fluttered into disarray, and then the flame leaped into the throat of the lantern and almost went out.

There was a loud and simultaneous cursing from many throats. The voice of Harry rose after the flurry, and, as the door was closed by José, the flame steadied and burned brightly in the throat of the chimney, and the white smoke rose from the stove and made a cloud against the ceiling of the shack.

"Keep your eye on that door, José!" shouted Harry Naylor. "I've told you before that that's your job. I tell you again. Watch that door! Or I'll make trouble come your way."

Another voice made comment, as José expressed himself with a shrug that might have been called apology, or amusement. It was the voice of Cullen: "If he had sense, he'd prop a stick against it from the inside. Then he could go to sleep, if he wished."

"You hear, José, put a stick against it!"

"I never thought of that," José responded meekly.

"He never thought of that!" sneered a chorus.

"Let him alone," Pike Naylor repeated.

The wind had fallen off, so that his words were startlingly distinct compared with the dimness of the preceding speakers. "Let him alone. Here the lot of you sit around like dolts . . . like ostriches you put your heads in the dirt and think that Geraldi can't see you. But he can!"

XV
"OUT OF THE PIT"

That exhibition of prescience made Geraldi actually start back in his place of concealment, but he realized, in another moment, that the old man could have no knowledge of him. It was merely out of the rancor of his suspicious heart that he had spoken. Yet he had a great effect upon his listeners. Cullen actually sprang up to his feet, throwing the card table into disorder, for which he was soundly cursed by the other players. Harry Naylor reached for the shoulder of a companion, as though about to thrust himself upward, also.

"What's the matter?" he yelled, enraged as he realized that it was a futile alarm.

"The matter is," Pike Naylor explained, "that you've sat down here like poor dolts, with this gent in the middle of you. You think that you got him safe? Why, he ain't no more safer than a boy in the middle of a lot of roarin' lions."

"All right, Dad," said Harry, settling back in his place, half sneering and half angered. "You tell us, will you? How could Geraldi get this here gent away from us?"

"I ain't a mind reader," Pike said. "How can I tell what a bright young gent like him would do? I'm old and my brain's pretty feeble. I been doin' the thinkin' for a flock of half-wits for so long that I can't no longer put things together very well. But suppose that he was to take a crowbar up the cliff in the back of us and start to work on one of them overhangin' rocks? He could send down ten tons that would smash us tolerable flat, I reckon."

The danger, as he named it, seemed so real that a groan broke out from several of the listeners.

"That," broke in Harry Naylor, "would be a fool's way of getting a man away from us. He'd simply be killing his friend along with the rest of us."

"Is Darcy his friend?" Pike asked. "He ain't his friend. Geraldi ain't had nothin' to do with him, before Darcy brought out the news of our money and stuff in the safe. Darcy ain't the sort that Geraldi would cotton to, and you all ought to know it." He paused and made a large, inclusive gesture, as though he took in all who were present and judged them to the bone. "No, Geraldi ain't a man that's easily pleased. The sort of a man that he would take up with, if he had a good chance, would be a man like me."

He made this astonishing statement with a great deal of pride, nodding his old head over it in reassurance of himself, so that Geraldi smiled a little, on the outside of the house, and then nodded in agreement with the other. Such a man as Pike Naylor, young or old, would have been a power that, united to his own, could have unlocked the treasure houses of the world.

"You mean," Harry Naylor said, "that he'd smash the whole lot of us for the sake of smearin' us out of his way, even if Darcy went under along with us?"

"Ain't it logical?" Pike asked, his terrible old eyes glittering at his son. "Ain't it better to kill twenty enemies than to save one friend? Besides, maybe some would live . . . Darcy amongst them."

He delivered himself of this frightful philosophy with utter complacency, but now Cullen spoke up with the terseness of one who understands his subject thoroughly and cannot be in doubt of what he says.

He declared: "I know Geraldi. I've known him for a long time, and I've hated him for a long time. I think all of you know that I'm as keen for his death as any of you, and keener, too, because he'll never leave off trailing me until he's caught me, since I double-crossed him in this last business between us."

He referred to his own treachery with such an indifferent air that Geraldi was amazed to hear him. It somewhat raised Cullen in his estimation to learn of the frankness with which the man could speak of his own shortcomings.

"Now," Cullen said, "though, as I say, I know all about the bad parts in Geraldi, I think that I know the good parts, also, and one of 'em is that he never will desert a friend in trouble."

"Look here," Harry Naylor broke in, "it's one thing to hear a lot of talk about a man who stands by his friends, but it's another thing to hear how a gent is gonna get such a fellow as Darcy away from us. No matter what Geraldi may want to do, what can he do?"

"I've told you one way," Pike Naylor insisted. "You can laugh at it, but it's a way. And he has other ways. He's young. He don't fear nothin' on earth. He'll find some way out, or else I'll be mighty disappointed in him."

"I could tell you a story," put in Cullen, "about Jimmy Geraldi. But it would take a long time, and I'll only brief it in. It's about a friend of Geraldi who went up in the hills with the Afghans and got away with enough to ransom a king and a whole family of princes. The Afghans caught him and took him back. They wanted to make such a fine example of him that they didn't kill him at once. They waited a while, turning over various ways, and not finding any way that seemed to them bad enough. While they were waiting, Geraldi slipped up there and took the prisoner away under the eyes of a thousand men. A thousand Afghans! For my part, I'd rather tackle a thousand wildcats. I don't mean to say he did it in open day or that they saw him do it. As a matter of fact, he managed it so that he had a good eight-hour start on them, and they never caught Geraldi."

"He got the gent away?" Harry Naylor asked, fascinated.

"Not all the distance. He died in the snows. Couldn't stand the route that Geraldi had mapped for them through the mountains. But the first part of the job was the important one for us to consider."

"What would you have us do?" Pike Naylor asked, whose eyes had burned with pleasure and excitement as he listened.

"I'd have us stop this game and face the wall around Darcy, and put two guards outside the shack to walk around it. That's my first idea."

"And a mighty good one," Pike agreed. "Let's do it."

"Hold on," broke in Harry. "We've got a fat pot here. We'll play this hand out and then maybe do what Cullen says. Set down, all of you. He ain't here this minute, anyway."

"That's what the gent said before the bullet hit him and the tree fell on him," Pike Naylor warned. "But go on with your ways. There ain't nothin' that should be done that shouldn't be done at once."

However, the players settled down to their game again, and Geraldi, hearing the betting and the drawing begin, went to the door and tried it gently with his hand.

The wind was blowing in great gusts that screamed over the quarry, and sometimes descended into it with big booming notes. It was a fierce gale that had sprung up. The intermissions between the blasts grew shorter and shorter;

the wind started to be one continual pressure, more than the pressure of hands.

It blew, moreover, directly against the cabin, and Geraldi, remembering the smallness of the stick that the Mexican had propped against the door to hold it in place, now stooped low and waited for a heavy blast. When it came, with a whoop like a wild animal, Geraldi gave the weight of his shoulder to the door, and felt the stick crunch beneath his effort and the hand of the wind.

Wide open flew the door, knocked the flame of the lantern up the chimney's throat and sent it flickering out, raised the cards from the table with a great rattling, and scattered the greenbacks that were piled before the gamblers.

On the wings of the darkness, Geraldi entered. He had charted in his mind the position of every man, but those positions instantly were altered.

He heard a confusion of oaths, of shouts, of interjections, of orders. Harry Naylor was bawling at the top of his voice: "José! José! Shut that door! Damn you, I'll certainly make you smart for this, you. . . ." The order ended in wild curses, half drowned by the yell of the wind and by other voices.

"Where's the lantern?"

"Gimme a match!"

"Stand here and make a shelter, will you, somebody? I got matches, but the wind. . . ."

"Get off my foot!"

"Mind Darcy, somebody!"

But Geraldi already was behind the prisoner and, feeling down his arms, reached the ropes that tied them. A touch of his knife made the hands free. Another touch, leaning forward and guiding the knife with his free hand, liberated the legs of the man, and Geraldi put his hands beneath the shoulders of his companion and lifted him to his feet.

"Hey!" yelled a voice close by. "Darcy! He's stood up! He's moved! Darcy. . . ."

In the darkness someone flung himself bodily at Geraldi, flung his weight blindly into the dark. Strong arms clasped the youth, and he raised the handle of his knife and brought down the butt of it on the head that was jammed against his ribs.

The arms relaxed, but the yell of the alarmist was taken up by others.

"Darcy's moved! What's happened?"

Then a shout of fury and despair: "Geraldi! Geraldi's in here with us! Block the door, will you, somebody? Lights! Lights!"

But Geraldi was already at the door, and dragging his companion out into the open force of the storm.

The numbed legs of Darcy seemed to regain their strength almost at once, and he struggled forward around the corner of the shack with his rescuer. Behind them, they dimly saw forms issue from the mouth of the shack. Then the door apparently was closed, and the lantern could be lighted, its flame struggling for a moment and sending dim and then stronger waves of light through the hut.

In the meantime, Geraldi had his man at the edge of the pit. A great flash of lightning burst at that moment like a flower of fire in the central sky; it showed them the rope end dangling before them, but it also showed them the figures of a dozen men running wildly here and there.

"Quick!" Geraldi shouted. "The rope, Darcy! Is there any strength in your hands?"

"There is . . . there's some. I gotta win, after you've done all of this."

"Tie it around your waist . . . the rope end. Tie it. Here, I'll do it. Now give three tugs on the rope. Naylor will haul you up, if there's strength enough even in those big arms of his, and I think there is. Climb with your feet and catch on where you can with your hands. Help poor Lamb Naylor as much as you can. There you go up. . . ."

"And you, Jimmy?"

"I'll manage. This is all planned. Work hard!"

Already Darcy was half clambering and half drawn above the head of his rescuer. And Geraldi was left alone in the pit, without a ladder for escape.

XVI
"WHAT MAKES HIM DO IT?"

He could not stand idle. Above his head, the rocks were sufficiently broken and rough to give him some chance of climbing, and, if he fell, the fall would not be far. He reached, found a handhold, drew himself up, gained footing likewise, and presently he was clambering slowly up.

Another long flash of the lightning glared at him, as it seemed to Geraldi, like a hostile eye. Perhaps he winced at the strength of it. At any rate, feet and his left hand lost their hold, and he dangled by one hand only over an abyss.

Looking up, he saw Darcy clambering over the edge of the cliff. From behind he heard a wailing cry in which he thought that he recognized the voice of Harry Cullen.

"The cliff! There they go now! There're away! It's Geraldi below!"

Grown desperate, he regained his hold with a struggle, his feet found places to cling to the rock, and he swarmed ahead, hardly waiting to be sure of each hold before he trusted his weight to it. Then he gained the ledge above, and rolled over flat on it as the lightning glared again. It showed enough of him to his enemies to cause a dozen bullets to whine about him. He heard them pounding on the rock. He heard the yelling of the Naylors, not like men, but like dogs on a trail.

Something cut him across the face, like the blow of a rapidly moving hand. He was half stunned by his exertions, but presently, as his mind re-awakened, he reached out, and found the rope end, which faithful Lambert Naylor had cast down again for him.

It raised him to his feet. He clutched the rope and, giving the signal, began to draw himself up, as Naylor pulled from above him. The thunder of the last lightning bolt still was pealing when the lightning bolt flashed out of heaven again, and Geraldi saw the strained, eager faces of his friends just above him, and behind them the tumbled clouds of the sky, swept and confused by the wind. Over his head, bullets whined from beneath.

Then he was at the quarry's edge. He was over it—and now he lay flat, gasping in the grass and the mud.

Big Naylor lifted him up. Half running by his own strength, half supported, staggering, by the power of The Lamb, he was taken toward the horses, mounted the black stallion, and took Darcy up behind him.

"The upper sentry?" Geraldi asked.

"When the lightning came and he seen me," Naylor said, "he run off. I guess he didn't like the look of my face, grinnin' at him in the dark. He won't bother us none again."

They gave the horses rein. It did not matter for the deluge that fell against them and whipped their faces, drenched and re-drenched them. For they were free from danger.

Steadily they rode on through the night. Again and yet again the lightning leaped across the sky. Then the thunder passed, the wind fell down, the great clouds were dimly seen parting above them and rolling heavily down the edges of the sky. And the stars shone through dimly, then more brightly as the last of the rain mist departed.

They went on. The soft ground sucked and popped under the feet of the horses. The slope rose before them. They were rising from the lower lands to the safety of the confused hills and of the mountains beyond them.

The changed wind now breathed from the very south, filled with the heat of the desert and blowing upon them so warmly that they were not aware of the coldness of their clothing, but only of the clinging wet.

They kept on without a pause, walking the horses, undesirous of speed, but wanting only to put behind them steadily a distance that pushed the Naylors away.

"Lamb," Geraldi said at last, "what will your friends and family do now?"

"I dunno," Lambert Naylor answered. "The rest of 'em will most likely want to quit and throw up the sponge and go home. But Pike and Harry, they're likely to want to stay on the trail till there ain't a ghost of a chance left to 'em."

"We'll let Gleason keep the horses, at least," Geraldi said. "For one thing, because he can use them, and for another because, if we go back in that direction, the whole Naylor tribe is likely to be there on our heels."

"True," Naylor agreed.

"Another thing, Lamb. What will they do when they come across Gleason again? They know by this time what he has done to help Darcy and me. Will they try to take it out of his hide?"

The giant laughed. "What would you do, if you was an ordinary gent, Jimmy, and you come across a *hombre* that took care of his own, the way you've took care of me, in the first chase, and then of Darcy in this one? Why, they ain't gonna hurt Gleason. They ain't gonna bring you back on 'em. It's bad enough to be huntin' you, without startin' you huntin' them. No, Jimmy, they ain't gonna lay a hand on Gleason's head. I'll promise you that, safe enough."

He said it with such emotion, that Geraldi sighed with

relief. And when, in the gray of the dawn, as the sun promised to rise clear and bright in the sky, they came upon a sheltered gully with plenty of small shrubbery in it, Geraldi made bold to halt and rest.

Darcy fairly fell from the saddle, and was told to sit on a rock, while Geraldi built the fire and Naylor got together the food they had brought with them in their saddlebags.

So breakfast was prepared, above all the necessary coffee, that Darcy drank with one hand steadying the other.

They let the fire burn high. Its heat dried their clothes and made it possible for them to roll in their blankets and go to sleep.

Naylor proposed to mount guard, but Geraldi would not hear of it. "I'm not sleepy," he said. "I couldn't sleep. And that's the reason that I'll walk up and down here for a while and look the countryside over."

He silenced all argument with an imperious wave of the hand and took his beat up, pacing swiftly back and forth along a sandy ridge above their camp. The black stallion, in spite of hunger and fatigue, followed him up and down in a more leisurely fashion, pausing now and then to gather a few mouthfuls of the grass.

The giant and Darcy lay side by side, their eyes instinctively turning up to watch the sentinel who marched above them.

"What do you make of him, Lamb?" Darcy asked.

"I dunno," said Naylor. "I dunno what to think. There he is, and that's all I know."

"He don't look down at us," Darcy murmured. "He's got his head turned. What's he thinkin' of? His girl, d'you think?"

"He's thinkin' that he wished he had the pair of us off of his hands," Naylor said sadly. "What right have we to be a weight on his back, now I ask you?"

"I dunno. Hardly none at all," said Darcy. "But I lie here and wonder, Lamb, as the sleep comes over me, did he give a whoop about me any of the time? Was it the fun of the game, or the rules of the game, that made him do what he done?"

"Nobody'll ever know," Lambert Naylor said. "He makes the rules of his own game."

About the Author

Max Brand is the best-known pen name of Frederick Faust, creator of Dr. Kildare, Destry, and many other fictional characters popular with readers and viewers worldwide. Faust wrote for a variety of audiences in many genres. His enormous output, totaling approximately thirty million words or the equivalent of 530 ordinary books, covered nearly every field: crime, fantasy, historical romance, espionage, Westerns, science fiction, adventure, animal stories, love, war, and fashionable society, big business and big medicine. Eighty motion pictures have been based on his work along with many radio and television programs. For good measure he also published four volumes of poetry. Perhaps no other author has reached more people in more different ways.

Born in Seattle in 1892, orphaned early, Faust grew up in the rural San Joaquin Valley of California. At Berkeley he became a student rebel and one-man literary movement, contributing prodigiously to all campus publications. Denied a degree because of unconventional conduct, he embarked on a series of adventures culminating in New York City where, after a period of near starvation, he received simultaneous recognition as a serious poet and successful author of fiction. Later, he traveled widely, making his home in New York, then in Florence, and finally in Los Angeles.

Once the United States entered the Second World War, Faust abandoned his lucrative writing career and his work as a screenwriter to serve as a war correspondent with the infantry in Italy, despite his fifty-one years and a bad heart. He was killed during a night attack on a hilltop village held by the German army. New books based on magazine serials or unpublished manuscripts or restored versions continue to appear so that, alive or dead, he has averaged a new book every four months for seventy-five years. Beyond this, some work by him is newly reprinted every week of every year in one or another format somewhere in the world. A great deal more about this author and his work can be found in *The Max Brand Companion* (Greenwood Press, 1997) edited by Jon Tuska and Vicki Piekarski. His next **Five Star Western** will be *The Lone Rider.*

36
9422M

447	470	493	516	539	562	585	608	63
448	471	494	517	540	563	586	609	63
449	472	495	518	541	564	587	610	63
450	473	496	519	542	565	588	611	63
451	474	497	520	543	566	589	612	63
452	475	498	521	544	567	590	613	63
453	476	499	522	545	568	591	614	63
454	477	500	523	546	569	592	615	63
455	478	501	524	547	570	593	616	63
456	479	502	525	548	571	594	617	6
457	480	503	526	549	572	595	618	
458	481	504	527	550	573	596	619	6
459	482	505	528	551	574	597	620	[illegible]
460	483	506	529	552	575	598	621	6
461	484	507	530	553	576	599	622	6
462	485	508	531	554	577	600	623	6
463	486	509	532	555	578	601	624	6
464	487	510	533	556	579	602	625	6
465	488	511	534	557	580	603	626	6
466	489	512	535	558	581	604	627	6
467	490	513	536	559	582	605	628	
468	491	514	537	560	583	606	629	
469	492	515	538	561	584	607	630	